WINGS OF FIRE

BOOK ONE
THE DRAGONET PROPHECY

BOOK TWO
THE LOST HEIR

BOOK THREE
THE HIDDEN KINGDOM

BOOK FOUR
THE DARK SECRET

BOOK FIVE
THE BRIGHTEST NIGHT

BOOK SIX
MOON RISING

BOOK SEVEN
WINTER TURNING

BOOK EIGHT
ESCAPING PERIL

BOOK NINE
TALONS OF POWER

BOOK TEN
DARKNESS OF DRAGONS

BOOK ELEVEN
THE LOST CONTINENT

BOOK TWELVE
THE HIVE QUEEN

BOOK THIRTEEN
THE POISON JUNGLE

BOOK FOURTEEN
THE DANGEROUS GIFT

BOOK FIFTEEN
THE FLAMES OF HOPE

BOOK SIXTEEN
THE HYBRID PRINCE

LEGENDS

DARKSTALKER
DRAGONSLAYER

WINGS OF FIRE

THE HYBRID PRINCE

by
TUI T. SUTHERLAND

SCHOLASTIC PRESS
NEW YORK

With special thanks to Ashley Mackenzie

Library of Congress Cataloging-in-Publication Data available

ISBN 978-93-5954-663-6

This reprint edition March 2026
Book design by Phil Falco

Printed in India at Shivam Offset Press, New Delhi

For the librarians, teachers, booksellers,
authors, students, and everyone else working to
protect our freedom to read – thank you

The Forgotten Isles
Court of Refuge

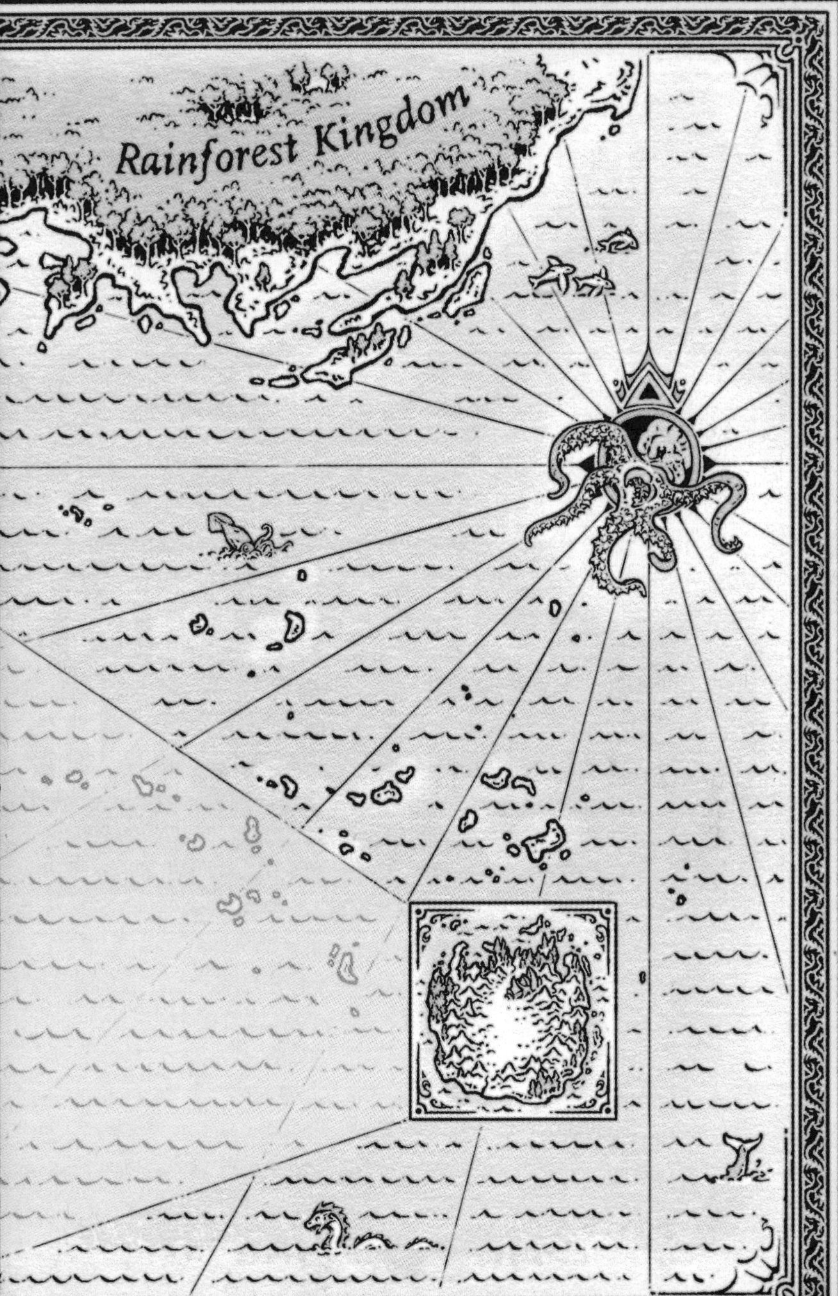
Rainforest Kingdom

A GUIDE TO THE

DRAGONS AND

OF PYRRHIA
PANTALA

SANDWINGS

Description: pale gold or white scales the color of desert sand; poisonous barbed tail; forked black tongues

Abilities: can survive a long time without water, poison enemies with the tips of their tails like scorpions, bury themselves for camouflage in the desert sand, breathe fire

Queen: Since the end of the War of SandWing Succession, Queen Thorn.

MUDWINGS

Description: thick, armored brown scales, sometimes with amber and gold underscales; large, flat heads with nostrils on top of the snout

Abilities: can breathe fire (if warm enough), hold their breath for up to an hour, blend into large mud puddles; usually very strong

Queen: Queen Moorhen

SKYWINGS

Description: red-gold or orange scales; enormous wings

Abilities: powerful fighters and fliers, can breathe fire

Queen: Queen Ruby

SEAWINGS

Description: blue or green or aquamarine scales; webs between their claws; gills on their necks; glow-in-the-dark stripes on their tails/snouts/underbellies

Abilities: can breathe underwater, see in the dark, create huge waves with one splash of their powerful tails; excellent swimmers

Queen: Queen Coral

ICEWINGS

Description: silvery scales like the moon or pale blue like ice; ridged claws to grip the ice; forked blue tongues; tails narrow to a whip-thin end

Abilities: can withstand subzero temperatures and bright light, exhale a deadly frostbreath

Queen: Queen Glacier, succeeded by Queen Snowfall

RAINWINGS

Description: scales constantly shift colors, usually bright like birds of paradise; prehensile tails

Abilities: can camouflage their scales to blend into their surroundings, shoot a deadly venom from their fangs

Queen: Queen Glory

HIVEWINGS

Description: red, yellow, and/or orange, but always mixed with some black scales; four wings

Abilities: vary from dragon to dragon; examples include deadly stingers that can extend from their wrists to stab their enemies, venom in their teeth or claws, or a paralyzing toxin that can immobilize their prey; others can spray boiling acid from a stinger on their tails

NIGHTWINGS

Description: purplish-black scales and scattered silver scales on the underside of their wings, like a night sky full of stars; forked black tongues

Abilities: can breathe fire, disappear into dark shadows, a limited few can read minds or foretell the future

Queen: Queen Glory (see recent scrolls on the NightWing Exodus and the RainWing Royal Challenge)

SILKWINGS

Description: SilkWing dragonets are born wingless, but go through a metamorphosis at age six, when they develop four huge wings and silk-spinning abilities; as beautiful and gentle as butterflies, with scales in any color under the sun, except black

Abilities: can spin silk from glands on their wrists to create webs or other woven articles; can detect vibrations with their antennae to assess threats; some are born with "flamesilk," an ability to spin threads of fire

LEAFWINGS

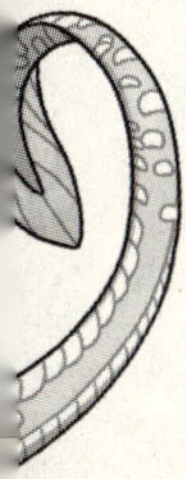

Description: green and/or brown scales and wings shaped like leaves

Abilities: can absorb energy from sunlight and are accomplished gardeners; some have unusual control over plants, a power known as leafspeak

Queen: Queen Sequoia

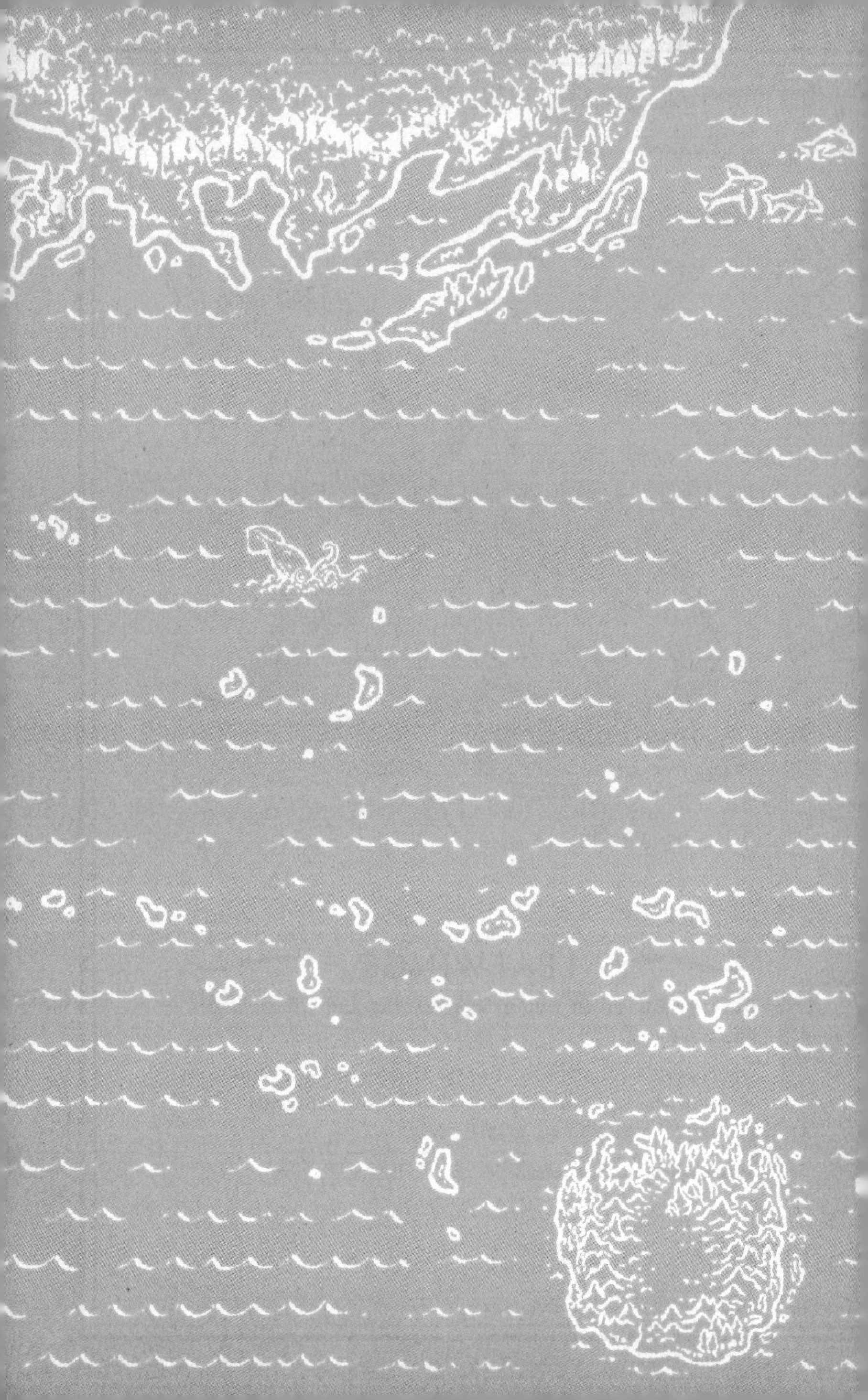

THE FORGOTTEN ISLES PROPHECY

Dear readers,

I know: What is this? This is not what normally goes here! WHERE is the new prophecy?

Well, it turns out the new prophecy is FULL OF CRYPTIC SPOILERS for this book (as one might expect from a prophecy! So inconvenient, dragons who can see the future!). Therefore, to preserve some mystery, we have decided not to put it here at the front of Book Sixteen. Never fear: The Forgotten Isles Prophecy will turn up eventually . . .

Happy reading!
With love and dragons,

PROLOGUE

Over three thousand years ago
in the forests bordering the Beetle and
Leaf Kingdoms on Pyrrhia . . .

"I don't see anything," Sorrel whispered.

"Keep your eyes on that cloud," Darkling whispered back. "They'll come from there."

Sorrel shifted his claws on the branch, flicking rain off his tail and his long, leaf-shaped wings. They'd been waiting in the misty drizzle for hours as the sun set and the sky went from pale gray to dark purple. There were so many gloomy clouds bunched together overhead that Sorrel had no idea which one Darkling meant or why she was so sure that was the one to watch.

And then — movement.

Darkling was right. Two dragon shapes dropped swiftly, silently from the clouds into the forest, barely flickers of shadows. Easy to miss if you weren't watching.

"They know about Harmony," Darkling said. "Come on." She leaped down to the forest floor, her BeetleWing scales shiny with raindrops, and Sorrel followed. Dread simmered through him. If other tribes had found out about the hidden village in the forest . . . did they also know what Queen

Euphoria and Queen Magnolia were planning? And if so, what would they do about it?

The sounds from the village were sleepy and peaceful, no louder than the rustling trees or chirping frogs around them. Darkling paused on the outskirts, scanning the shadows, then caught Sorrel's eye. After a moment, he saw them, too: two dragons perched like vultures in one of the vast oaks, peering down. The NightWing was barely visible, and the SkyWing beside him was so still she seemed like a strange, twisted branch of the tree.

Darkling and Sorrel crept closer, and gradually Sorrel's ears picked up their whispers.

"See?" hissed the NightWing. "Look at this abomination. BeetleWings *and* LeafWings, which is bad enough, but look closer, Precipice. This place has fugitives from *every* tribe." Sorrel recognized Bloodshed's voice and his heart sank even further.

"Seems like a violation of the Accords," the SkyWing agreed. She angled her head toward the village. A glimmer of moonlight reflected off something in her talons — one of the weird little things Precipice carried everywhere.

"It's grotesque," Bloodshed growled.

"It's illegal," Precipice said in a measured voice. "We have to tell the other Queens' Claws."

"We can't trust Sorrel or Darkling." Bloodshed lashed his tail. "They kept this from us. They know what their queens are up to. They must be punished."

"I'm sure the other Claws will agree," Precipice said.

Sorrel shivered. This was bad. There were nine dragons in the council of the Queens' Claws, one representing each tribe. They kept the peace by shaping and upholding the Accords of Dragonkind. If Bloodshed and Precipice thought the village was illegal . . . then Darkling and Sorrel would have to work fast to get the other tribes on their side, if they could.

But the village doesn't *break the Accords,* Sorrel thought, his claws sinking into the damp moss below him. *It's not hurting anyone. Harmony is just a safe place for any dragon to live. What's wrong with that?*

"This place undermines all of us." Bloodshed pointed a claw at one of the village houses. Outside it, a small white dragonet with leaf-shaped wings was playing with a blue-and-gold BeetleWing. An older dragonet, pale green with icicle spikes around his head, was sorting berries while he watched them.

"For example, I'm sure the IceWings would be *very* interested to know where that banished family went," Bloodshed said viciously. "They were supposed to suffer and die outside the Ice Kingdom. Not cozy up to *LeafWings* and live happily ever after in a forest village full of monsters."

Sorrel had been with Queen Magnolia the day two desperate IceWings came to her, pleading for refuge in the Leaf Kingdom. What was she supposed to do — drive them out? Kill them herself? She wasn't that kind of queen. Of course she had let them stay.

And then of course other dragons had followed, drawn by the promise of safety. That was all they wanted.

Sorrel didn't understand how anyone could look at Harmony, at these peaceful dragons living together and taking care of one another, and see a threat.

"My queen may not care," Precipice said pensively, "as long as the SkyWings here never try to return to our kingdom." She turned the object in her talons over, adjusting something without looking at it. She always did this at their meetings, too; her claws needed things to hold or move or work on while she thought.

Maybe we can talk to Precipice. Sometimes she listens. If we get her away from Bloodshed and tell her our side . . . maybe there's a chance.

"Your queen *should* care," Bloodshed spat. "This is only the beginning. Euphoria and Magnolia have bigger, more dangerous plans."

He knows, Sorrel thought with a stab of despair. *He'll turn them all against us.*

"Like what?" Precipice asked.

"Shhh," said the NightWing, and they fell silent for a long moment. Sorrel stopped himself from shivering. He was behind the dragons, pressed into a hollow between tree roots on the forest floor. There was no way Bloodshed could know he and Darkling were there.

Unless he's been a mind reader all along without telling us.

But he couldn't be. One of the rules of the Accords was that the NightWings couldn't appoint a mind reader to the Queens' Claws. No animus dragons or flamescales or leafspeakers were allowed either. And none of them could use any of their regular powers during their meetings. That was only fair.

Finally Bloodshed spoke, his voice laced with quiet menace.

"I'll tell you somewhere safe," he said. "But trust me, both tribes must be punished."

"Then we'll call for a trial, and they'll be judged by the laws of the Accords." Precipice slid her little creation into her traveling bag.

"No," said Bloodshed. "That's not enough." The NightWing hunched forward, glaring at the village. "We must burn this place to the ground."

"Not on our own," Precipice said. "We should report back to our queens and see what they want us to do."

"Fine," Bloodshed spat. "But no matter what the other tribes say, these dragons cannot be allowed to survive."

In a span of heartbeats, with a muffled snap of wings, they were gone.

Sorrel turned his head quietly to look at Darkling. She was crouched in the shadow of the oak, angry tears in her eyes.

"We'll get to the other Claws before they do," he said. "I'm sure we can get the RainWings on our side. The SeaWings, too, I think."

She shook her head. "It doesn't matter. You heard Bloodshed. He's not going to worry about the law or getting the queens to agree. He's going to come back with an army to kill everyone in Harmony." She flared her venom-tipped claws and hissed softly. "But he'll have to go through me."

Sorrel dug his talons into the carpet of moss underfoot. "What if we hide them instead? So there's no one here when the army comes? We can send them somewhere safe."

"Where?" Darkling demanded. "There *isn't* anywhere to hide from the queens on this continent."

"Then maybe there's somewhere else," Sorrel said. The drizzle was turning to rain, slipping wet tendrils between his scales. "Not on this continent. A safe place far away from the queens who want to kill them." He took one of Darkling's cold talons in his.

"We just have to find it."

PART ONE

ESCAPE FROM JADE MOUNTAIN

CHAPTER 1

My sister is a murderer.

Lightning flashed all around Umber, flickering inside the clouds like a battlefield full of smoke and dragon fire. The rain hadn't started yet, but the air was heavy with the scent of it.

She killed two dragons while trying to kill another. And she still kept trying — she wasn't going to stop, no matter how many dragons got hurt.

She's dangerous, and she's in danger. And she's my responsibility.

This was never supposed to be in Umber's talons. He was the little brother of his sibling group, the last-hatched and the smallest. He was hilarious jokes and cheerful suggestions and following orders and being agreeable. He was definitely not "shelter a murderer and figure out where she'll be safe" or "mastermind the fugitive from justice plan" or "make sure she doesn't kill again, because something's definitely wrong in there, good luck!"

But I don't have a choice.

She's my sister, and I'll do anything for her.

He could see Sora's shape winging furiously ahead of him into the darker and darker clouds. She hadn't stopped since they'd left the school, or even looked back to make sure he was behind her.

"Sora!" Umber called. "Sora, wait!"

Imagine if I lost her already. We just left the school; I just *promised to keep her safe — and keep everyone safe from her.*

He still couldn't believe his sister — quiet, sad, shattered Sora — was the one who'd set off a dragonflame cactus that killed two students.

Why hadn't he seen how unhappy she was?

Because she's been unhappy for so long, he answered himself. *Ever since Crane died.* He'd thought the school would make everything better for all of them — him, Sora, and their brother Marsh. He'd dreamed about how happy they would be. They'd be with their brother Clay. They'd meet new dragons and learn how to live in peace after growing up in a world at war.

But Sora brought the war to school with her. He understood some of that — he missed Crane, too. If he'd met an IceWing who looked like the memory of Crane's killer in his head, he might have snapped like Sora had.

Even then, he couldn't imagine trying to kill someone or his next step being "set off an explosion." He didn't ever want to fight another battle. He definitely didn't want to hurt anyone. He felt Sora's grief, but he'd never understand how she could put all the other innocent dragons in danger.

I wish she'd told me. Or Clay. We could have found her a new clawmate and gotten her away from Icicle. We could have helped her find peace. I think . . . I hope.

Will I ever see Clay again? Or any of my other siblings?

A gust of cold, wet air knocked him sideways, spraying raindrops in his face. He righted himself, shaking his head, and spotted Sora diving toward the trees below. Was this the rainforest? He couldn't tell how far they'd gone. He spiraled into a dive to follow her.

It took him a panicked few moments to find her; her brown scales blended with the shadows under the trees. But he heard her soft sobs below the sound of the branches thrashing, and he slipped through the undergrowth to her side.

She lifted her head as he brushed her wing, then buried her face in her talons again.

"Sora," he said, twining his tail with hers. "Where are we going?"

"Home," she said. She tipped her snout to give him a puzzled, tearful look. "Of course home. To Reed and Pheasant. Marsh will find us there."

Back to our siblings. To our big brother and sister, who have always taken care of us.

"Sora, we can't go home," he protested.

"I know we can't *stay* there," she said, "but we have to go talk to them — to tell them — to explain. Then they can come with us wherever we go. We can all be together, like we should be."

"We can't do that to them," Umber said, although he wanted so badly to go to Reed right now. He wanted his big-wings to say *it'll be all right* and *I'll sort this out, don't worry* and *oh sure, homicidal sisters are perfectly normal, don't fret, everyone's got one.* But it wouldn't be fair to Reed and Pheasant. "For one thing, they work for Queen Moorhen now — we'd get caught before we made it into the palace. And even if we did get to them, they should turn us in out of loyalty to her."

"Turn *me* in," she said, her eyes dark pools. "They wouldn't do that."

"You're probably right," he said. "But if they run off with us, they lose everything — and if we all get caught, they'd be in trouble, too. I don't want to put them in danger, do you?"

"They wouldn't *lose everything*!" she protested. "We'd have each other — brothers and sisters! That's all we need!"

She wasn't wrong. That was how MudWings lived; you stayed with your sibling group your whole life.

Umber realized he was already thinking like the other dragons at Jade Mountain. He was imagining families like other dragon tribes had, with falling in love, and dragonets you took care of, and work that wasn't "fight a war until you die." He'd *been* imagining it ever since he got to the school. A future with someone like Qibli, studying and maybe teaching and choosing his own path.

I'm never going to see Qibli again either.

He pushed that thought away. *That was a crush. Sora is my family.*

"You have me," he said. "I'll always be your brother. But we can't go back to the Mud Kingdom. We have to hide somewhere that the IceWings won't find us."

"It's not fair," Sora said in a trembling voice. "Icicle killed Crane and then I didn't even actually kill her and now we have to hide from her forever?"

Umber didn't know how to answer that. It wasn't only about Icicle — Sora had killed a SkyWing and a NightWing who had tribes and families that would want justice. Moorhen was a good queen. She wouldn't risk another war to protect Sora when Sora was guilty.

Should I convince Sora to turn herself in?

What if I did, and they executed her? I'd never forgive myself.

Sora's not evil, she's just . . . wounded, in a way that's hard to see.

"Maybe Clay's friend would take us in?" Sora suggested. "The one who's the queen of the RainWings now?"

Glory has to answer to her NightWing subjects, too, Umber thought. *She's one of the queens who will need Sora to be punished.*

"Let's find our own place," he said. "Maybe south?" *The opposite direction from the Mud Kingdom and Sky Kingdom.* "I think there are islands south of the rainforest. Maybe we can find one where we'll be safe and no one will ever know we're there."

Sora let out a long sigh. After a moment, she stood up. The rain was pouring through the trees now, sliding off leaves and sending sudden chilling cascades down Umber's spine.

"Fine," she said. "South. But I still don't think this is fair."

She took off again and he followed, trusting her uncanny sense of direction. Sora was always their navigator on long flights, but this time they were going off the map of the known world. Umber didn't know what they would find, or whether there actually were habitable islands there. He just wanted to get Sora far away from other dragons.

I'm not sure what's happening inside her head. She seemed genuinely remorseful about hurting Tamarin, and he was pretty sure she felt guilty about accidentally killing Carnelian and Bigtail. But she had still tried to kill Icicle a second time. The war was still raging in Sora's mind, and Umber wasn't sure who else she might hurt.

Somewhere far away, somewhere peaceful, where she can rest and get better. That's what they needed.

Then maybe one day they could come back, when all the war and death was far behind them, and Sora could atone for what she did.

Umber glanced over his shoulder, although the dark and the storm made it impossible to see the mountains they'd left behind. Rain pelted in his eyes as he thought of the future he'd dreamed of — studying with his winglet, making friends, living without the shadow of the war over everything.

That was all gone now.

He turned away and flew after Sora.

The next morning they crossed out of the rainforest and flew over a stretch of choppy water. The sky was still gray and overcast, and beady-eyed seagulls darted around them, screaming indignantly when Umber tried to catch one. He was so hungry, but Sora flew as though she had no plan to ever stop.

The southern coast of the continent rippled with inlets and wetlands full of mangroves that reminded Umber of home. But they didn't stop to sink their claws into the mud, even for a moment. They flew on, out into the wild ocean sky and over clusters of tiny islands, most of them no more than rocks.

Finally, around midmorning, they spotted a larger island covered in greenery. It was small enough that Umber could see the whole thing from the air, but bigger than the overgrown boulders they'd seen so far. He followed Sora down to land on the pebbly beach. Tiny crabs, no bigger than the tip of his claw, darted away in a flurry of movement and vanished into the sand.

Other than that, nothing moved except the waves crashing behind them and the jungle swaying ahead of them. Tangles of vines hid the interior.

Sora flumped down and covered her head with her wings.

Is this it? Umber wondered. *Do we live here now?*

"Excellent choice. So rustic," he tried to joke. "Great, uh . . . sand. Plus nonstop soothing ocean noises! Very peaceful. I always say, *any* neighbors are *too many* neighbors, am I right?"

Sora did not respond.

"Much calmer than the academy anyway?" he offered.

Maybe this was what Sora needed — space to breathe and be alone.

Alone. Umber sighed. That wasn't what he wanted at all. He loved other dragons; he loved meeting new ones and being in busy, noisy groups. But this wasn't about him; this was about taking care of Sora. Although he wasn't doing a very good job of that so far, as she still had her head under her wings and seemed to be finding him the opposite of funny.

He walked up the beach to the line of trees and peered in. Shadows, branches moving, ominous rustling. The very distinct, creeping feeling he was being watched.

As his eyes adjusted, he noticed a scratch on one of the closest trees — something that looked like a gouge left by a claw. He turned and saw another on a tree some distance to his right, and then another farther along.

Were there other dragons here?

He followed the clawmarks (if that's what they were), finding one every few trees until he reached what seemed to be the halfway point of the beach. To his left, the island curved away out of sight, and to his right, a stretch of craggy rocks trailed into the ocean and cut off the view beyond.

And here, at the midpoint, the clawmarks changed. Umber felt a chill run through his scales.

There were words carved into the trees.

NOT SAFE HERE, the jagged letters read.

KEEP GOING.

Umber felt as if sharp-taloned little birds were scuttling between his shoulder blades and crawling out to his wingtips.

Who left this message? Why isn't it safe here?

Does "keep going" mean there is *somewhere safe to go?*

He turned and ran back to where he'd left Sora — but as he came closer, he realized she wasn't there anymore. The beach was empty.

"Sora!" he shouted. "SORA!"

He found the churned-up sand where they had both landed and the depression where she'd dug herself in to rest. His own talonprints were still there, heading toward the trees . . . and here was another patch of scattered sand as if Sora had taken off.

Did she . . . leave without me? He looked up, but the sky was still and overcast. *She wouldn't do that, would she?*

Something howled from deep in the jungle and Umber spun toward the trees. Maybe she'd gone in there to look for food.

He flew up the beach and crossed the tree line, shoving aside the damp branches and strangling creeper vines. It was worlds colder in the shadowy jungle. Every tree seemed to lean toward him and he kept feeling tendrils (or snakes, *it's probably not snakes don't think about snakes*) coiling around his talons as he edged farther in.

"*You* get it," he heard Sora say, in such a normal conversational tone that he felt off-balance for a moment. "I see what you're thinking. You'd have tried to kill her, too."

"Sora?" he called.

There was a pause, and then he heard her whisper, *"He doesn't get it."*

He followed her voice until he found her a little farther in, perched high up in the canopy, on a branch of a tree that had twisted itself around another tree until the one underneath was dead.

"It's just war, right?" Sora was saying. "They kill someone we love, now it's our turn to kill them."

"Sora, who are you talking to?" Umber asked, tilting his head back.

She glanced down at him, then flicked her tail impatiently at the canopy around her.

The shadows were full of eyes.

Eyes gleaming yellow and green in the dark, eyes that blinked slowly as they drew closer. Eyes sunk deep in shaggy skulls, glowering under heavy brows.

Monkeys? Umber thought, but these were the largest, hairiest, most sinister-looking monkeys he had ever seen — twice the size of Winter's scavenger, and covered in heavy, dense gray fur. One jumped to the end of Sora's branch, grinned down at Umber, and yawned to show off teeth as huge as a full-grown dragon's claws. Its face was striped red and blue and its growl was low and muttering.

"My point exactly," Sora said to it.

"Sora," Umber said cautiously. "I think we should get out of here." He would deal with *my sister thinks she can converse with menacing monkeys* once they were well out of range of those teeth.

"Yeah, obviously," Sora scoffed. "This island belongs to them." She snapped her wings out, and the gathering crowd hissed. "I'm not *rude*, I don't *pick fights* with creatures who *haven't* wronged me or, you know, murdered my loved ones." She snorted and leaped into the air, flying up through the leaves into the sky.

"Come onnnn, Umber!" her voice trailed back to him.

The eyes all turned to Umber.

"Uh. Sorry," he said, taking a step backward. He couldn't fly out the way Sora had gone. If he tried, he'd have to go straight through the crowd of monkeys, which would make him an easy target for anything large and shaggy that felt like jumping on him and maybe biting off his ears or whatever shaggy teethy monsters liked to do.

"I'll just . . . go," he said.

One of the creatures let out an ear-piercing shriek and threw itself down the tree toward him, faster than any animal should be able to move. Umber turned and bolted back toward the beach, tripping over every branch and smashing his head and wings into tree trunks as he tried to run.

He didn't look back, even when the howling felt as though it was right on his heels, and as soon as he hit the open beach he flung himself into the air. He hoped he was just imagining the graze of teeth against his back talons.

The trees shook with angry growls as he soared out of their reach.

Sora was up in the sky, doing little flips around a wisp of cloud.

"There's another island that way," she said, pointing. "Let's go check it out!"

Umber followed her, exhausted, his heart pounding.

Is she all right? he wondered. *That wasn't normal, was it?*

Maybe they were both just tired and overemotional. She probably didn't *really* think she'd been having a conversation with the monkeys. She didn't realize she'd left him in danger; she would never do that on purpose. *Right?*

The next island was all rocks and it was covered in angry, giant-beaked birds defending their nests. Sora and Umber circled a few times without landing, and Umber thought he saw an arrow scratched into a few of the rocks, pointing south.

The island after that looked promising at first, muddy and crisscrossed with little rivers, but as they got closer Umber spotted another message spelled out in rocks on the beach. **NOT SAFE.**

KEEP GOING.

"Sora," he said tentatively.

"I see it," she said. "Let's not land here."

"I wonder where someone wants us to 'keep going' *to*," he said.

"I guess we'll find out," she said with a shrug, which was quite a bit more casual than Umber felt about it.

They flew over three more islands (and several rock

formations and a lot of ocean) with similar messages, until finally it started growing dark. Umber's wings ached and his heart ached and his stomach was *so empty*.

"I think — I think I need to rest," he said.

Sora pointed to a crescent-shaped island off to their right. The two arms of the island curved around a bay that glimmered with phosphorescent jellyfish and silvery reflections of the moons. The sand was soft and warm under their talons as they landed. Umber didn't see any messages, and even if there was one, he was too exhausted to "keep going" tonight.

He collapsed to the beach and dragged sand around him with his wings. Sora walked up and down the shoreline, frowning, then came over and studied the nest he was making. Finally she dug herself in next to him and rested her chin on his shoulder.

Her breathing slowed and evened out, and he felt her warmth spread through his cold scales. For a moment, he could pretend they were back in the swamps, with Marsh and Crane and Pheasant curled up beside them and Reed standing watch for any danger. For a moment, everything felt normal and safe.

He was almost asleep when he heard her whisper, "Thank you for coming with me, Umber."

This is why I left Jade Mountain Academy with her, he thought. *She's my sister and I'll always protect her. That's what brothers and sisters do.*

His heart finally calmed down, and under the rising moons, he fell asleep.

In his dreams, he walked through long empty halls in an unfamiliar place, looking for Sora — or Clay, or Reed, or anyone he knew. He could hear laughter echoing in the distance, but he couldn't find anyone. Room after room was empty, filled with nothing but echoes.

Something brushed his ankle, and when he looked down, he realized there were hundreds of snakes covering the floor. All at once the room was wall-to-wall snakes, slithering and hissing and sliding and winding around and around and around his ankles.

He tried to back away, to turn and run, to leap into the air, but a giant python had him in its grip, and it dragged him ruthlessly into the hissing scales. The snakes rose around him like a wave — like water rising, rushing into his mouth.

Umber woke up with a start, choking on seawater.

A huge tentacle was wrapped around his front leg, dragging him into the ocean.

CHAPTER 2

"Sora!" Umber screamed, clawing at the wet sand below him. A wave swamped over his head and he came up sputtering. "Sora, help!" He tried to dig into the ground with his talons, but his claws slipped right through the sand. A trail of helpless gouges followed him into the sea.

He thrashed his wings and struggled, but the tentacle was a vise of stone around his ankle. It was impossible to shake, relentless as it dragged him toward a huge dark shape under the water. Umber saw the glint of teeth and more tentacles swarming around it.

A kraken. He'd heard of the legendary sea monsters, large enough to eat an entire adult dragon, but he'd thought they were only a story — a tale told to scare little SeaWings.

"Sora!" Umber screamed again. He twisted to look back at where he'd been sleeping.

His sister was awake. She was sitting up, staring at him, frozen in terror.

"Sora, help me!" Umber cried.

She didn't move. He could see the horror on her face and the look in her eyes that meant she was sinking away from what was happening in front of her. She was only partly here; part of her was trapped in a terrible memory.

She can't help me. She's too lost.

Another wave crashed over him, and when he surfaced, he was too far out to touch the bottom anymore. The kraken had been moving slowly before, trying to sneak him off the beach without waking him; now it towed him so quickly that water went up his snout and his wings tangled around him.

I can't leave Sora alone. I can't let her lose another sibling right in front of her eyes.

He took a deep breath and dove under, clawing at the tentacle. His talons couldn't pierce the rubbery skin or dislodge its grip. The maw of gleaming teeth drew closer.

I'm going to die, Umber thought. He wasn't sure if he was crying; his eyes were already stinging from the salt water. *I'm going to die, and Sora is going to watch it happen, and then she'll never be herself again.*

I left Jade Mountain for nothing.

I did nothing with my life, and now it's over.

The water surged strangely forward and then, suddenly, strong wings wrapped around him. Warm scales pressed against his back, and a talon reached past his face and rested gently on the kraken's arm. The kraken stopped pulling, letting Umber float for a moment in the water.

Sora?

No . . . that's not my sister.

The dragon beside him was a bit bigger than Sora or Umber, maybe the size of Reed or Clay. The scales Umber could see were dappled dark red and gold with hints of green.

A RainWing?

The kraken's tentacle rippled from the stranger's talon down toward the large, dark eye. And then . . . it let go.

The tentacle withdrew and the kraken faded back into the depths of the ocean.

Umber felt the stranger's arms close around him. Red-gold-green wings unfurled in his peripheral vision as the other dragon swam toward the surface, carrying Umber to safety.

They staggered onto the beach and Umber collapsed with a *flump* in the wet sand.

A face appeared above him, silhouetted by the moons overhead. Maybe Umber was delirious from nearly dying, but it looked like the kindest, most handsome, noblest face he'd ever seen in his whole almost-too-short life.

"Are you all right?" the dragon asked.

Even his *voice* was kind and handsome and noble. The most perfect voice in the world. As if the moons could sing. (Umber was definitely a little delirious.)

The stranger took Umber's front talon in both of his and studied the ring of marks left by the kraken. "I'm so sorry I didn't save you sooner."

"How?" Umber breathed. "I mean — who are you?" He felt as though he should sit up, but he also didn't want to move and have those warm talons let go of him. Also, the world seemed to be doing a bit of a weird swooping in and out thing.

"My name's Mulberry," said the other dragon.

"Mulberry," he echoed. *Perfect name. Amazing name.* "I'm Umber."

Mulberry gave him a shy sideways smile. "Hi, Umber."

"Thank you," Umber said. "For saving me. I'm so lucky you exist. I mean, that you're here. Lucky that you were here."

Mulberry looked back down at Umber's claws and let go *(reluctantly? maybe reluctantly?)*. "Oh, I . . . I've kind of been watching you."

"Watching us?" Umber asked. He sat up slowly, shaking wet sand off his wings, but carefully, so that none would get on Mulberry. "Why?"

"It's what I do," Mulberry said. His tail traced a worried pattern in the sand behind him. "I'm supposed to make sure any dragons who come this way are safe. That's why I should have gotten here sooner. I knew the kraken sometimes hunts in this bay — I should have been more watchful. I'm sorry."

"Hey, no, you saved me. You were amazing." Umber tentatively nudged one of Mulberry's wings with his, which was when he realized for the first time that Mulberry's wings were different from his own. They were shaped like . . . like giant *leaves*. Most of his scales were dark red edged with gold, with flecks of gold and green and warm autumn orange here and there. Gold scales lined his dark green eyes.

This wasn't a RainWing; Mulberry was something else.

"How did you actually — I mean, what did you do?" Umber asked. "To scare the kraken away? Do you have an 'enemies, quake in fear' face you're hiding really well right now?" He couldn't imagine running away from Mulberry's face. It was the kind of face someone would want to look at forever.

Mulberry laughed. "I didn't scare it," he said. "I asked it to let you go."

"Whaaaaaaaa," Umber said incoherently. "What?! You can speak kraken?"

"No, I can sort of, um . . . sense what it's feeling? And share my feelings with it? So I just felt *please don't take this one*, and it heard me and let you go. Does that make sense?"

"No," Umber said promptly. "Not even a little."

"We think it's kind of like how LeafWings can communicate with plants," Mulberry said. "Like leafspeak, but I have it with, um, everything?" He waved his talons in a sweet, bewildered way.

"What's a LeafWing?" Umber asked. He still felt sort of shaky and unreal, as if his body couldn't quite believe he wasn't dead right now. He was *here*, the sand was *real* below his talons, he could have a conversation, and yet his heart was still pounding and he felt not entirely there at all.

"Oh, right," Mulberry said. "You're from Pyrrhia. LeafWings are a tribe of dragons from the other continent, Pantala."

"Other — is that where you're from? Are you a LeafWing?"

"Sort of; more like half a LeafWing," Mulberry said. "I'm not from either continent. I'm from a safe place, not far from here. I'm — I'm supposed to bring you there, if that's what you need. A safe place to hide, I mean."

Umber looked down the beach toward Sora. His sister was still crouched where they'd been sleeping, now with her head buried under her wings. She didn't seem to have noticed that Umber had been rescued.

"How did you know?" he asked softly.

Mulberry gave him a sympathetic look. "Most dragons who come this way are looking for somewhere to be safe. There's a lot to run away from, back there." He gestured north with one of his wings. "I've found so many dragons fleeing from wars on both continents. Is that why you're here?"

Umber glanced at Sora again and sighed. He wanted nothing more than to say, *yes, that's it, please take us, please tell me how to help her, please let me rest.* He wanted to follow this kind-eyed dragon anywhere he went.

"No," he said sadly. "We can't go with you. I'm sorry. My sister — she's not safe to be with other dragons right now. I'm afraid she might hurt someone else."

Mulberry was watching him intently. "But I can't leave you," he said. "It's dangerous everywhere else. The Court of Refuge doesn't care what you're running from; they'll take you in and keep you safe, whatever it is."

"But it's *her,*" Umber said helplessly. "It's inside her. I can't promise — I don't know what to do, and if she hurt anyone —"

Mulberry reached over and covered Umber's talon with his own. "We can help you," he said. "I know we can."

Umber looked down at Mulberry's warm, gold-tipped claws wrapped around his. "Your magic. Can you — um, can you sense what other dragons are feeling, too?"

"Sometimes." Mulberry ducked his head. "I mean, yes, usually."

Ha ha, whoops. So it doesn't even have to be written all over my face that I like him. "Could you try it with Sora?" Umber said in a rush. "I don't know what's happening inside her head, but maybe you can tell whether she's too dangerous to bring back to your dragons?" *Maybe she just needs to be away from IceWings. Maybe if she never sees anyone like Icicle again, she'll be all right.*

"Sure," Mulberry said. "Absolutely. Let me try." He picked up an orange silk sling bag from the sand and settled it over one shoulder. Umber could see that it had several different fruits in it; he guessed that Mulberry had dropped it before flying into the ocean to save him.

Umber led Mulberry back along the beach and paused next to his sister. She looked like a petrified statue, as though she'd tensed every muscle in her body against the outside world and was planning to stay that way forever.

"Sora," he said gently, brushing one of her wings. "Sora, it's all right. I'm here."

"Not really," she mumbled. "It's not real, none of this is real."

"The kraken didn't take me," Umber said. He felt more anchored to the world once he said it out loud. He tried shaking her lightly. "Sora, this dragon saved me. His name is Mulberry and he might be able to help us. Sora, come back."

"May I?" Mulberry asked.

Umber stepped back with a helpless gesture. Mulberry rested his talons lightly on Sora's wings, above her head.

A moment passed, and then another, and then Sora's scales began to ripple gently, just like the kraken's tentacle. Her wings shivered, and slowly they opened. Mulberry stepped back as she lifted her head. Her expression was confused but calmer than Umber had seen it in months.

"Umber?" she said. "I thought you were gone."

"I'm here," Umber said again. "This is Mulberry."

"You feel . . . safe," Sora said wonderingly to Mulberry. "What tribe are you?"

"I'm a hybrid," Mulberry said, unfurling his wings. "First-generation LeafWing-SkyWing. My parents met at the Court of Refuge after they'd both escaped different wars."

"SkyWings," Sora said excitedly. "You're our allies in the war! Umber, we can hide with them!"

Umber noticed that she didn't ask what a LeafWing was or anything about the Court of Refuge. "Sora, the war is over," he said. "Remember?"

She frowned at him.

"There's no war in the Court of Refuge," Mulberry said. "We can protect you." He turned to Umber. "I sense no malevolence in her; only fear and confusion. It doesn't scare me. You would both be welcome with open wings."

"Are you sure?" Umber asked. His heart felt balanced on

a cliff edge. Could this be real? A real place where he wouldn't be alone, where Sora would be safe? How could somewhere like that exist and nobody knew about it?

"A-million-times-over sure," Mulberry said, and his smile was firelight and blankets and leaves in the wind, warmth in the cold and shelter in the rain. He held out his talon and Umber clasped it, his heart racing. "Come with me."

CHAPTER 3

It was a long flight to the Court of Refuge: two days of flying over many islands and long stretches of sea with no land in sight. Umber wasn't sure he would ever have found it on his own, even with the "keep going" messages.

He asked Mulberry about those the first night, when they stopped to sleep on an island that was barely a sandbar in the ocean. They'd caught a couple of fish to share, and Mulberry was showing them how to dry seaweed over the fire so they could eat that, too.

"Have you left messages on all these islands?" Umber asked, flicking his tail at the dark sea out beyond the waves. "Aren't you worried that evil dragons might see them and come find you?"

Mulberry paused with a sheet of seaweed draped over his claws. He looked out to sea, where Umber had pointed, with an expression like the entire concept of evil dragons had never occurred to him.

"Maybe a little," he said finally. "But that's why I'm on watch. I'm supposed to figure out which dragons are threats and which ones need our help. It would be hard to find the Court of Refuge without me." He nudged Umber with his tail. "I'll make sure no one follows you, don't worry."

Who might come after us? Umber thought. *IceWings? Queen Ruby? Glory? None of those are* evil. He glanced at Sora, who was picking apart a crab she had roasted. *But neither is my sister.*

"It's not only you, is it?" Umber asked Mulberry. "Watching all these islands alone?"

He didn't know how to interpret the expression that crossed Mulberry's face. Worry, maybe — worry that rested like twenty krakens on Mulberry's shoulders.

"It's just me right now," he said. "It's my responsibility."

"Maybe I can help you?" Umber offered. "Once Sora is settled, maybe I can come back out here with you and be a watcher, too? I'd love to help other dragons get to safety."

"Oh," Mulberry said, setting the seaweed down without meeting Umber's eyes. "Um, that's a really sweet offer. Thank you." Something about the way he said it sounded more like a no than a yes, though.

Did I say something wrong? Umber wondered. *Maybe he doesn't like whatever feelings he's picking up from me.* Puzzled and a little sad, he dug one of his front talons into the sand and unearthed a pale pink shell.

As he was picking it up, Mulberry reached over and covered Umber's talon with his. A wave of anxious kindness swept through Umber, spreading like the ripples he'd seen in the kraken's tentacle and Sora's wings. There were no specific words, but the feeling was *warmth, curiosity, gentleness,* and *no, no, I really like you, too.*

He looked up in surprise and Mulberry let go of him quickly, as though he'd said too much, even though he hadn't said anything at all.

"Are there a lot of SkyWings where we're going?" Sora asked, tossing aside her dismembered crab carcass. "And MudWings?"

"More SkyWings than MudWings right now," Mulberry said, smiling at her. "But everyone is welcome. Dragons have been coming to our island for centuries, so there are a lot of hybrids — some whose families go so far back they don't look like any specific tribe anymore."

Sora pulled her wings closer. "Hybrids," she echoed softly. Umber knew there were more hybrids in Pyrrhia now; the war had brought tribes into contact that normally stayed far apart. The one he knew for sure himself was Sunny, but he'd seen a few in battles and he suspected he'd met others without realizing it.

"Wait, centuries?" Umber asked. "The Court of Refuge is that old?"

"It hasn't always been called that," Mulberry explained. "That's kind of a new name. But there have been dragons here for over three thousand years. Maybe someone at court can give you a history lesson, if you're curious."

"Do you have scrolls?" Umber asked. "Sora loves scrolls."

"We do," Mulberry said, shooting her an anxious smile. Sora was staring moodily out at the sea and missed it.

"You know, that's enough questions for tonight. Let's play a game," Umber said. He wanted to make Mulberry smile for real, and maybe it would help bring Sora back to earth, too. "My brothers and sisters play this all the time." He flipped the shell he'd found into Mulberry's talons. "Now you say a favorite food and flip it to Sora, and then she has to name one and flip it to me. If you can't think of another food, you have to suggest a new theme instead. It should go quickly, without thinking too long."

"Tuna," Mulberry said, tossing the shell to Sora.

"Gross," she said. "Crocodile."

"Crocodile is *much* more gross than tuna!" Mulberry protested.

Umber caught the shell, laughing. "Blackberries."

"Ugh, such a coward's answer," Sora said, rolling her eyes.

"Says the dragon who *eats* all the blackberries but never crawls through the bramble thickets to pick them," Umber teased. "It's *absolutely* as hazardous as wrestling crocodiles!"

"I like blackberries, too," Mulberry said. He flipped the shell to Sora again. "Carrots."

"What is wrong with you two?" Sora asked. "Bear."

"Yeah, right. We had bear *once* at a campfire in the mountains with SkyWings," Umber said. "And I felt bad about it because bears are kind of cute, actually."

"Well, I liked it," Sora said.

"I've never had bear," Mulberry said. "We don't have bears anywhere in the, um — Isle." Umber noticed the pause before "Isle," as though there was another name for it, or a word Mulberry was leaving out.

"Cheese," Umber said, flipping the shell to Mulberry.

"Yesssssssss," Mulberry said fervently as Sora rolled her eyes again. "Ice cream."

"What?" Sora said, catching the shell. "What are those two words together?"

"You've never had ice cream?" Mulberry said, fluttering his wings. "It's *amazing*. We mash bananas and milk together and freeze it and add things and there are more steps I don't know, but the first step was I had to bring ice from the southern snowplace to make it, and now we have it on special occasions and it's my favorite thing. One of our IceWings taught us how to make it a few years ago."

Sora leaped to her feet, showering them both with sand, and stormed off to the other end of the sandbar.

"Oh no," Mulberry said. His face was picturesquely woeful. "I'm so sorry. What did I say?"

"She has a problem with IceWings," Umber said. "It's not you." He picked up the shell from where Sora had dropped it and placed it gently in Mulberry's palm. "I can't wait to try ice cream."

"I — I hope you like the Court of Refuge," Mulberry said, closing his claws around the shell.

I'll like anywhere you are, Umber thought. He knew he shouldn't say that out loud; he'd just met this dragon. *The court turned out someone like you, so it must be pretty great*. He couldn't say that either. His first impression didn't seem to be changing. Mulberry still had the kindest face Umber had ever seen.

"I hope the Court of Refuge likes *us*," he finally managed to say.

"They will," Mulberry said. "It's really a good place. A safe place."

Umber tilted his head. "You don't have to convince me," he said. "I trust you."

Was it his imagination, or did Mulberry flinch? *Is there something he's not telling me?*

"We should get some sleep," Mulberry said. "Long flight tomorrow."

"Sure," Umber said. He watched Mulberry turn in a circle a few times before curling up and closing his eyes.

Umber felt uneasy . . . but Mulberry had saved his life; of course he trusted him. Whatever wasn't being said, Umber would find it out soon enough, surely. And it wasn't as though he and Sora had anywhere else to go.

It'll be all right. Whatever it is, we'll face it together.

Me and Sora.

And me and Mulberry.

On the third day of flying they reached an island that was much bigger than any of the ones he'd seen before. Umber couldn't see an end to it in any direction. It might as well have been as big as the continent behind them, except Mulberry assured him it was less than a quarter the size of Pyrrhia.

They flew over rugged coastline, then a forest noisy with

clicks, squawks, and howls, and finally up into a range of mountains that looked as though the land had been crumpled by huge talons. These mountains weren't as tall as the Claws of the Clouds. The only snow was on peaks in the far distance; they were mostly brown, with scatterings of green here and there.

Mulberry led them into a crevasse between mountain folds, twisting right and then left and then right again. And there, at the end, was a wall as tall as the mountains itself, filling the entire canyon. It was the same color as the canyon around it, a sort of rusty reddish brown, as if it had grown right out of the landscape. Square, rough-cut windows dotted the wall all the way to the top, and Umber saw curious dragon faces peeking out of several of them.

At the base of the wall was an archway with no door, and standing just inside the archway was a tall statue of a dragon.

No door? Umber thought as he swooped down behind Mulberry. *Then how do they seal this off when they're attacked? How do they keep out enemy dragons?*

Maybe they don't need one because there are no enemy dragons here, he thought with a weird little jump of hope in his chest. Maybe this place would be peaceful, like Jade Mountain Academy.

Or . . . like Jade Mountain Academy should have been, if it weren't for Sora. The flicker of hope faded as he glanced over at his sister.

Mulberry landed in front of the archway instead of flying through it, resting his talons in a scrubby patch of grass near a dried-up streambed. Umber and Sora touched down beside him.

"The Court of Refuge is through there," Mulberry said, and Umber didn't think he was imagining the thread of worry in Mulberry's voice. He definitely wasn't imagining the chorus of whispers coming from the windows overhead.

Carved above the door, but scuffed as though someone had ineffectively chiseled at it, were the words FOR THE SAFETY AND PROTECTION OF ALL.

That's reassuring, Umber thought. *Especially if "all" really means every dragon . . . no matter what they did.*

Suddenly the statue in the shadow of the arch stirred, and Umber realized it wasn't a statue at all. She was an adult SkyWing, with dark red scales and a lean, angular face, wearing a gold circlet on her head and thin chains of gold in her ears and around her ankles.

"Mulberry," she said reverently, as though his arrival was the most glorious thing that had ever happened to the world. "You found new friends for us."

"This is Umber and his sister Sora," Mulberry said. "And this is my mother, Queen Beryl." He hesitated as Beryl lifted one talon toward them. "Mother . . . I think we should —"

"Sora, what a lovely name," Beryl interrupted him. Umber's sister was already walking toward the archway, and Umber felt a shiver at the way her eyes and Beryl's were both shining. "Welcome to the Court of Refuge. We're so happy you're here."

"Me too," Sora said shyly, stepping through the arch.

Beryl wrapped one wing around her protectively. "How

wonderful that Mulberry found you," she said to Umber. "Let me show you both around." She spread her other wing toward the light at the far end of the archway and smiled.

Umber took a step forward and Mulberry reached to catch his wrist.

"Wait —" Mulberry said. "Maybe this isn't —"

"Mulberry," Beryl said in a fond but reproving tone, as though he had taken the last cookie without asking.

"What is it?" Umber asked Mulberry softly. "Did you change your mind about Sora? Is she too dangerous to bring here?"

"It's . . ." Mulberry pressed his claws into his forehead, closing his eyes. "No, no, nothing."

"Don't worry," Umber said, patting Mulberry's scales where they touched his. "If we don't fit in, or if you start to worry about her, we'll just leave. I promise. We won't cause trouble."

"Come on, Umber!" Sora called. She was already halfway down the tunnel, light and shadow from the other side streaked across her scales.

Umber clambered up the slope and stepped through the arch, following his sister, like he always would. Beryl smiled down at him and rested one of her elegant red talons on his head.

"Yes," she said. "So very, very happy you are here."

CHAPTER 4

Umber had met some sinister dragons in his time, so he felt experienced enough to say there was nothing *sinister* about Queen Beryl. She seemed genuinely pleased to see him and Sora; she was also over-the-moons proud of Mulberry. *Intense*, maybe, was the word instead. She was certainly . . . intense.

"Come on, darling," she said, beckoning to her son. "The king is waiting."

"King?" Umber said, startled. Beside him, Mulberry leaned in to accept a hug and a gentle pat on the head from his mother.

"Mulberry's father and I are blessed to be the current rulers of the court," Beryl explained.

"Together?" Sora said from the other end of the tunnel.

"We are devoted to doing what's best for our dragon community," the queen said with her serene intensity. "They need us."

"So you're actually *Prince* Mulberry," Umber joked as Beryl swept away toward Sora. "I notice you didn't mention that before."

"Gah, ack, no," Mulberry said, wrinkling his snout. "Don't think of me that way! I'm not fancy; I'm *so* normal."

"Mulberry!" shrieked at least six different voices as they reached the end of the tunnel. Umber blinked, briefly blinded by the sun, and when his eyes adjusted, Mulberry was surrounded by a crowd of excited dragons. Fluttering wings of all different colors barged into the space between them, shoving Umber away.

"What did you see this time?"

"What did you bring back?"

"Any new birds?"

"Any news from the continents?"

Umber thought it was sort of strange that they were asking Mulberry for news instead of him or Sora, but he got the impression these dragons wanted to talk to Mulberry more than they actually wanted answers to their questions. Their expressions were almost as adoring as Beryl's.

And their wings — he'd never seen some of these wing shapes before. There were green leaf-shaped wings like Mulberry's, but also some in rose and orange and aquamarine shaped like butterfly wings and others that flickered with black diamond trace patterns like dragonflies. There was a dark blue NightWing with webbed talons and pale blue patterns along his wings. A dragon with a SandWing barb on her tail had wings that rippled into different colors, purple to yellow and back again. And there were dragons whose tribe — or tribes — he couldn't begin to guess.

Mulberry stood at the center of the whirlwind, giving

each dragon a moment in the sunlight of his smile, holding the talons that reached out to him and leaning into each hug. He looked so sweetly happy to see each and every one of them. *He's like this with everyone,* Umber thought. *Kind and friendly. It's not just with me.*

I have to remember that. I mustn't read into the way he looks at me.

He was probably also imagining the hint of exhaustion behind Mulberry's eyes. Or it was normal, after they'd flown so far in the last few days. Mulberry was probably tired, but happy to be home with all his friends. Relieved to hand over the responsibility of Umber and Sora to someone else.

Umber couldn't let himself feel that relief. Sora was his responsibility all the time, even with Queen Beryl's wing around her. He turned and saw the two of them standing by a statue in the courtyard — an actual statue this time.

The courtyard was sunny and dotted with fountains and fruit trees. Oranges, cherries, lemons, and plums glowed like jewels in the trees around him. The space stretched away from the entrance tunnel for several dragon lengths until it ended in a startlingly huge castle that seemed to glitter in the sunshine.

Umber had been to Queen Moorhen's palace and the SandWing stronghold where Queen Thorn now ruled. He'd thought both were impressive but much too big. The mud sleephouse where he'd grown up with his siblings was just the right size for six dragons who liked being together. Walking around the Mud Kingdom palace, Umber had wondered if Queen Moorhen often lost her siblings in the winding halls, and whether all that space made her feel lonely.

This castle was as large as Thorn's stronghold, maybe larger. Instead of mud or yellow bricks, it was made of warm brown wood that was polished until it glowed. The shape was unusual, too, with loops and edges like extra wings or giant scales poking out from all the sides. It filled the valley between two mountain peaks, and the sky beyond it was clear, sunny, and the bluest color Umber had ever seen.

"Is it absolutely terrible back on the continent?" Beryl asked Sora as Umber approached them.

"Yes," Sora said fervently.

"No, it isn't," Umber interjected. "It's so much better than it used to be. The war is over. There's a new SandWing queen and a new SkyWing queen and a wonderful new school and everyone's at peace now."

Sora gave Beryl a very clear "he doesn't know anything" look, but Beryl had transferred her intense gaze to Umber.

"New SkyWing queen?" she asked. Her tail flipped slowly from side to side.

"Yes — her name is Ruby?" Umber offered. He wondered how long ago Beryl had left Pyrrhia and whether she'd once lived in the SkyWing palace. Did she know Scarlet or Ruby? "Scarlet disappeared; no one knows where she is."

"Hmmmm," Beryl said. Umber didn't know how to interpret the small, satisfied smile on her face. "I don't remember a princess named Ruby. But how delightful to hear of Scarlet's dethroning in my own lifetime. You'll have to give me all the details later."

"Who's this, Your Majesty?" Sora asked, pointing at the statue. It was abstractly carved of blue-gray stone, but it was still clearly a SeaWing, posed with her talons outstretched toward the castle as though it were the sun and she was making it rise. Shells that shimmered deep blue, pale green, and silver were embedded along the lines of her wings and along the cheekbones of her serene face, like the incandescent Aquatic patterns Umber had noticed on Tsunami and Turtle.

"That's Waterfall," Beryl said reverently. She rested one talon on the base of the statue, where the name was carved. "She built our palace almost two thousand years ago and enchanted it to stand forever."

"Enchanted?" Umber echoed, startled.

"She was an *animus*?" Sora breathed.

"Why would a SeaWing animus come here?" Umber asked.

"Because she needed the Court of Refuge, and it needed her," Beryl said. "It calls to anyone who seeks a haven. It is the only good place in this whole world. As long as *we* are in charge of it, that is."

Umber didn't want to argue with the queen only moments after arriving, but he thought of Queen Moorhen's sunlit palace, of the Diamond Spray Delta where he'd grown up with his brothers and sisters, and of Jade Mountain Academy and all the care that had gone into building it. *Maybe one day she'll see them,* he thought, *and then she'll know there can be other safe places. At least . . . for some dragons.*

He glanced at Sora, who really did need a place like this. *I hope she can be happy here. I hope it brings her peace.*

Beryl cocked her head. "Here they come," she said. "Hold still."

Now Umber heard something, too: a strange whirring sound coming toward them, like a coil of rattlesnakes descending from the clouds.

"What is it?" Sora whispered, edging closer to Umber.

"Think of it as an official welcome," Beryl said in a bored voice. "We can't turn them off, so everyone has to put up with it."

Something small zipped up in front of Umber's face and he jumped backward.

It was a tiny metal dragon, flashing gold and copper in the sunlight, with its wings beating a hundred flaps a minute. It was small enough to trap between his talons, if it ever stopped moving long enough for him to catch it. But it never stopped: like a hummingbird, it darted around him, studying him with bright silver eyes.

Then suddenly there were seven more, buzzing in sharp circles around Umber and Sora. Two of them flickered down to poke at Umber's wrists and ankles, tapping his scales lightly with their gold claws and clicking their jaws at one another as though they were puzzled.

"Whoa," Umber said, lifting one of his talons so the

little creatures could examine it. "They're so small! Can they talk?"

"Name," barked the one hovering in front of his snout.

"Oh, they can! That's amazing! I'm Umber," he answered. "What about you? What's your name?"

"No questions," the little dragon snapped. "Category?"

"Um." He glanced at Beryl. "MudWing?"

"Category Four," Beryl said. "Don't worry, it doesn't mean anything. They just want a number; nobody knows why, so we make them up."

"Four," echoed the creature. It darted over to Sora. "Name."

"I don't like it," Sora said anxiously. She backed away from the metal dragon, trying to hide behind Umber's wings. "Go away! Leave me alone!"

"Oh dear, no," Beryl said. "Don't make it mad. They're harmless as long as you don't antagonize them."

The one that had spoken pressed closer to Sora, eyes narrowing. "Name and category," it said again, and Umber thought he heard a little extra buzz under the question.

"She's Sora," Umber said. "Uh, I don't know, Category Ten? What happens if they do get mad?"

"Nothing permanent," Beryl said, which Umber thought was kind of an alarming answer. The four around him were now tapping his tail and wings as though they were taking measurements. Sora swiped at one as it dove toward her, but it evaded her claws easily.

"Sora, just let it do whatever it's doing," he said. "It only tickles a little. They're not scary."

Sora hissed at the one fluttering around her tail.

"Do they have names?" Umber asked Beryl. "Are they alive? Can you talk to them?"

She shrugged. "I don't think so. They don't respond to anyone, and as soon as they're done, they'll disappear back into the castle. They're not that interesting, really."

Umber wildly disagreed; he'd never seen anything so weird and shiny and clever. And each tiny dragon was a little different. One had metallic pink scales between the gold, another shimmered dark green and coppery orange, and he saw blue and purple flickering under other wings.

"If they're not alive — are they magic? Did Waterfall enchant these, too?" Umber asked.

"No," Beryl said tightly. "These have been here since the first settlers."

Sora swatted at another little dragon and this time it swerved around and jabbed her talon with its claws. She let out a little gasp and slammed her eyes shut, freezing in place.

"Are you all right?" Umber asked. Three of the little dragons landed on her and started walking from nose to tail and wingtip to wingtip, clicking their teeth. Sora didn't move or open her eyes. "Sora?" He reached for her talon and another tiny dragon swooped down and batted him away.

"She's fine," Beryl said. "Give it a moment." With a whir of metal wings, the little dragons suddenly rose into the air and flew off toward the castle. "See? All done."

"But what are they?" Sora blurted, opening her eyes. "Why are they here?"

"Nobody knows," Beryl said with an elegant shrug. "Or cares. Let's go find the king." She set off toward the castle. Umber noticed that she kept glancing up into the fruit trees as she passed them, as though she might spot the king among the oranges.

"Did it hurt you?" Umber asked Sora quietly.

She held out the talon it had touched. A small red dot shone in her palm, like a tiny drop of blood.

"It's all right," she said. "They're gone. Everything's fine now." She pulled away from him and hurried after Beryl.

Umber glanced back at Mulberry, but the prince was still swarmed by dragons trying to get his attention. Two of the miniature metal dragons were there, too, circling Mulberry and humming at each other, wings catching the sunlight in little flickers.

What are they doing? Umber wondered. *What do they want? What does "category" mean?*

What did they do to Sora?

As he turned to follow Beryl, he saw a flash of light overhead and realized they hadn't all gone back into the castle. Three of them were still out here, perched in the highest branches of the fruit trees that lined the path.

And all three of them had their eerie silver eyes pinned on his sister.

CHAPTER 5

Umber's unease faded as they stepped through the open front door of the castle. Sunshine poured through skylights high above them, making the walls glow like the warm brown scales of his MudWing siblings around a campfire. It felt like being gently hugged by a tree.

A pattern of rainbow opals dotted the floor, leading in looping paths out each of the five doors and up the grand spiraling staircase ahead of them. The staircase looked as if it had grown there, and like it was still growing, toward distant floors and sunlit balconies and silken bridges to other towers. Columns like tree trunks dotted the grand hall, covered with carved dragon scales and dappled with engraved leaves, raindrops, jellyfish, and butterflies.

On four of the columns, a large scroll hung tucked into the scales, with a dragon's face painted on it. The dragon was pale rose pink with glittering gold scales along her snout, silvery IceWing spikes around her head, and ice-blue eyes. The words below her face said: NORTHERN LIGHTS CONCERT: NEXT TWO-FULL-MOONS NIGHT!

Umber saw Sora narrow her eyes at the nearest one. *It's just an IceWing hybrid, Sora — please don't get upset*. He felt a panicked impulse to distract her, but the queen spoke before he could think of how.

"Hmmm," Beryl said, shooting a look at the ceiling. "Let's try the throne room."

As they followed her up the stairs, Umber thought he saw a flash of phosphorescent green dart along an empty balcony overhead. Curious faces peered out of doorways at them and they passed a trio of small, multicolored dragonets playing on a curve of the stairs. Umber noticed that two of the dragonets didn't have wings at all. Dragons with no wings! How did they survive? He wondered if they had winged siblings who took care of them.

"Sora," he whispered. "Are you all right?"

"You don't need to keep asking me that," she said. "You're not my bigwings, Umber."

"I know," he said, feeling awkward. He didn't mean to annoy her. *But Reed isn't here. No one is here but me*.

Five spirals above the ground level, the staircase opened onto a lobby in front of two grand doors. Each had a gold rectangular plate embedded in it, etched with the form of a dragon. The one on the left looked more or less like Beryl, and the one on the right had the leaf-like wings Umber had seen on Mulberry and some of the dragons outside.

A few dragons were waiting drowsily in the lobby area. When they saw Umber and Sora, their faces lit up.

"New dragons?" one of them said eagerly.

"Does that mean Mulberry is back?" asked another.

Beryl waved one of her wings with a gentle nod and the waiting dragons all went galloping away down the stairs.

Going to find Mulberry instead of even saying hello to us, Umber thought. *Is that weird?*

"Mulberry is very special," Beryl said to Umber, which made him worry a bit about what his face was doing. "Very beloved. There's no one else like him."

"Right," he said. "Of course. I see that."

Beryl nudged the doors open and led the way into a cavernous throne room. Two thrones sat on a dais at the far end, but strangely spaced, as though a third throne to the left had been removed. Sunlight poured through tall stained glass windows, drifting green and blue puddles of light along the floor. More dragon scale columns towered around them, shooting up into the rafters, where garlands of leaves hung in whispering thickets.

In fact, the whole room felt like it was whispering, even though it was empty as far as Umber could see.

"Not two," murmured the leaves. "Not two, but three, and nobody knows."

"Come meet our newcomers, darling," Beryl said, ushering Umber and Sora forward with her wings.

"Is it safe," the leaves hissed back. "Is it wise." A rustle shivered along the branches. "Might break everything . . ."

"They won't break anything," Beryl said in a no-nonsense voice. "They're perfectly harmless."

But we're not, Umber thought with a stab of guilt. *Sora's not. She's a murderer.*

A dragon suddenly surged out of the foliage, swarming along one of the rafters overhead like a cloud of furious hornets. He stopped directly above them and glared down.

"This is King Snakeroot," Beryl said calmly. "Darling, this is Umber and Sora."

Snakeroot's scales were forest green and his wings were the same leaf shape as Mulberry's. That was the only resemblance Umber could see. While Mulberry radiated warmth and kindness, his father seemed to fill the air with invisible spikes and traps and the weight of a thousand eyes. A jagged round scar like a dragonflame cactus slashed across one of his wings.

"Dangerous," snarled the king.

"Don't mind him," Beryl said, patting Sora's shoulder. "He's quite brilliant. A wonderful king, the best the court has ever had."

"Has it had other kings?" Umber asked.

"Oh, we don't like to dwell on the past," Beryl said.

Snakeroot abruptly thudded to the ground in front of Umber, his tail lashing. "Why does he ask?" the king snapped. "See, dangerous! You stay away from the hybrid prince!"

Umber flinched back. *The hybrid prince — does he mean Mulberry?*

"Tsk, love, stop scaring them," Beryl said, inserting

herself between Umber and the king and nudging Snakeroot toward the thrones. "They're just a pair of innocent MudWing dragonets. You're being very dramatic, dear."

Some wild flame went out in Snakeroot's eyes. He looked at Beryl and sagged like a melting clay statue. "Yes," he agreed. "Of course I am. Most ridiculous." He climbed slowly onto one of the thrones and lay down. "It's not them," he muttered, closing his eyes. "Is it them? Who breaks it? How soon?"

"Well," Beryl said, patting his shoulder, "that's gone worse."

"Is he all right?" Sora asked, and the gentleness in her voice made her sound like Umber's sister again, the way he remembered her from before the war. "Did something bad happen to him?"

"No," Beryl said, "no, no. He's very strong. He lost his mother when he was too young to remember her and then his father brought him here. We've held the throne for about two years now and everything has been perfect. Right, dear?"

Snakeroot grunted.

CRASH! went something out in the lobby. *BANG! CRASH!*

Snakeroot jolted upright and Sora darted behind Beryl, trembling.

Umber didn't know whether to run toward it or away. Was something terrifying happening? Something that would endanger Sora? Then they should clearly run away — but did someone need help? Then shouldn't he go see what was happening?

Reed would know. If Umber's bigwings were here, he could

follow whatever Reed did and know it was the right choice. Again he was seized by the feeling that as the littlest brother, he was all wrong for this job. *I shouldn't be the one making decisions or taking care of Sora.*

"What was that?" Sora whimpered.

Beryl rolled her eyes as another *CRASH* echoed through the room. With a grumbling sigh, Snakeroot climbed up to the top of his throne and flew back into the rafters.

"Nothing to worry about," Beryl said, shaking out her wings. She stepped off the dais and marched toward the giant doors. "It's just our ghost."

CHAPTER 6

"Wait, what?" Umber said. "Sorry, did you say — *ghost*?"

Beryl threw open the doors as Umber and Sora caught up to her. The waiting room looked as though it had been trampled by extremely grumpy wild boars. The couches were both overturned, startled legs pointing toward the ceiling and cushions escaping down the stairs. All the posters had been shredded into whirls of ragged snow. And everything was covered in splatters of gory purple goop. For a moment, Umber had the horrified thought that some of these strange dragons must bleed purple blood and one of them had been murdered — until he stepped on a giant smashed fruit and realized it was only mystery-fruit guts.

Umber couldn't believe someone had made such a mess in such a short amount of time.

But perhaps for *ghosts*, anything was possible.

"You don't mean *literally* a ghost, do you?" he asked. "Like . . . a dead dragon who haunts the palace from beyond the grave?"

"It's VERY ANNOYING," Beryl said loudly. "And ENTIRELY POINTLESS, I might add."

Do ghosts normally have a point? Umber wondered.

They stepped gingerly out into the disaster. Sora kept blinking and blinking, like she needed the scene in front of her to disappear. Umber wondered whether it reminded her too much of the cave she blew up, where Carnelian and Bigtail had died. *Maybe somewhere in there she's feeling guilty?*

Umber glanced back and discovered that the ghost had smeared the purple fruit guts on the gold doors as well. Wait — those were words. Whoever it was had left a message.

Over Queen Beryl's face it said *LIAR*.

And over King Snakeroot's, it said *THIEF*.

By the three moons, what was happening?

"Why would the, uh . . . ghost write that?" Umber asked Beryl, pointing to the doors.

Beryl frowned. "Perhaps because it knows that *nothing it does* will make *any difference*," she said. "Because everyone else LOVES US. QUOKKA! QUOKKA!"

Sora gave Umber a worried look and he tried to convey *I have no idea* with his face. Maybe this was how dragons in the Court of Refuge dealt with rage: by shouting nonsense syllables at the sky?

Beryl swept over to the stairwell and bellowed upward. "QUOKKA!"

"I'm here!" A small dragon scurried down the stairs and

came to a stumbling halt in front of the queen. "Sorry, sorry, I'm here." Her eyes widened as she saw the mess, and then Umber and Sora. "Oh — oh, hi!"

"Quokka, get these two settled, and then clean this up," Beryl said. "Sora, Umber, I'll find you later." She spread her wings and vaulted over the balcony, sailing up toward the sky and out of view.

The little dragon — Quokka, Umber gathered — sighed and picked up one of the ripped posters. She looked about the same age as Sora and Umber, but he couldn't guess which tribe she was from. Her scales were brownish yellow, like a lion, with speckles of gold and dark blue, and her wings were shaped like his, but her snout looked more like a SandWing's. She didn't have a venom barb, though; what she did have were some strange blobby spikes along her spine, shaped a bit like rose thorns. Her eyes were also dark blue, almost black, crinkled around the edges as if she smiled a lot, although the rest of her face looked tired.

"Can I help?" Umber asked, setting one of the benches upright. "I'm Umber, and this is my sister Sora."

"Oh, thank you, that's so nice of you," Quokka said. She smiled at Sora. "You look like someone who maybe loves scrolls as much as I do — do you? I could show you the library? It's my favorite place."

Sora's face softened. "Yes, please!"

"I always feel safe in a library." Quokka turned her smile on Umber as he picked up another overturned bench. "You're so kind; don't worry about this."

"You shouldn't have to clean it up alone," he said.

"Oh, I do — it's, um." Quokka paused awkwardly. "A little bit my fault?"

Umber blinked at her. "The *ghost*? Is your fault?"

"My responsibility," Quokka said in a rush. "That's what I mean." She nervously twitched an orange cushion back into place.

"Why?" Umber asked. *If a dead dragon is haunting the palace . . . did this friendly dragon kill someone?*

"We're not supposed to talk about it," Quokka said. "Don't worry about it! Are you hungry? I bet you're hungry; let's start there!" She bundled a torn banner into the corner and hurried toward the stairwell.

I don't understand. Umber didn't know how to line up this beautiful place or the warmth of dragons like Mulberry, Quokka, and Beryl with the weirdness of the mad king, the metal dragons, and ghosts nobody could talk about. *Are we safe? Should we stay here? Will Sora be OK here?*

How do I decide? What's the right thing to do?

How did Reed always know how to take care of us?

Hatching memories were naturally a bit fuzzy, but Umber was sure he could remember Reed's strong claws cracking his shell and drawing him into the light and warmth of his siblings. His earliest memories were of Reed's talons bringing him earthworms and moles to eat. He remembered Reed leading them through the mud village of the Diamond Spray Delta as tiny dragonets, helping them learn to communicate, choosing their names, finding them shelter, even though he was no older than the rest of them.

Umber had never thought about how scary that must have been for a dragonet, to have five siblings to take care of from the moment of hatching. Reed never seemed scared. He never hesitated, never got them lost, never let them go hungry.

I have to be like him now, for Sora.

But I'm not sure about anything.

Maybe they could find another dragon here to be their new Reed — someone to take care of both him and Sora. Someone to tell him what to do and what to think and whether they were safe.

Umber was already sure he'd happily follow Mulberry anywhere he led, but the prince was too busy and had too many other dragons around him. So perhaps Quokka could be the dragon they needed. She seemed kind and patient already, just like Reed.

The castle had more than one dining hall, Quokka explained as she flew them to another floor and then trotted down a long sunlit corridor. There was one in the orchards on the ground level for SilkWing dragonets ("For *what*?" Sora said, but Quokka was talking too quickly to hear her) and other vegetarians. Another was at the top of a tower, mainly used for dragons to practice hunting birds in flight.

But Quokka's favorite was the Gathering, which turned out to be a room shaped a bit like a bowl, with tables of food in the center, a pool of water at one end, skylights overhead, and deep steps all around the edges. Arches stood open to the air on two sides, letting in warm breezes and flying dragons.

The steps were lined with jewel-toned cushions and woven silk rugs where dragons could sit together while they ate. It felt so strongly MudWing to Umber; it reminded him of all the rooms in the palace that were designed for sibling groups.

"This is where everyone brings anything extra," Quokka said, flicking her tail at the tables. "So there's always enough to share." She picked up a bowl of mystery stew, added a few shakes of yellow powder from a pouch around her neck, and offered it to Sora. "Especially from the cooking classes."

"How long have you been here?" Umber asked, watching her season another bowl with the powder and hand it to him. They climbed up to one of the higher steps and settled on a trio of cheerful sea-green cushions.

"Oh, my whole life," Quokka said. "I'm a WildWing."

Sora paused midbite to stare at her. "A what?" she asked quietly.

"Um . . . that's what we call the descendants from the first dragons here," Quokka said. "Or the ones who've been here for so many generations that we don't look like any particular tribe anymore."

"Who were the first dragons here?" Umber asked as he ate. "How long ago?"

"Um — they — it's," Quokka stammered, getting flustered again. "A really long time, thousands of years. Um, RainWings, SeaWings, BeetleWings, LeafWings, mostly, in that first group."

"LeafWings and *Beetle*Wings," Sora echoed in a puzzled voice.

"That's amazing," Umber said. "That all those different tribes came together to find a safe place like this."

"Right," Quokka said. "They did . . . that."

A storm of dragon wings came flapping up to one of the arches from outside. Umber turned to look and realized it was a crowd following Mulberry into the Gathering. His heart did a jump-skip-gallop-around-in-wild-circles thing as Mulberry came in, spotted Umber, and smiled across the distance at him. He hoped his return smile looked cool and not absolutely bananas.

The prince made his way to the center tables, greeting everyone as he went, and started unpacking his sunset-colored sling bag. Dragons gathered around his wings and leaned on the other side of the table with shining eyes. The fruits and fish he laid out looked ordinary enough to Umber, but each one was greeted with *ooohs* and questions and admiring remarks. All of which made Mulberry look deeply, adorably embarrassed.

"Why is everyone like that?" Sora whispered to Quokka. "I mean, *so obsessed* with Mulberry?"

"Oh, he's very special," Quokka said. "There's no one else like him."

Umber shivered. He was pretty sure those were the exact words Beryl had used.

"Hello, hey now, who is this?" a loud voice demanded. Umber turned to find a short, stocky dragon with muscular shoulders swaggering up to him, flanked by two other dragons like bodyguards.

"New dragons," Quokka said. "Leave them alone, Taipan."

"Scrawny," scoffed the new dragon, looking Umber up and down. Umber had no idea what tribe he might be — which he guessed meant he must be a WildWing, like Quokka. His wings were the familiar Pyrrhia shape, but he was bright green and black in blobby stripes, and he was covered all over in those weird, sharp rose thorn spikes, like the ones on Quokka's spine. Two equally sharp, bristly horns rose from the top of his skull and another from his snout like a rhinoceros. His eyes, small and yellow-green, glared out from the thicket of spikes as he strutted in a circle around Umber, studying him from talons to tail.

"I'm Umber, and this is my sister Sora," Umber greeted him.

"MudWings, I see." The spiky dragon chuckled unpleasantly. "New subjects for you, Dugong!" He cut his bristly gaze over to the dragon on his left.

"Uh, right," Dugong responded, blinking. "Yeah. You better, uh, listen to me."

"Oh, very regal," said the third dragon in a deeply bored voice. "Seriously pathetic, Dugong."

"You're *such* a waste of noble blood, Dugong," added the first dragon.

"Literally tragic," said the third.

"Royal, poke him with the Toughen Up Stick."

The third dragon — Royal, presumably — produced a blunt club from a harness on his back and jabbed Dugong hard in the side with it.

Dugong hunched his shoulders. Umber wanted to reach

out and comfort him somehow, but he got a strong feeling that he shouldn't, and he wasn't sure why. He wanted to say "hey, that's mean!" but he felt like it wasn't his place to say anything. Was it?

His sister Pheasant would have said it. She never stayed quiet when she thought someone was being treated unfairly. She'd once jumped into a fight between *SkyWings* because the bigger SkyWing called the littler one a worm. She'd confronted their MudWing section commander several times about how the Diamond Spray Delta troops were treated as more expendable than the ones from wealthier villages. Umber was always happy to back her up, with all his brothers and sisters around him — but saying something himself, alone and surrounded by strangers, felt impossible.

He glanced back at Mulberry, but the prince was hard to see behind the crowd of admirers still hanging on his every word. He didn't seem to be paying attention to whatever was going on here.

"Sorry, Taipan," Dugong mumbled. "Sorry, Royal."

Royal sighed loudly. "Oh, an *apology*," he said. "Much better. *So* tough." Royal had the strange butterfly-shaped wings, with interwoven stripes of black and orange, and a dark purple underbelly. His snout was unusually long and his eyes were narrow slits of blue.

"It's nice to meet you, Dugong. Are you a MudWing?" Umber asked, trying to shift the conversation onto friendlier ground. Dugong looked like he might be a MudWing, or distantly related to them: his face was broad and his scales were tree-bark brown, although there were patches of dark green and dark blue on his wings, and a few of the same unusual WildWing spikes jutted out from his spine. Dugong was also bigger than his two friends, even though he hunched his shoulders and behaved as though they might squash him under his talons.

"He's from the *true* MudWing royal bloodline," Taipan said challengingly.

"What does that mean?" Sora said, bristling.

"Spikes and spiders, Taipan," Quokka said. "Nobody here cares who's ruling the MudWings. Although you'd be a great king, Dugong; don't listen to them."

"I'm just sizing up our new arrivals, Quokka," said the spiky dragon. "You can take that one away and leave her brother with us." Taipan puffed up his chest and took a step closer to Umber. "We'll make sure he's properly welcomed."

"Oh, no, thanks," Umber said. "I should stay with my sister."

"Why?" Taipan demanded. "Do we make you nervous?"

Not as nervous as Sora does, Umber thought. *You're loud and hostile, but I know how many dragons she's killed.* His head was starting to feel a little woozy — maybe from all the flying? or the stress of a new place? — and he did not know how to talk to this angry dragon to make him less angry.

"Can we please not fight?" Quokka said, twitching her wings and taking Umber's bowl. "We were just about to leave anyway."

"No, no, don't run away," Taipan said. He grinned with

all his teeth and crowded into Umber's personal space. "We have a few questions for you, MudWing."

"Sure," Umber offered. "I'm happy to answer anything — I just want to stay near my sister."

"Fine, I'm lying," Taipan spat. "It's only one question." He leaned closer. "Are you the useful kind of MudWing — or not?"

His mouth hinged open terrifyingly, like a cobra or a RainWing, and with a roar, he blasted Umber with fire.

CHAPTER 7

Umber was small and Umber was "the friendly one" and Umber was "too quick to trust strangers who might be spies," according to his siblings, but he was not slow and, thanks to Reed's endless training drills and his years in the war, he was a better fighter than most dragons expected at first glance.

His battle instincts kicked in before his conscious thought. While his brain was still going *ACK THAT DRAGON IS TRYING TO SET ME ON FIRE WHO WOULD DO THAT WHAT A JERK!*, his body was already ducking and rolling under the flame, shoving Sora up the steps to safety, grabbing one of the rugs, and flinging it over Taipan's head.

HE SHOT FIRE! AT ME! ON PURPOSE! IN A WOODEN ROOM FULL OF FLAMMABLE CUSHIONS AND OTHER DRAGONS! A JERK AND BY THE WAY NOT VERY SMART EITHER! Umber's brain kept shrieking as he wrestled Taipan to the floor, smothering the flames with the rug and beating the ones that escaped with his tail.

WATCH OUT FOR HIS FRIEEEEEEEENDS yelled his brain a moment after Umber had grabbed the Toughen Up

Stick out of Royal's harness, knocked Royal's feet out from under him, and whirled to point it at Dugong, who stood blinking in befuddled shock.

WE'RE BEING ATTACKED FIGHT EVERYONE OR JUMP OUT THE WINDOW GET SORA TO SAFETY THERE'S DANGER EVERYWHEEEEEEEEEERE!!!!!! his brain continued as Umber caught his breath and realized that silence had fallen across the Gathering. Under his feet, Taipan was thrashing about in the rug like a bundled-up crocodile, roaring furious incoherent curses, but at least smart enough to realize he shouldn't set fire to the thing wrapped around him.

"Ow," Royal said in an offended, dignified way, climbing to his feet. "There was no need to drag *me* into this. And thanks *so* much for *your* help, *Dugong.* More like *do-nothing,* as usual."

"Wild stars," Quokka breathed. She sidled up next to Umber and eyed where he'd pinned the rug down with his talons. "I've never seen anyone take down Taipan so fast."

"Why did he do that?" Umber asked her. "Why would anyone attack a stranger for no reason?" *Is this proof that it isn't safe here?* What if most of the dragons in the Court of Refuge were like Taipan? Unpredictable and perhaps a little evil?

But Mulberry's not like that at all.

Mulberry, in fact, was hurrying across the room to him, his face frantic with worry as he brushed past all the dragons in his way.

"Oh no," Mulberry cried. "Are you all right?"

Umber nodded, but he was starting to feel sort of disconnected from the rest of himself. It was as though too many strange things had happened today, and this was the last one his brain could handle, so it was absolutely done, going to bed, right to the bottom of the swamp, no more thoughts or decisions coming anytime soon, sorry everyone, peace out.

Mulberry swept one wing over Umber's back, enclosing him in warmth. *It'll be all right, it'll be all right* radiated through Umber from everywhere their scales were touching.

"Taipan!" Mulberry barked at the thrashing rug shape, which abruptly stopped thrashing at the sound of the prince's voice. "What did you *do*?"

"And *why*?" Umber added.

The rug growled something angry.

"You can let him out," Mulberry said to Umber. "He won't pick a fight again with everyone watching."

Umber wasn't sure he agreed with that theory, but what was he going to do, say no to Mulberry? Stand on this rug for the rest of eternity? He ducked his head and stepped back, and the prince pulled him closer as Taipan exploded out of the rug.

"How dare you," Taipan snarled. The fabric caught and snagged on his thorn spikes and he struggled to cast the rug aside. "How *dare* you!"

"You attacked him," Quokka pointed out. Royal shot her a look and she stuck her tongue out at him.

"So what?!" Taipan snapped. "I wasn't going to *kill* him. I was just checking if he's fireproof!"

"You could have *asked*," Umber pointed out. "There are

much easier ways to get that answer than *setting someone on fire*."

He realized that the crowd of dragons had followed Mulberry over and were now standing around watching this uncomfortable scene. Their faces were fascinating, or at least, they would be if Umber could get his brain to focus on them. Most of them looked as if they were trying to mirror whatever expression was on Mulberry's face, although some of them were studying Umber with suspicion instead.

He looked around for Sora. She was still perched two steps up where he had shoved her in the middle of the fight, but she looked fine. Not worried, not upset, maybe curious and a little tired. He wished he could read her expression. Really, he wished he understood anything happening inside her.

"Go away," Mulberry said to Taipan with quiet authority. "If you try to hurt Umber again, you'll have me to answer to."

"What do you care?" Taipan growled as Mulberry nudged Umber toward the nearest doorway. "Hey! What do you care?!" Mulberry ignored him, and the crowd was starting to murmur now.

Why does *he care?* Umber's thoughts were a blur of confusion. *He has so many friends. He doesn't need me. He could just leave me to fend for myself.*

"I'm so sorry," Mulberry said anxiously. "I didn't think anything like that would happen so fast. Taipan's a bully, but he usually waits a few days before picking a fight with newcomers. Don't worry, Umber. I'm here. I'm not leaving you," he added, and Umber remembered Mulberry's power.

Not that he could do anything about the worried spiral of his thoughts.

"Sora," he said. "I have to —"

"She's right behind us," Mulberry said, glancing back. "Quokka's bringing her. But we should keep moving, because if I stop anywhere, I tend to get . . . hmmm, *cornered* feels like the wrong word."

"Ensnared," Umber offered as they reached the empty corridor. "Engulfed. Adored. Pedestal-ed."

"Is it that bad?" Mulberry said, looking mortified. "I promise they'll calm down in a day or two; they just haven't seen me in a while."

"Are they like that with everyone who comes back after leaving the court?" Umber asked shrewdly. "I bet not." Mulberry's face fell, far more than Umber expected. "I'm sorry, I'm only joking," Umber said, nudging his side. "I totally understand why they think you're so awesome."

"It's not really me," Mulberry said. "I mean, it's not about who I am, it's just what I do and, I guess . . . kind of who they think I am."

"How are those two different?" Umber asked. "Who you are and who they think you are?"

"I don't know . . . . They think I'm, sort of, doing magic? And that maybe I could teach it to them, except honestly I'm not doing anything on purpose and I can't pass it along. So I keep thinking eventually they'll realize that and then decide it's unfair and be so mad at me."

"I can't imagine anyone being mad at you," Umber said.

"I bet they would love you even if you weren't magic."

Mulberry looked down at his talons and didn't answer. They had traveled down a long spiral to an entirely new corridor, which had no windows and was maybe underground. Umber glanced around at the doors evenly lining the new hallway. Many of them were decorated with swirls of paint and dragon names. Behind him, he could hear Quokka's and Sora's voices chatting — well, mostly Quokka's.

"Where are we going?" he asked.

"To find you and Sora a room," Mulberry said. "Most dragons live here in the castle, although there are other options if you don't like it."

"Thank the moons," Umber said fervently. "I will sleep anywhere. I'm *so tired* I nearly fell asleep while sitting on Taipan." His eyes were drooping and the hallway seemed *very* blurry. Why would anyone make their hallways so blurry? And unstable, too; it was decidedly wibble-wobbling under his talons. That was a poor engineering decision if Umber ever saw one. Hallways should stay still! They should not wibble-wobble!

Mulberry laughed. "Here — there should be open rooms along here." He steered Umber around a bend and they found a row of undecorated doors. Mulberry knocked on one and, when there was no answer, opened it cautiously.

The room was very bare, containing nothing but two sleep rugs, and like the corridor, it had no windows. The walls and floor and ceiling were all the same smooth pale wood; it would feel a bit like sleeping in a box, Umber thought.

He had a sharp, sudden stab of memory: walking into his cave at Jade Mountain Academy for the first time and meeting Turtle, his clawmate. That cave had clearly been decorated with them in mind, with scrolls for Turtle and little cartoon drawings of Umber's siblings that must have been left for him by Clay and welcome notes for both of them. He'd been so happy and so excited — the war was over, everyone was at peace, and he could finally go to school and make friends like a regular dragonet.

"Oh no, it made you so sad!" Mulberry took one of Umber's talons in his. "I'm sorry! We can find you a completely different room! Different sleep rugs? We can build you a different castle!"

Umber laughed through the pinpricks of tears in his eyes. "It's not the room," he said. "This is great. I mean it, I'm happy to sleep anywhere." He glanced along the hall, but Sora and Quokka were still a ways back. Lowering his voice, he added, "I just miss where we came from, that's all."

"But you had to leave for a reason, right?" Mulberry asked. "You *had* to."

"Yes, because of Sora," Umber said. "But if she's all right here, maybe one day I could go back to see my other siblings again. I want them to know we're safe." *If we* are *safe. Maybe I could bring them here one day — they could meet Mulberry and see the court and we could all be together again.*

"Oh. I . . . didn't realize you'd want to do that," Mulberry said.

"Not immediately," Umber said. "Maybe not at all! I'm so

grateful, I really am. Thank you for bringing us here. If you hadn't, we'd have been eaten by krakens or very grumpy monkeys by now."

"Mandrills," Mulberry said distractedly. "I don't think they actually eat dragons."

"Where do you sleep?" Umber asked, hoping to chase the wistful look off Mulberry's face. None of the doors they'd passed had cheerfully declared "Mulberry!" on them.

"Near my parents," Mulberry said with a sigh. "In one of the towers, surrounded by guards and locks. They can be a little overprotective."

Umber wanted to ask about the king, or maybe the ghost, or the metal dragons, but that was when Sora caught up. She bundled straight past him into the room and threw herself down on one of the rugs.

"Hey, that's the one I wanted!" Umber protested.

"No, it isn't! You only wanted it because I chose it first!" Sora said, and then they both started laughing, because this was the same fight they'd had at every camp for years. Reed would get so cross with them because "don't we have enough dragons to fight without fighting each other" and "WHO LITERALLY CARES SLEEP ANYWHERE."

"I'll come find you for breakfast?" Quokka asked from the doorway.

"Thanks, Quokka," Sora said, burrowing sleepily into the rug.

"Thank you both," Umber said. Mulberry lifted one talon as though he meant to — Umber wasn't sure. Hug Umber good night? But instead the prince gave a sort of awkward wave and backed away.

"Sleep well," he said, and hurried off down the hall before Umber even had the door closed.

Sora was already snoring lightly. Umber dragged the second rug across the room and arranged it next to hers, then curled up so their wings were touching.

Maybe I'll see Clay tonight, he thought. Clay and his friends had a magic object at the Academy that they could use to appear in dragons' dreams. Umber knew he'd used it to talk to Queen Moorhen once during the war. Surely he would try to reach Umber with it sooner or later.

They hadn't slept properly in days, so the dreamvisitor probably wouldn't have been able to work on him yet. But tonight — maybe tonight Umber would be able to tell Clay where they were and that they were safe.

That thought made him feel a little better as he drifted into sleep, worrying over the strangeness of the day.

I hope Sora will be all right.

I hope this place is safe for us.

I hope we made the right choice coming here.

CHAPTER 8

The next morning Quokka woke them by charging into their room and immediately tripping over Umber.

"Eeep!" she said, flailing upright again. "You moved your sleep rug! That's OK, of course you can do that. Sorry for landing on your head! Wait, I'm here for a reason. The king and queen want to see you!" she said to Umber. "Both of you but mostly you. Right away!"

"Why?" Umber asked. "Am I in trouble?"

"Oh, I . . . I don't think so," Quokka said, her wings drooping a little. "I mean, why would you be in trouble, right? You're great. Everything's great! And if it's not, don't worry, I'm here for you no matter what."

Umber shook himself as he stood up. He still felt a little blurry, like he hadn't quite come all the way out of the deep sleep he'd been in.

He couldn't remember any dreams, especially any with Clay in them. Maybe he'd been too tired. He sighed. Maybe he'd see Clay tonight or the night after instead.

"What's this?" Sora asked, picking up a piece of paper that must have been shoved under their door overnight. She squinted at the spiky, manic handwriting as she read it out loud. "'Beryl and Snakeroot are imposters and traitors. They stole the thrones from the rightful' — hey!" she protested as Quokka whisked the paper out of her hands.

"Ignore that!" Quokka said. "Ignore it, nothing to see, forget you saw that, never mention it again."

"*Did* they steal the throne from someone?" Umber asked.

"That's, um, one interpretation," Quokka said, shredding the paper nervously between her claws, "and we *really* shouldn't talk about it."

"Who'd they steal it from?" Sora asked.

"The ghost?" Umber jumped in. "Is that why it's haunting them?"

"No, no, she was never — that's silly," Quokka said, cutting herself off. "All right, off we go!" She barreled away down the hall fast enough to escape any more questions.

She, Umber thought. That was new information. Umber wondered about ghosts all the way to the throne room. He'd heard plenty of ghost stories around MudWing campfires, but he'd never really *believed* any of them. Like most MudWings, he believed that after death you were reborn in a new life along with all of your siblings, so you'd always be together. He knew he'd see Crane again one day, although they wouldn't remember any of this life.

But if this castle had a real ghost, did that change his idea of the afterlife? Was she a dragon who couldn't move on to be reborn? Was there something she had to do first?

And why did she hate Queen Beryl and King Snakeroot so much? What had happened when they took the thrones?

He wondered if the ghost was ever visible to other dragons, or if she could move things without appearing. It was weird to think she might be there in the corridor with them, invisibly watching.

He glanced behind him and saw two of the little metal dragons — one silver, one copper — zip from the sill above his door to a rafter overhead. Had they been there all night? Were they following him and Sora?

The lobby outside the throne room was tidy again, the royal gold faces gleaming and polished as if they'd never been touched by a speck of purple fruit. Beryl and Snakeroot waved from their thrones as Quokka opened the doors. The king looked much more awake than he had before; he even smiled as they approached.

"Hel*lo*, little MudWings." Queen Beryl clasped her front talons together. She was wearing different jewelry today: strings of emeralds and cascades of winking opals. "Umber, dear, you neglected to mention yesterday what a *skilled* warrior you are. Quokka, go fetch these two some breakfast."

"Oh, she doesn't have to —" Umber started, but Quokka had already whisked away. "Um. Thank you, Your Majesty. I promise I'm nothing special."

"Well, it's just what we need," Snakeroot said. His green talons curled around the edge of his throne. "We have an elite guard called the King's Teeth and, between you and me, they're a bit of a mess. Disorganized, lazy. They fight like they've never seen a battle and don't know which end of a sword to poke someone with."

"We want you to train them," Beryl said with a glittering smile. "We need them to be strong warriors who can protect us, fight off our enemies, stand around the throne looking imposing, all of that."

Umber's heart sank. He'd hoped he was done with fighting, ideally forever. "A guard?" he echoed. "Is that — do you really need one? All the way out here?"

"There's danger everywhere," the king said, staring into his eyes. "Especially for those on the thrones."

"But who would attack you?" Umber asked. He hoped he didn't have to train soldiers to fight off ghosts. He had no idea where one would even start.

Beryl rose from her throne and beckoned him to the nearest open window. It took Umber a moment to realize they were looking out the far side of the palace, beyond the valley. Instead of orchards and mountains, this window overlooked a vast, dry-looking plain tufted with yellow grasses and thorny little trees. Large reddish rock formations dotted the landscape, but otherwise it was flat and sunbaked.

"There's something out there," Beryl murmured. She narrowed her eyes at the horizon, tracking a solitary hawk across the sky. "Plotting against us. Lying in wait . . . biding their time." One of her claws pinned a ladybug on the windowsill. "One day they will strike, and we must be ready."

Umber shifted his wings uncomfortably.

"Will you help us be ready, Umber?" asked the queen, turning her searing gold eyes on him.

"I — can try," he said, "but what is it?" *Is it real,* was what he really wanted to ask, but he didn't dare. "I mean, it's just that, um, we can train better if we know what we might . . . have to fight?"

"Be ready for anything," she said intently. "Venom, fire, ice, night attacks."

"Poison in our food," Snakeroot added. "Knives in the dark. Camouflage scales. Silk that burns and chokes."

"Dragons who want *my throne,*" Beryl finished.

Umber felt as though he'd been in a safe river that had suddenly swept him into the wild ocean, where sharks swarmed just under the surface and solid land was vanishing into the distance.

"OK," he said. It seemed like the only safe thing to say.

"What about me, Your Majesty?" Sora asked softly. "I was a soldier, too."

Don't make her fight again, Umber prayed, looking up into Beryl's face. *She needs rest, not more danger — but if I say that, Sora will be furious with me.*

"Mulberry suggested you might prefer an assignment in the library, Sora," said the queen. "Do you disagree?"

Sora flicked her tail and smiled — a real smile, as far as Umber could tell. "No, I agree with him," she said, to Umber's relief. "I'd like that."

* * *

Three days passed in a blur of new names and faces. After each training session, Umber wrote down every name and any details about each dragon he'd learned that day, and then he studied them at night, his head aching.

Goana: WildWing, three rings of black stripes on her tail, hums to herself while training. He'd asked her what she was humming and she'd confessed she was trying to write a song. She had two little brothers who watched their training from a window overhead. Umber made himself a note to ask their names.

Raspberry: HiveWing-LeafWing-RainWing hybrid, color-changing scales except for permanently dark pink wings, three pet snails. When he wasn't training, Raspberry worked in the vegetable gardens and took home scraps of carrots and cabbage for his pets, who were the most enormous snails Umber had ever seen.

Tarakihi: WildWing, webbed talons, maybe the clumsiest dragon I've ever met, probably should not be given weaponry. Tarakihi managed to trip over his spear in every drill and spent half his time apologizing to everyone. Umber actually wondered if he was doing it on purpose to get kicked out of the King's Teeth. He suspected Tarakihi would be happiest if he could somehow turn birdwatching into a job, since that was what he seemed to be doing every time he fell over.

Umber hoped memorizing all their names would help, but he couldn't convince himself that he should be in charge of all these dragons. He tried to lead training exercises just like Reed's, but he wasn't used to ordering other dragons around, or shouting to be heard, or telling anyone they were doing something wrong. He kept catching himself in the middle of an exercise just standing still, with all the King's Teeth staring at him, because he was waiting for someone else to announce the next drill.

This was all wrong for him. He'd never wanted to lead a squadron of soldiers. More important, he didn't want to teach anyone to fight. He wanted this place to be safe and peaceful, a refuge from war.

He couldn't understand what Beryl was afraid of. Nobody else would tell him either; all anyone would say was "we don't talk about that." It made him wonder what anyone *did* talk about here, when everything interesting seemed to be off the table.

Questions clearly made other dragons in the court nervous, but even in normal conversations, most of them seemed perpetually stressed. Everyone was jumpy when the king or queen was nearby. Most dragons acted tense and worried around the King's Teeth as well.

He wished he could ask Mulberry any of his million questions, but every time he saw the prince, there were dragons around him — sometimes only a couple, sometimes a crowd, but always absorbing all of Mulberry's attention. Umber tried not to think about Mulberry too much. How could he possibly compete with all the dragons who adored him? Probably Mulberry wasn't thinking about him either . . . although sometimes their eyes would catch across a courtyard, as though Mulberry was looking for him, too.

On the plus side, Sora seemed happy. She loved being in

the library all day, and at night she would tell him about the new scrolls she'd found. Quokka went with her everywhere and did all the talking when Sora was too shy.

There were IceWings here, but most of them were hybrids who couldn't possibly have been in the war. Sora didn't mention any of them. Umber watched her for a reaction whenever they saw one, but there was nothing visible. She acted totally normal — but then again, he hadn't noticed anything strange about her at school either, before she'd tried to murder Icicle.

Possibly he was terrible at this. Marsh had always been closest with Sora; they were both quiet and nervous and found the other comforting. Umber clearly wasn't comforting. When he tried to be, mostly Sora just looked annoyed. He wondered if she wished Marsh were here instead of him.

He also wondered if Clay had already forgotten about him. Even after three nights of normal sleep, there was no sign of him or anyone else using the dreamvisitor to look for Umber. Umber tried not to admit to himself how much that hurt his feelings.

In the late afternoon of his fourth day at the Court of Refuge, Umber found a trio of pools on a balcony. Two of them were busy with SeaWing hybrids, so he slipped into the third, empty one and sighed as the cool water washed the grit from between his scales. It was so much hotter and drier here than in the Diamond Spray Delta. There were no soothing mud puddles to roll in, no mists or rain so far. He missed the willows and cypresses with their long trailing branches, the warbling chorus of frogs all night, the smell of rain on the way; he even missed the coils of snakes in the trees.

All right, maybe not the snakes. If he was honest, what he really missed was his siblings. And he missed his new friends at Jade Mountain Academy — Turtle, Qibli, Winter, Kinkajou, and Moon. The winglet of dragonets who should have been his new team, his new best friends forever.

He looked up at the bright, hot, blazingly blue sky, blinking back tears, and saw a flash of red dart past, heading toward the plain beyond the castle.

Mulberry?

Mulberry alone and leaving the crowded court.

Umber clambered out of the pool, shook his wings vigorously, and took off after him. This was his chance. He'd catch up to Mulberry and ask all his questions.

The prince's scales shone in the sunlight as he flew, reflecting flashes like hummingbirds of rubies and gold and emeralds. He was faster than Umber, but he kept pausing to do little flips in the air or diving loops through the clouds. Umber wasn't sure why for a while. Was Mulberry looking for something?

Except it didn't look purposeful; it looked . . . happy? As though Mulberry had been set free and couldn't help dancing about it.

Maybe after all those dragons looking at him all the time, he's just thrilled to be alone.

Umber's wingbeats faltered. Perhaps he shouldn't be

following him. What if Mulberry wasn't happy to see him? Perhaps he would rather be left alone.

But Umber wasn't one of the dragons who'd been following Mulberry around. He'd barely seen him in days. Maybe instead Mulberry would be *extra* happy to see him, out here where they could be alone together? They could fly and loop and spin through the clouds side by side. Umber could show him the games his siblings would play in the sky. He was pretty sure Mulberry would like those. And if he seemed bothered, Umber would leave.

He put on a burst of speed, trying to catch up. They were approaching the edge of the northwest mountains now, where the flat brown-gold grassland below started to slope into furrowed ridges of frowning foothills. Umber hoped they were going to the forest on the other side of the mountains — surely it would be cooler there. Maybe there would even be mud!

Up ahead, a dark line slashed across the grass, running parallel to the mountains in both directions. As he got closer, Umber could see that it was a line of charred trees and burnt grass — as though a dragon had drawn a border in fire all around the valley. Mulberry flew over it without even stopping to look, so it must have been there long enough that it didn't surprise him.

Mysterious, Umber thought, and then he realized he might be close enough now for Mulberry to hear him. "Mulberry!" he called. "Mulberry, wait!"

He saw the prince tilt his head as though wondering where the sound was coming from.

"Mulberry!" Umber called again. "It's me! Behind you!"

He caught a wind current to soar over the dark line — but as he reached it, something slammed him forcefully backward.

Umber let out a yelp of pain, clutching his snout and flailing his wings to stay aloft. *What — what hit me?*

The sky around him was empty. There wasn't so much as a bird nearby.

Umber cautiously winged forward again . . .

. . . and *SLAM* was thrown back once more, this time with needles of lightning pain shooting through his wings.

"Umber, stop!"

A blur of autumn red hurtled toward him, talons outstretched. Through the pain and the spinning sky, Umber tried to reach back.

New sparks of agony sizzled down his claws, his arms, his shoulders. He felt himself falling, surrounded by the sound of distant insistent buzzing, his wings too numb to move.

Warm scales, flashes of green and gold and red, tails tangling, giant leaves trying to slow his fall . . .

The buzz circling his head, words echoing loud and painful, like metal bars struck together:

"NO ONE LEAVES THE DUNGEON ISLE, PRISONER."

And Mulberry's voice saying, "I'm sorry. I'm sorry, Umber. I'm sorry," over and over, as Umber dropped into darkness.

PART TWO

THE DUNGEON ISLE

CHAPTER 9

Umber woke up slowly, like flying through smothering gray clouds toward a pale clear sky somewhere far overhead. His head was resting on something soft and he could hear the distant hum of drowsy bumblebees.

"I thought you left this morning," said a quiet, unfamiliar voice nearby.

"I should have, but I didn't want to leave without seeing him." That one he knew; that was Mulberry. Umber tried to open his eyes, but his eyelids felt like enormous manatees were lying on top of them.

"He's all right. It just takes a while to heal from trying to cross the Barrier three times."

"That's my fault," Mulberry said sadly. "I should have warned him — I should have told him before I ever brought him here."

"You're not allowed to," said the other voice. "Those are the Court of Refuge rules. Your parents' rules."

"I know, but it's not fair. He wouldn't have come if he'd known."

Umber tried to focus on each part of his body separately. Claws . . . talons . . . tail . . . legs . . . wings. Cautiously he reached his senses out along his wings. They didn't hurt, but they both felt a little numb.

Reed used to make them all do this meditation together. It was meant to calm them down and check for injuries, and it usually ended with Umber secretly poking Pheasant with his tail, swearing it wasn't him, and getting tackled so everyone wound up in a noisy, laughing pile.

Umber felt a tear roll down his snout, but even though he could *feel* his limbs, he couldn't yet seem to *move* them to wipe it away.

"Oh no." Someone gently brushed his face. "Does that mean he's awake? Umber?"

"Here," said the unfamiliar voice. There was a rustling and a small snap near his head, and a sharp, clean smell swept through his nose, clearing away the cobwebs in his brain. He inhaled and opened his eyes.

Wow, it couldn't be good for his heart to return from trauma to the sight of Mulberry's kind, worried face again.

"Hey there," Umber said, smiling despite himself.

"How do you feel?" Mulberry asked, clasping one of Umber's talons in his.

"Confused?" Umber said. "And embarrassed. Listen, that's your limit. Next time I'm in mortal peril, it's someone else's turn to save me."

Mulberry gave a choked laugh and ducked his head. "I'll try to remember. But it was really Paua who did all the work to heal you." He nodded at the dragon on the other side of the bed.

Paua looked closer to a SeaWing than anyone else Umber had seen here, but she had some of the thorny spikes along her tail, so he wondered if that meant she was a WildWing. Her scales were sapphire blue and iridescent silver in curling patterns along her sides and wings, and her talons were webbed.

"He's exaggerating," she said tranquilly. She kept her eyes on the side table, moving jars around as if she preferred not to be noticed. "The best cure is rest."

"Thank you, Paua," Umber said. She kind of flickered her wings and nodded without looking at him. "I don't know how you healed me so quickly."

Mulberry made a rueful face. "It's . . . been a while, actually."

"A while?" Umber echoed. He glanced at the sun filtering through the far windows. "What — what does that mean? How long?"

"We kept you asleep so you could heal," Paua said.

"Like . . . overnight?" Umber said. Mulberry's face got, if possible, even more rueful. "Wait, more than a day? Multiple days? How many days?"

"We try not to count the passage of time here," Paua said.

That was an entirely other new weird thing, and Umber only had the energy for one weird thing at a time. "But Sora," he said, trying to sit up. "She's been alone — has anyone been watching her? Is she —" He didn't know how to finish that sentence. *Is she OK,* yes, but also, *is she freaking out, is she talking to anyone, is she acting strange, is anyone mysteriously dead?*

"She's great," Mulberry said. "Don't worry at all; she fits right in."

"I'm sure she'll be here to see you soon," Paua said. "She comes every day. Much like certain other dragons, who have more important things to do." She shot a significant look at Mulberry, who ignored her.

The room was long and sunny, with multiple windows and several beds separated by gauzy curtains, although Umber seemed to be the only patient there. He tried to find that reassuring. Maybe dragons didn't get hit by invisible lightning every day here.

Wait. *What* had happened to him? He frowned, trying to remember.

Bzzzt went something overhead. Umber looked up and saw five of the metal dragons clustered on a rafter above him. They saw him looking and rattled their wings fiercely. *BZZZBZZBZZZ.*

"Did I make them mad?" he asked Mulberry. "Is that what happened? What did I do?"

Paua snorted.

"Yes," Mulberry said awkwardly. "But it wasn't your fault! It was mine. I should have told you — I'm so sorry, Umber."

A memory came bubbling up — a clicking, clanging voice, or many voices together . . .

"No one leaves the Dungeon Isle," Umber remembered,

and saying the words felt like piling stones onto his own wings. *"Prisoner."* He met Mulberry's eyes. "That's me? I'm a prisoner here?"

"Everyone is," Mulberry said, looking so sad and so guilty at the same time. "This place was originally built to be a prison, thousands of years ago. The first settlers were actually prisoners, sent here from Pyrrhia and trapped with magic. Not just for them, but for future generations and anyone else who comes here. The Barrier stops anyone from leaving."

"And those little guys," Umber said, pointing up at the metal dragons. They *buzz-rattled* grumpily at him again. "They're like . . . guards?"

"We assume so," Paua said. "Enchanted to keep an eye on us."

"So no one can leave this island? Ever?" Umber glanced at Paua and she nodded. "But . . . *you* can," he said to Mulberry.

"Right," Mulberry said miserably. "Just me. Nobody knows why."

Suddenly a few things made a lot more sense. "That's the magic you were talking about. The reason everyone keeps saying you're special — why everyone follows you around. They're hoping it'll spread to them?"

"Well, I wouldn't say that," Paua said. "Most dragons have given up on trying to leave. Hardly anyone ever tests the Barrier like you did. They love Mulberry for lots of other reasons, not just because they want his magic."

"Yeah." Umber let his head fall back on the pillow. He felt

very tired and incredibly overwhelmed. "That makes sense to me."

"You can be furious with me," Mulberry said. His wings drooped along the floor, like the last fallen leaves of autumn. "I deserve it. I tricked you into coming here."

Umber wrinkled his snout at him. "No, you didn't. You offered me and Sora a safe place to live where other dragons would help take care of us. That was all true. You just didn't mention that we'd never get to leave again."

"I should have." Mulberry covered his face with his talons. "And now you'll never see your family again, and it's my fault."

That didn't feel real yet. It couldn't be true that Reed and Pheasant and Marsh and Clay were gone from his life forever. It couldn't be real, so Umber didn't believe it, not really.

"Hey, hey." Umber reached up and tugged one of Mulberry's talons toward him. "You were following orders, right? The rules of the court? I know all about what that's like. That's me, too; I've always done what I'm told. You had to."

There was a loud *HISSSSSSS* and something went *SMASH!* behind a curtain farther down the room.

"Oh, for crying out loud," Paua said, jumping to her feet and hurrying off toward the sound. "That BETTER NOT HAVE BEEN A JAR OF MEDICINE!"

Umber blinked at Mulberry. "Ghost?" he asked.

"Ghost," Mulberry confirmed.

"Did I say something to offend the ghost?" Umber asked.

"The ghost," Mulberry said wryly, "exists in a sort of perpetual state of offendedness."

A roll of bandages came sailing over from a different curtained area and bonked Mulberry on the head. Through the silky curtains, Umber thought he saw a flash of phosphorescent green.

"Sorry," Mulberry said, picking up the bandages. "What I *meant* to say is that the ghost would like us to *think* a little harder about 'following orders' and how to say no to ones that we think are wrong. She leaves me notes to this effect almost every night. And I do read them! I promise!" he called, covering his head.

There were no further missiles or crashing sounds. Mulberry lowered his talons. "She's not wrong," he added. "It's really hard to argue with my parents, but . . . I could try harder."

"Not if it gets you in trouble," Paua said, coming back to Umber's bedside. "You have to stay safe."

Mulberry shrugged. "Who's safer than me?"

"Um . . . Paua?" Umber said cautiously. "Either I'm hallucinating, or there is an octopus on your head."

"Oh!" Paua laughed, reaching up to lift the little octopus into her talons. It was a smooth pale color, like driftwood, and it blinked enormous sweet eyes at Umber as she set it on the bed. "He's real. This is Blob."

Blob meandered over Umber's scales and wrapped two tentacles gently around his neck, snuggling into him.

"Oh my gosh," Umber breathed. "I love him."

"My great-great-great-some-number-of-greats-grandfather Fathom made him for my great-great-great-whatever-great-grandmother," Paua said. "And then he got passed down in the family, and Waterfall brought Blob with her when she came here."

"Waterfall — the animus dragon who made the castle?" Umber asked. "You're related to her?"

The smile dropped off Paua's face like a soldier falling from a battle in the sky. "Yes," she said. "But before you ask, no, I have no animus powers myself."

"I don't know much about animus dragons," Umber said apologetically. "I'm just wondering, if Waterfall was here and knew about the prison, couldn't she cast a spell to un-prison the island? I mean, why couldn't her magic break the first magic and set everyone free?"

"She tried," Mulberry said. "According to our records, she tried everything. The original animus dragon who enchanted the prison must have made it invulnerable to any other animus magic."

Oh, Umber thought. *Maybe other animus spells can't reach in here from outside. Maybe that's why no one has found me with the dreamvisitor.*

"And yet everyone keeps hoping a new animus dragon will hatch who can change everything," Paua said with a sigh.

Mulberry reached over Umber to touch one of her talons. "You're amazing the way you are," he said. "You help dragons all the time, all day long."

"Not as much as I could if I had animus magic!" Paua flicked her tail at the window. "Waterfall changed everything here. She built this castle, enchanted water sources that will never run dry, planted orchards where before nothing would grow. She couldn't set everyone free, but she made this place beautiful and safe. Imagine what I could do with magic like that."

She fell silent, fiddling with her claws. Umber was trying to think of what to say when a wadded-up ball of paper came flying over the partitions and bounced into his lap. Paua rolled her eyes, picked it up, unwrinkled it, and scanned the note scribbled on it.

"Yes, I *know*!" she called. "Thanks *so* much for the input!"

"You all have a very weird relationship with this ghost," Umber said to Mulberry.

"Tell me about it," Mulberry said, and his voice was so mildly exasperated that it made Umber laugh. Mulberry smiled down at him, but his eyes were still worried. "Aren't you mad at me?"

"I can't imagine being mad at you," Umber said truthfully. "I do have some other questions, though."

"Anything," Mulberry said.

"OK — for one, what is your mother so scared of that she's having me train the King's Teeth?"

"Oh," Mulberry said, wincing. "Um. We're not allowed to talk about that."

Umber raised an eyebrow at him.

"I know, I'm sorry!" Mulberry clutched his head.

"Mulberry," Paua said suddenly, whipping toward the door. "Someone's coming. It could be one of your parents." She flapped her wings, which made Blob startle in alarm and clamber up Umber's snout to the top of his head.

"I have to go," Mulberry said in a hurried whisper, taking a step away from Umber. "I promise I'll be back as soon as I can."

"Wait, why?" Umber asked. "Where?"

"Don't worry," Mulberry said. He started to reach for Umber again and visibly stopped himself. "I'll try to tell you more next time." He glanced toward the exit, bounded across the room, and pressed something on the far wall. A hidden door slid open; Mulberry slipped through and was gone.

Paua took a nervous breath as the talonsteps echoing from the hallway reached the infirmary and stepped inside. A light jingle of jewelry chains accompanied the heavy tread down the length of the room, until finally King Snakeroot stood at the foot of the bed, peering down his long green nose at Umber. Paua sank into a low bow.

"H-hi," Umber said. "Your Majesty." Should he get out of bed to greet him? Paua reached out and put one talon on his arm, as if making sure he didn't exert himself. The icy look on Snakeroot's face made Umber kind of wish he *didn't* have an adorable octopus draped over his forehead.

"Have either of you seen my son?" Snakeroot asked in a deathly calm voice.

"I thought he left for island patrol this morning," Paua said. "Isn't it overdue?"

"It *is* overdue, Paua," said Snakeroot. "Mulberry hasn't patrolled the outer isles since this young MudWing arrived, and as we all know, that makes everyone very anxious."

"I'm sure he's on his way now," Paua said. "He's so responsible. And brave. Always thinking of the community. Like his parents."

"Yes," Snakeroot said, twitching his long green tail. "If only *everyone* took after their most accomplished ancestors."

Paua's claws tightened on the bedsheet beside Umber and she bowed her head a little deeper.

"It's true Mulberry always has been very responsible," Snakeroot said. "And yet. I hear rumors that he has been here, sitting beside this bed and this unconscious dragon, every day for *hours*."

Every day? Umber thought. *To see* me?

"He really does not have time for that," said the king. "He is very special and has much to do. *No one* is allowed to monopolize his attention, no matter who they are."

"Of course," Paua agreed. "I will tell him so if I see him."

Snakeroot turned his dark green eyes on Umber. "You will, too. Stop distracting the prince."

"I didn't mean to," Umber said. This felt a little unfair; he *had* been unconscious, after all.

"Hmmm," Snakeroot said, glaring around at the rest of the room. "Well, if he hasn't been here today, perhaps he did leave this morning, as he was instructed." His eyes snapped back to Umber. "Will you be fit for training my guards again tomorrow?"

"I wouldn't recommend it yet, Your Majesty," Paua answered.

The king sighed. "Very well. Send him along as soon as you think he *is* ready. Heal quicker, MudWing." He shook out his wings, folded them back, and stalked out of the infirmary.

Paua exhaled and climbed to her feet again.

"That was too close. You must be hungry," she said, handing Umber a plate of ruby-orange fruit from the side table. "You've had nothing but broth this whole time."

How long was that? he wondered. How much time had he lost? Had he been asleep for weeks? How could he find out? Maybe Sora had been keeping track.

"I'll go see what else the kitchen has," Paua said. She patted his talon and glided out of the infirmary.

He realized she had dropped the note from the ghost on the floor by the bed. Carefully holding Blob in place, he leaned over and scooped it up.

It said, in the ghost's spiky handwriting:

YEAH, IMAGINE! YOU COULD HELP OVERTHROW
THE TRAITORS WHO STOLE THE THRONE!
OH WAIT . . . YOU COULD DO THAT WITHOUT MAGIC!

Huh.

Umber stared down at the plate of fruit, suddenly too exhausted to eat.

This is a prison. We're trapped here forever.

With angry ghosts and dangerous royalty and secrets no one can talk about.

It still didn't feel real, even though the memory of his Barrier encounter was getting clearer in his head.

What do we do? What can *I do?*

Nothing, was the obvious answer. Umber was nobody and this was a situation far beyond him. Dragons here had been wrestling with it for centuries; they must have tried every possible solution to escape. *He* certainly wasn't going to come up with the one new idea that worked.

He'd have to accept this life the way it was, like the others had. It wasn't so terrible, was it? Sort of weird and unsettling, and he had to be a soldier again, and the king seemed mad at him for some reason . . . but it could be worse, right?

We're stuck here.

I'm going to be responsible for Sora all by myself for the rest of our lives.

I'm never going to see my siblings again.

Umber buried his face in his talons. A moment passed.

There was a soft *whump* nearby.

"I wouldn't eat that if I were you," said a voice he'd never heard before.

Umber blinked up at the dragon perched on the end of his bed and knew immediately that he was looking into the eyes of the ghost.

CHAPTER 10

Umber and the ghost stared at each other for a long moment.

"Hello?" Umber said tentatively.

"It's covered in sleep powder," she said. "They use that stuff LIBERALLY around here. For newcomers, patients, dragonets, anyone with an opinion. Keeps everyone quiet and slow. Dragons can't fight back if they're ASLEEP."

He glanced down at his fruit and noticed there was, in fact, a dusting of yellow powder over the whole plate. It looked like the powder Quokka had put on their food on the first day — was that why he and Sora had fallen asleep right after eating?

For newcomers . . . maybe so we wouldn't ask too many questions or notice that we couldn't leave.

Did he believe the ghost?

Before he could decide, she seized his plate and flung all the fruit out the window. Umber hoped it didn't land on any unsuspecting dragons, although in the Court of Refuge they would probably be like, *no, no, we don't talk about the papaya from the sky.*

"There," she said, handing the plate back to him with an air of satisfaction.

She looked like a WildWing, spiky all over like Taipan, but dappled gold and dark blue and black with streaks of phosphorescent green striping her Pyrrhian-style wings. The shape of her face was a lot like Quokka's, but a fierce, scowly version. She was smaller than him but he wasn't sure she was younger; she gave off a bristly air of being a thousand times older and tougher and grumpier than him. She didn't look anything like he'd expected a ghost to look.

"I'm Umber," he said.

"Yeah, OBVIOUSLY I know that," she said. "I live in the WALLS, I know EVERYTHING."

"Sure," he said. "I mean, mostly I said that because I was kind of hoping you'd tell me *your* name. Or — oh no, I'm sorry; have you forgotten it?"

She stared at him like he had twelve cows on his head instead of one perfectly normal octopus. "Why would I have forgotten my name?"

"Because you're —" Suddenly Umber very much regretted the direction of this conversation, even though it had started as normally as possible. He couldn't say "dead" to a ghost, could he? He had no idea what ghosts knew and didn't know! "A ghost?" he finished awkwardly.

She picked up the roll of bandages and threw it at his head. Blob flung out a tentacle and caught it neatly out of the air.

"I'M NOT A GHOST!" she yelled. "AAAAAARGH!"

"I'm sorry!" Umber cried, scrambling out of the bed. The not-a-ghost grabbed the nearest curtain, yanked it down, and started ripping it to pieces. "Everyone said you were a ghost!"

"Why would you BELIEVE *THEM* instead of ME?" She kicked over a bench and then picked it up again and shook it furiously.

"I do believe you," he said helplessly. It was true: there was nothing ghostly about this angry whirlwind-of-chaos dragon. She wasn't invisible or translucent or ethereal or wafting or any of the other ways he had imagined her. She was as solid and real as him, maybe more so.

"Oh, good," she said, dropping the bench. "Because I'm right about everything else, too, and you should listen to me about ALL OF IT."

"But why does everyone think you're dead?" he asked.

"They DON'T!" She eyed another curtain with a ferocious look. "Weasels and cowards!! They know PERFECTLY WELL that I am alive and that I refuse to die!" She left the curtain in peace and pointed at him, flaring her wings. "The traitors declared me a ghost because they wanted me dead but FAILED to kill me. They've forbidden anyone to talk to me or listen to me, but it doesn't work! I'm still here and EVERYONE KNOWS IT. I won't let them forget me! I will *never* let them forget what they did!"

"What did they do?" Umber asked.

She cast a dark look at the doorway. "If you really want to know, come with me right now, before Paua gets back."

"Uh — is this a one-way trip?" Umber asked. "I mean, will I be able to come back here?"

She made a face like she was trying to squash a different face underneath. "For your sister, yes, yes, I know. Yes, it'll be fine. You'll be back before dark. Paua will cover for you." She glanced around at the mess she'd made. "She'll be able to guess who took you," she added with a grin.

"I'm — not sure I —"

"Why, what was YOUR brilliant plan?" she demanded. "Lie in bed and be depressed and do nothing? Accept your boring fate?"

That . . . kind of had been his plan, Umber had to admit to himself.

"I know you don't want to be stuck here," she said, "and neither do I. So let's DO SOMETHING ABOUT IT! Let's figure something out! Or have ideas! Let's make everyone pay attention! Or if that doesn't work, let's BREAK EVERYTHING!" She pulled down the curtain she'd previously spared and started shredding it with angry muttering noises.

"Three moons," Umber said. "All right, I'll come with you if you stop destroying Paua's infirmary." He untangled Blob from his ears and gently set the octopus on the bed, patting blankets into a nest around it. "Can I ask where we're going?"

"To answer two of your questions," she said, tossing aside the half-shredded curtain. "One: What is the queen so scared of — besides ME, of course, as she should be. And two, because I know you're thinking it: What did the original prisoners do to deserve a magical forever prison?"

"How about three?" he offered. "The third one being: What's your name?"

She grinned again with all her teeth. "It's Platypus. And if you laugh at that, I will literally murder you."

"I wouldn't!" he protested. He didn't even know what *platypus* meant or why it might be funny.

He also didn't know if it was a *great* idea to follow Platypus the chaos dragon through the secret door where Mulberry had gone, but he did it anyway. There was something about her that he couldn't say no to, and she was the first dragon to offer him real answers.

He just really, really hoped this didn't end with him as a ghost, too.

The secret door led to a whole maze of secret passages behind the walls and over the ceilings of the castle. It was like an entire second world slipped right behind the world he knew.

"Did Waterfall put all of this here on purpose?" he asked as Platypus peeked through a spyhole into the throne room.

"Not exactly," she said. "She made this a kind of . . . adaptive castle. So if a new room is needed for a vital purpose, it will grow like a new branch of a tree. Or, in this case, when I really needed secret passageways, the castle grew them for me."

"Just for you?" Umber asked.

"There are a couple other dragons who know about some of them," she said. "This way." She slid aside a section of wall and started down a long flight of stone stairs. As the light faded behind them, Umber discovered that Platypus's green scales glowed in the dark. It was enough for him to see a few steps in front of him, so he didn't trip when the stairs flattened into a tunnel, or when they turned into stairs again.

It went on forever, stairs tunnel stairs tunnel stairs *up* more tunnel stairs down again tunnel tunnel tunnel. The eeriness of the blue-green light in a sea of darkness on a never-ending path made Umber start to wonder if he'd actually died at the Barrier, and everything since had been a dream, and this was his passage into being a ghost.

Tail, talons, wings, shoulders, head. He breathed into each part of his body, doing Reed's meditation. *Tail. Talons. Legs. Wings*. He was real, this was real.

"Platypus?" he said. "Why does Quokka say she's responsible for you?"

The dragon in front of him hissed and lashed her spiky tail so hard he had to jump back a step to avoid getting smacked in the face. She twisted her head around to scowl at him.

"She doesn't have to do that," Platypus growled. "She could live in the walls with me! She could fight back instead of smiling and bowing and doing what she's told!"

"But isn't that true of all the dragons in the court?" Umber asked. "Why does Queen Beryl always call Quokka in particular to clean up the mess you make?"

Platypus exhaled furiously. "Quokka is my sister," she said, turning away and stomping forward again.

"Oh," Umber said. Now he understood. If Sora suddenly

became an angry living ghost in the ceiling who occasionally smashed things, he'd feel like he had to clean up after her, too.

"Beryl is trying to punish me by pushing her around like that," Platypus added. "But it doesn't work, because I don't care."

"I see," Umber said.

"I don't!" Platypus insisted. "She could have come with me! She still could! She chose this, not me!"

"I'm sorry," Umber said.

"It's fine." Platypus kicked a pebble out of her way. "One day everyone will listen and rise up and throw Beryl and Snakeroot off their stolen thrones, and then I can come out of the walls and we'll be normal sisters again. Here we are."

The tunnel opened at last into a cave — a round, dome-like space with a rough stone bench running all around the wall. Across from the tunnel entrance was another tunnel, slanting up toward distant sunlight. And equidistant between the two tunnels was a solid stone door, with silvery glowing letters on it that said: MEMORY ROOM.

"What is this place?" Umber asked, touching the bench with one of his claws. The stone was cold as ice; the whole space sent shivers through his scales. And it was silent. He had gotten used to the murmurs of the court and the odd cries of the birds in the orchards. Here there was no sound, nothing but a deep muffling void, as though they had stepped out of time and space.

"Well, here's my theory," Platypus said. "I think the first

prisoners were required to come here sometimes to relive their crimes. Like, as a punishment or reminder of what they'd done or whatever." She sat down in front of the Memory Room door.

Umber stared at her. "So — more magic?" he said. "Like the Barrier?"

"Right," she said. "It's kind of intense. Be prepared for that." She opened the door and gestured at the darkness beyond like *enough said, off you go!*

"Um — can you tell me anything else?" Umber asked. "Will I be in there very long?"

"It won't seem long to you," she said. "But every minute that passes in there is a hundred years out here."

"What?!" Umber cried.

Platypus started laughing. "That was amazing! You really believed me!" She snorted gleefully. "OK, no more questions, get in there."

"But now I don't know *what* to believe," Umber protested.

"You'll see," she said. "Just remember it all happened thousands of years ago. It's not happening to you, and you didn't do it, no matter how it makes you feel. And it'll be over soon."

Umber took a step closer and craned his neck to see inside. But there was nothing *to* see: only darkness, deeper than any night.

Well, there were much easier ways for Platypus to kill him, if that was what she was trying to do.

And *someone* other than her had put this here.

And — although he didn't want to admit this to himself — he appreciated being told what to do, clearly and simply, in this very confusing place.

Umber took a deep breath and stepped into the Memory Room.

CHAPTER 11

He didn't hear the door close. He didn't see the light disappear; the darkness was just there, all around him, all at once.

The surface under his talons felt different. Instead of rough stone, it was polished smooth as glass. Maybe it *was* glass? He reached out and felt one wingtip brush a wall that also seemed to be glass, or solid quicksilver, or —

He blinked, and he was standing in the palace of the SkyWings.

He recognized it, and yet this wasn't Ruby's palace, the one he'd visited after the war. It was in the same place — he could see sharp mountains in the moonlight beyond the balcony where he stood. But the shape of the palace below him was smaller, rougher, and covered less of the mountain. There was no arena, and fewer towers. No statues of Scarlet overlooking everyone; no gold embedded in the walls.

This was the Sky Kingdom long ago, in the early days when the palace was first being built.

The balcony led into a throne room, where Umber found himself facing a huge dragon throne carved from dark wood and embedded with gems. It was artfully surrounded by exquisite gifts: a silken tapestry portrait of a golden-orange SkyWing in a crown, a carved wooden sculpture of a dragon about to take flight, an obsidian orb that glittered with flecks of starlight, a necklace of symmetrical oval pink pearls, a perfect miniature tree covered in perfect miniature apples.

Gifts from the other tribes, Umber realized. He counted eight of them. Pyrrhia had seven tribes now . . . so this must be a time when BeetleWings and LeafWings still lived here. *If the tribes are exchanging art honoring each other's queens, there must be peace between the kingdoms.* That was the dream of Jade Mountain Academy: a world where dragons coexisted and there was no war.

A whisper of dread drifted through him. Something was about to go terribly wrong, and there was nothing he could do but watch.

Two SkyWings entered the room. Neither acknowledged his presence; he guessed he was watching what happened but was invisible to them. One of them was tall and glamorous and looked like the dragon in the tapestry, including the glittering crown. The other had darker orange scales and the face of someone who was always doing math problems with part of her brain. Around her neck she wore a necklace of nine different claws. Umber wasn't close enough to be sure, but they each looked as if they came from a different animal — crocodile, polar bear, eagle, if he had to guess a few. She also wore odd twisty metal earrings and beaten copper wristbands, and there was something clipped to each wristband.

Umber squinted. They looked like even smaller versions of the Dungeon Isle's little metal guards.

The queen climbed onto the throne and settled like a watchful lioness, looking down at the other dragon. Umber felt a strange, powerful wave of admiration for her: *Behold this glorious queen. Behold how great and generous and wise and benevolent she was. The greatest queen who ever lived.*

That's magic at work, Umber realized with the logical side of him. *Part of this enchantment is making me feel that way about her.*

"We'll sort this out, Precipice," said the SkyWing queen. "Go set a meeting with the NightWings."

"Yes, Queen Falcon." The other dragon glanced around the empty throne room. "I'll summon some guards for you."

The queen waved one of her talons dismissively. "Not necessary, but thank you."

"But . . . sorry to mention it, Your Majesty," Precipice said, "but your sister was acting odd earlier."

"I'm not worried about Summit," the queen said. "She's not strong enough to challenge me for the throne. You may go, dear."

"All right. Be careful." Precipice glanced around again, then headed for the balcony, walking right through Umber's tail, which was not his favorite thing that had ever happened. She spread her wings and flew off into the night sky.

The queen plucked one of the miniature apples from the tree and ate it in one bite.

Glorious queen, thrummed Umber's heart. *The best queen.*

Not as great as Moorhen, he tried to tell himself stubbornly. That only seemed to intensify the magic.

Kindest queen. She took a scroll from a table beside the throne and started to read, coiling her tail around herself. *A queen for all time. A queen who could have reigned for years of peace and prosperity.*

Something moved on the empty ceiling.

Uh-oh, Umber thought, his stomach twisting. He didn't want to see this, but now he was frozen in place, unable to move or turn away.

The wall rippled as a shadow slipped down from the ceiling behind the queen's throne. Umber caught a glimpse of the outline of a dragon, scales shifting from one camouflage to another.

It crept closer and closer to the queen.

Umber wanted so badly to yell a warning, but he couldn't. *This happened thousands of years ago,* he reminded himself. *No one can change it now.*

Wings fluttered just outside the balcony, and the queen looked up sharply. "Yes?" she called. "Who's there?"

The camouflaged dragon struck.

He wrestled the queen to the floor, a coil of thorn-covered vine around her neck, as another dragon slipped over the balcony railing and ran toward him.

The new dragon was dark purple, with wings somewhere between a SilkWing and a HiveWing that folded back neatly along her spine. A BeetleWing, Umber guessed. She leaped onto the queen and helped pin her down.

Cowards, hissed the magic in Umber's heart. *Murderers.*

"You're sure about this, Darkling?" whispered the RainWing at the queen's throat.

"Yes," said the BeetleWing. "We have our orders. No mercy, Lemur." She raised one talon, and Umber saw glittering spots of dark liquid on the ends of her claws. "This is the only way."

Her claws slashed down, carving vicious lines across the queen's throat. The SkyWing queen flailed, trying to throw her attackers off — but as her wounds bubbled scarlet and black, her movements grew weaker, and finally she stopped moving altogether.

The queen was dead.

"One down," said Darkling. "Now we go after the NightWing queen."

They fled to the balcony and away into the night sky.

The scene began to fade, but Umber still couldn't move. He stood there, trapped in place, forced to stare at the dead SkyWing queen as the walls and throne and night sounds ebbed slowly away. The queen was the last to disappear, and then Umber finally felt himself released from the magic.

He could see the Memory Room now. The walls and floor were smooth green glass that reflected him blurrily in every direction; the ceiling was obsidian and the light seemed to come from below him. In the center of the room was a stone pedestal about as tall as his shoulder, with a shallow basin on top of it. It reminded him of the birdbaths in the orchards around the court, but this was dry and empty.

Umber had the strange feeling that the room was waiting for him to do something . . . as though the magic was lingering around the edges, ready to draw him back in.

If he stood here long enough, would another scene begin? Would he have to watch those dragons murder another queen? Or the same one, again and again in a loop?

Neither of those sounded appealing. He backed toward the door, hoping there wasn't a catch in the magic that he was missing. The waiting feeling hung there, like fog crowding in between his scales. But nothing happened as he touched the handle; nothing happened as he pushed the door open and stumbled back out into the cave.

"You survived!" Platypus cried, popping off the bench next to the door. "That's pretty rare; only like one in twenty dragons makes it out of there."

"What?" Umber's wings were shaking. He sat down, then decided lying down sounded even better. He curled into a tight ball and closed his eyes. "Are you messing with me?"

"Yes, always," Platypus said. "It's a *Memory* Room, not a MURDER room, don't worry. Oh wow, I wish I had a murder room. Wouldn't that be useful? Think of all the things I could accomplish with a murder room! Stop making that face, I'm just kidding. MOSTLY kidding."

"Does everyone see the same thing in there?" Umber asked, deciding to ignore most of that.

"The pink tarantulas? Doing a kick line and singing about how regicide is justified?"

Umber cracked open one eye to look at her sternly.

"OK, all right, not the time," she said. "Yes, as far as I know, everyone gets the same scene of a RainWing and a BeetleWing murdering the SkyWing queen."

"Is that really what happened?" Umber asked. "All the RainWings I've met are so nonviolent. And the SilkWings at the court seem really mellow, too, except maybe Royal. They seem like the last dragons who would break a peace between the tribes by assassinating a queen."

"That's what the history scrolls say." Platypus shrugged. "There was a peace treaty between all the tribes — the Accords of Dragonkind, very fancy and serious — and some council of dragons called the Queens' Claws with one representative from each tribe."

"Really?" Umber said. "That sounds great."

"Sure, until it ALL WENT WRONG," Platypus said dramatically. "Apparently some of them decided to secretly kill the queens of the other tribes, as you saw in there. But turns out they weren't very good at it, because right after the SkyWing queen's murder, they were caught and sent here."

"Why would they do that?" Umber sat up again, rubbing his head. "If there was peace — why would they ruin it? That's awful."

"Yup. Hence: PRISON FOREVER," Platypus declared, flinging out her wings.

"For the assassins on the council?" Umber asked. "How did they survive?"

"No, no," she said. "For them, their families, and in the case of the BeetleWing and the LeafWing, their entire tribes."

"What?!" Umber stared at her. "Is that another joke? Their *entire tribes*?"

"No, it's true," she said. "A bunch of them escaped to Pantala, but the rest were sent here. That's why, as you may have noticed, there are no BeetleWings or LeafWings on Pyrrhia."

"Why just those two tribes?" Umber said. "Why not the RainWings, too? I mean, that was a RainWing helping to kill the queen, wasn't it?"

Platypus shrugged again. "WHO KNOWS," she said. "That's not in the Memory Room! But the *important thing* is that we *both agree* that *throwing rightful leaders off their thrones* is *very bad*, right?"

"Um," he said. "I have to admit I'm nervous about how you said that."

"Great!" she said. "So let's go meet the rightful leaders of the Court of Refuge!" She bounded toward the other tunnel, the one that led up toward sunlight.

Umber climbed to his feet and followed her. His head was spinning, and he couldn't get the image of the murder out of his head. It did explain why the other tribes would want to punish them so severely. Assassinating queens was the kind of thing that set off wars, as Umber well knew from the War of SandWing Succession that he'd fought in all his life.

But what he'd seen still didn't make sense to him.

Why had they killed her?

Were they just evil?

Were they trying to start a war? One of them said something about orders . . . so did their queens know?

His brain was going in circles around these questions as he stepped out of the tunnel into the blinding sunlight, and so it took him a moment to notice the half circle of dragons around him, pointing spears in his direction.

"Stop right there," someone said. "In the name of the true court, we hereby claim you as our hostage."

CHAPTER 12

"*Do* we?" said another voice. "The last time we tried to take a hostage was a miserable failure."

"That's because they didn't want that dragon back," said the first voice. Umber's eyes were starting to adjust to the bright sun. He could see that the dragon talking was a WildWing, covered with the thorny spikes from nose to tail. "Understandably; he was terribly dull. This one looks much more interesting. I bet they'll be mad if we keep him."

"You think?" said a third voice hopefully. "Maybe they'll give us the throne back in exchange for his life?"

"Ha ha ha. They wouldn't even give us a half-eaten coyote in exchange for *anyone*," the second voice pointed out.

Except maybe Mulberry, Umber thought.

"He just thought 'except maybe Mulberry,'" said a fourth dragon, sounding kind of bored about it. Startled, Umber turned to find her. *A mind reader?* He'd begun to think those were a NightWing myth. She gazed back at him impassively. She had butterfly wings dotted with silver crescents like little moons, so she was a hybrid, not a full NightWing. Her scales were a deep blue-black, except for two silver teardrops by her eyes. *Just like Moon's,* Umber thought. *What does that mean?*

"Well, sure," said the second voice. "I mean, that's pretty obvious, strange dragon, but the prince hasn't deigned to wander into any of our clever traps, so."

"You can't take Umber hostage anyway because he's my guest," Platypus said. "Also, yeah, Beryl and Snakeroot wouldn't give you anything for him. Sorry."

"Ah, well," said the WildWing, pulling back her spear. "Always worth a try."

They were out on the yellow plain, the castle in the distance behind them, and the wind was hot and dusty. The tunnel emerged from one of the larger rock formations, and Umber wondered whether it had been there before dragons put a Memory Room under it, or whether they'd created the rock somehow to mark where the Memory Room was.

"These three you don't need to worry about," Platypus said to Umber, pointing to the dragons on the right half of the circle.

"Hey," said one of them, a roly-poly brown WildWing with a SandWing barbed tail, dark green freckles across his snout, and a sweet grin. "I'm scary sometimes."

"That's Wollemi," Platypus said. "He's scary never. He won't even sneak into the castle to break stuff with me. The NightWing-SilkWing is Crescent; she doesn't believe in secrets. You would think a mind reader would have been helpful at stopping a traitorous conspiracy, but it turns out, NOT SO MUCH."

"They avoided me, you know that," Crescent said, rolling her eyes. "And frankly that was fine with me, because their brains were very boring."

"And this is Glowworm — he's just a HiveWing," Platypus said. Glowworm, an older, yellow-and-black adult with worried eyes, nodded politely at Umber. "The three you *really* need to meet are these over here: the elected Triumvirate, rightful leaders of the Court of Refuge."

"Elected?" Umber echoed, surprised. He'd heard the word in the context of MudWing families, like when he and his siblings voted on which river to fish in or who should get to be their navigator on a long flight (Sora always won). But elected . . . leaders?

"Yes! The court used to be fair," Platypus said furiously. "There was a system! We voted peacefully and chose who made the decisions and then they cycled out and we voted in new ones and IT WAS FAIR AND NOW IT ISN'T."

"Who *are* you yelling at," said Crescent. "All of us here agree with you."

"Yeah," said Wollemi. "Or else we wouldn't be living in scrubby caves, eating nothing but dingoes."

Platypus pointed to the WildWing who'd suggested taking Umber hostage. "This is Tuatara, who's probably the oldest WildWing at court, and also the smartest."

"Thank you, dear," Tuatara said, tipping her head at Umber.

"And this is Horizon." Platypus gave a little bow at the dragon next to her, whose scales were dappled red and blue.

"His parents were a SkyWing and a SeaWing who ran away from Pyrrhia so they wouldn't have to fight each other in the war. It's very epic." She took Umber's shoulders and turned him all the way to the left to see the last dragon. "And this is Monarch."

Monarch was a beautiful orange SilkWing with long antennae and blue and white markings along her wings and by her eyes. She looked like she hadn't slept in a really long time. She had scars around her ankles and along her throat, and one of her back claws was missing.

"It's my fault," she said wistfully to Umber. "I'm afraid I have a habit of losing kingdoms."

"It is NOT your fault!" Platypus shouted. "It is BERYL AND SNAKEROOT'S FAULT for being LYING WORMS and STEALING THE THRONE with their SNEAKY GOONS."

"Have you met a dragon named Royal yet?" Monarch asked Umber. "Is he all right?"

"Oh," Umber said, feeling awkward. He sensed that *yes, but he's a jerk* was not the polite thing to say. "I met him briefly. He seemed . . . fine." *Don't mention the Toughen Up Stick. Don't even think about the — oops.*

Crescent met his eyes and gave him a little "yeah, I heard that, but I'll spare you" smile.

Glowworm sidled around the circle to take one of Monarch's talons in his. "Everyone has said he's all right," he said to her. "Don't worry. I know we never liked Taipan, but being his friend will keep Royal safe."

"So this is it," Platypus said to Umber. She spread her talons at the six dragons in a "ta-da!" gesture. "THIS is why the king is having you train his little army of thugs. In case the terrifying Triumvirate suddenly attack."

Umber looked doubtfully around the circle. These were not exactly the most intimidating dragons he'd ever seen. Were Beryl and Snakeroot really afraid of them?

And did that mean . . . would he have to fight them one day?

"So I had this GREAT idea," Platypus went on, "which is maybe you could train your merry band of soldiers ALL WRONG. Like, teach them to hold their spears from the wrong end and accidentally fall off walls and bonk each other in the snout when they're doing formations. And then they'd be super easy to defeat! You can do that, right?"

"I don't think so?" Umber said. "I mean, I'm not sure how I would plausibly train anyone to fall off walls."

"Well, some other kind of sabotage, then," Platypus said. "We can't let them feel like they're winning, Umber. They have to wake up every morning wondering what we'll do next. We have to be fighting them all the time, in all the ways!"

"OK, I — I'll think about it," he said. What he meant was *I need to think about whether I agree with you,* but she must have thought he meant *I'll think about how to help you,* because the hopeful look that spread across her face was heartbreaking.

Had she really been living in the walls for two years,

causing chaos and leaving notes and being treated like a ghost by everyone? All because she believed so much in the possibility of a fairer system and better leaders?

"I should get back to the infirmary," he said. The exertion of the long walk and the stress of the Memory Room were starting to hit him rather intensely.

He'd wanted answers to his questions, but now that he had them, he didn't know what to do with them.

Could he picture himself helping Platypus to overthrow Beryl and Snakeroot? But if it didn't work — wouldn't that put Sora in danger, and shouldn't she be his first priority?

But if Beryl ordered him to fight these dragons, how could he do it? Now that he'd met them and knew their story, wouldn't he rather protect them?

And they were all trapped here on this island. Sooner or later, he was sure, Beryl would want him to attack them, and there was no way for anyone to escape.

He wished he could ask Mulberry what *he* thought Umber should do. But the prince was gone now, on island patrol for who knew how long. And presumably he would be on his parents' side, so it probably wasn't even safe to ask him.

Umber waved to the exiled dragons and followed Platypus back into the tunnel, thinking over what he could do next.

There's one other dragon I can talk to . . . if I let myself start trusting her as a sister again.

The walk back up to the castle was *not* fun, and he spent the night and the entire next day in bed recovering. He took the sleep powder gratefully and let himself swim in and out of consciousness, interspersed with blurry visits from Paua, who was very cross with him for getting up and "running around after phantoms." She wouldn't let him tell her anything about where he'd been or what he'd seen.

The day after that, he felt well enough to walk around again. This time he asked Paua humbly if he could go see Sora in the library, and she agreed, as long as he came back within an hour and had nothing to do with ghosts while he was gone.

The library, like the Gathering, was set up perfectly for MudWings, with corners full of cushions for groups of dragons to sit and read together. It was three stories tall, with an open central area so dragons could fly from floor to floor, and the ceiling was made of glass so sunlight could come through but the scrolls were safe from the weather.

Umber wandered the warren of shelves until he finally found Sora on the second floor, curled up by a window, reading a scroll. For a moment, he hesitated. She looked the way he always pictured her: his quiet, shy sister, who loved to read and study old maps and recommend scrolls and share her favorite scenes with her brothers and sisters. She should never have been sent to war.

Maybe none of us should have.

He would do anything for Queen Moorhen, and more important, he would do anything for Reed, but when he thought about the war now, he couldn't stop wondering what the point of it was. To install one SandWing on the throne instead of another? What did that have to do with him or Sora or any other MudWing?

If Sora had managed to put all that behind her — maybe he shouldn't drag her into this.

But before he could leave again, she looked up and spotted him.

"Umber!" She waved her tail at the cushion next to her. "You're up!"

"I'm trying," he said with a smile. Sora threw both her wings and arms around him as he sat down and hugged him tightly.

"I wouldn't say I was worried," she said, "but three moons, did you sleep for a long time!"

"Did they tell you why?" Umber asked. "Do you know about the Barrier? That this place is a prison?"

"*Was* a prison," she said. "But it doesn't feel like one anymore." She waved one of her wings at the beautiful library around them.

"Except nobody can leave," he said.

Sora shrugged. "Why would we want to?"

To see our brothers and sister again, Umber thought, but if Sora was happy, he didn't want to ruin it. Instead he said, "I learned something interesting about the original prisoners. Have you found anything about them in your reading?"

She shook her head. "Not yet. Tell me."

He explained about the Memory Room and the scene in the SkyWing palace, leaving out the details about Platypus for now. "So I guess now I know *what* happened three thousand years ago," he said, "but I still don't feel like I understand *why*."

"That sounds horrible to watch," Sora said. She traced the edges of her scroll with her claws. "I can't believe they left something like that here. Just to torture the prisoners even more?"

"I don't know," Umber said. "Maybe to remind them what a terrible thing they did? The magic in the room tries really hard to make you love the queen. So it's, like, emotionally devastating when she dies — maybe that's what the dragons felt who built this prison? And they wanted to make sure the prisoners felt it, too?"

"It's only a piece of the story, though," Sora said intently. "The BeetleWing and the RainWing, they must have had a *reason* for what they did. The rest of the story is missing."

Umber felt a worry headache starting. It hadn't occurred to him that Sora might identify with the two murderers in the scene. "But . . . even if they did have a reason," he said cautiously, "it was still wrong to kill the queen. Like, wrong because murder is always wrong. And also because of all the terrible things that followed — the peace falling apart, entire tribes being driven out of Pyrrhia, this prison. No matter why they did it, they shouldn't have."

Sora lifted her gaze from the scroll to the window, staring out at the mountains with a faraway look. "Right," she said.

"Do you know anything about animus magic?" he asked, hoping to steer the conversation back to safer ground.

"A little," Sora said. "Moon was reading a scroll about it, so I borrowed it, too."

"Did you see anything about how to break an animus spell?"

"It depends on the spell," Sora said. His strategy was working. Her face was back to an expression Umber had seen a lot before: she was trying to remember all the scrolls she'd read. "Like, how it was worded and what object was used for the enchantment."

"Object?"

"Every animus spell requires an object to enchant," Sora said. "It can't be like, enchant this whole continent or create a prison out of thin air — it must be something solid to focus the magic. I think. And it must still exist, because I'm pretty sure if the object is destroyed, the spell would break — oh, unless destroying the object is written into the spell, like: 'when I crush this grape all my enemies will die,' that kind of thing."

"An animus dragon could do that?!" Umber cried. "That's so scary!"

"I don't know!" Sora said. "I've never met one; I'm just telling you what I read!"

"SHHHHHH," said a dragon somewhere else in the library.

Umber lowered his voice again. "OK, so maybe we can find whatever they enchanted and set it on fire, and then everyone will be free."

"Or we can just do whatever Mulberry did," Sora said. "I mean, why can he cross the border?"

"He doesn't know," Umber said. "He said nobody knows." Sora was right — if they could figure that out, maybe the answer would work for other dragons, too. But Umber didn't want to be like one of Mulberry's followers, only trying to get something out of him.

"Beware," breathed a voice overhead.

Umber and Sora both jumped. Umber spread his wings to shield her as they looked up.

Perched on top of the bookshelf, squeezed between it and the ceiling, was King Snakeroot, his eyes glittering. His green wings hung like enormous leaves over the scrolls.

"Beware," he whispered again. "Beware, beware the hybrid prince."

"Um . . . hi, Your Majesty," Umber said.

"When the claws are at his throat," Snakeroot hissed.

"Y-yes, sir?"

The LeafWing lashed his tail, knocking scrolls to the ground, and finally swarmed off along the shelves to another shadowy corner of the stacks.

"He's a little alarming," Umber whispered to Sora.

"Hey, if you're allowed out of bed," she said, grabbing his arm, "you should come to the Northern Lights concert tonight!"

"The what?"

"You *have* to," Sora said, her eyes shining. "You've missed two already and Aurora is — I don't even know how to describe her. She's magic, but like, real, like a real dragon who can make magic with only words and music. Her music makes me feel sane, Umber."

"Oh, wow," Umber said. He hadn't seen Sora this excited in — maybe ever? "That sounds amazing."

"When I'm listening to her, there's finally something else in my head. Something besides Crane and Icicle and all the terrible things I keep trying to push down. It's as if she says all the things I'm feeling and I understand myself. I can stop worrying and I can breathe and be happy, even just for a moment. That probably doesn't make sense."

"No, it does," Umber said, catching her talons and squeezing them. He had a flash of memory — the posters in the grand entrance hall; weren't those of Aurora? Wasn't she a SkyWing-IceWing hybrid?

If Sora didn't care about that . . . if she was this excited about an IceWing . . . then he really needed to see this miracle.

He smiled at Sora. "I would love to come with you."

CHAPTER 13

Umber could hear thrumming through the rock underfoot. The crowd around them had started dancing already on their way to their seats, wings loose, tails swinging, smiles everywhere.

The concert amphitheater was outdoors, at the far end of the castle, with the huge expanse of the plains and distant mountains and the whole starlit sky as a backdrop beyond the stage. Flames trapped in tall glass lanterns bordered the stage, shifting from pink to blue to purple as the fire danced. Vines of plants with small flowers that glowed in the dark were woven all along the benches and stairs; it looked as though there were fireflies everywhere.

A dragon sat on a platform between the lights upstage, playing drums as the audience arrived. The beat reminded Umber of MudWing festivals, where they'd meet other sibling groups under the moons. Sora, Marsh, and Reed always got tired and went to bed early, but Umber, Crane, and Pheasant loved meeting new dragons and dancing until they couldn't feel their talons anymore.

Umber glanced over at Sora. She'd woven herself a necklace of reeds and small paper cranes, winking white and gold in the shifting lights. Her eyes were shining.

Sitting next to Sora was Quokka, and on his other side was Paua, with Blob nestled on her shoulder. "If you're going to the concert," Paua had warned him, "I'll have to tell the king you're well enough to start training again tomorrow."

Umber was dreading it, but he didn't think he could put it off any longer anyway.

"Here she comes!" Sora cried, seizing Umber's arm. The drumbeat had changed, the tempo rising, and now everyone was looking up as a silvery figure descended from the sky.

It *was* the dragon from the posters, glittering ice and breathing small bursts of blue fire as she glided down to the stage. She stepped toward the audience and began to sing in an ethereal voice.

I want to fly through the fire
I want to touch the lights in the sky
I want to breathe in the gold and the green
I wish we could be seen
Could be free

Sora — and every other dragon in the theater — was standing on her seat, singing along. Umber had never seen anything like it. He hadn't even known all these dragons could be so happy. Nobody looked worried about saying the wrong thing or breaking the rules. It made him realize even more how nervous they usually were around the court — how careful.

Up in the royal box, the king and queen were watching.

"Let's hear it for my amazing brother, Borealis," Aurora called, sweeping one wing toward the drummer. The crowd roared. "And, of course, for our wonderful king and queen." She bowed toward the royal box. The drums rose again, and she kept singing.

Mother kept you in your place
Blades of ice, frozen face
Father blazing deep inside
Fire hidden, burning wide
All of that is in me, too
The ice, the fire, searing through
I feel it
I feel it all the time
The constant eyes, the endless frowns
And I just want to burn it down

"Burn it down!" the audience screamed. Blob waved half of his tentacles in delight.

All the nights when I can't breathe
Heart too fast, mind full speed
Talons stealing all my air
Never, ever show you care
Hold your smile through all the lies
I dream it
I dream of open skies
The prison bars, the ones in charge
They can never hold us down

A gust of snowflakes suddenly whirled across the audience. Startled, Umber caught one in his talons — but it wasn't snow. It was a tiny, folded piece of paper. He knew before he even unfolded it that it would be a note from Platypus. An entire snowstorm of ghostly notes blanketed the singing dragons. The one in his claws said:

WAKE UP! FIGHT BACK!

He caught another one, which said:

IT DOESN'T HAVE TO BE LIKE THIS.

They're saying the same thing, he realized suddenly. *The notes and the song. Is Aurora doing that on purpose? Does she know?*

Suddenly the queen was looming next to Paua, glaring at Umber.

"Do something about this," she hissed, catching a talonful of notes out of the air and crumpling them. She looked more angry than he'd ever seen her . . . as menacing as Snakeroot.

"M-me?" Umber said. He scrambled to his feet. What did she mean — clean it up? Hide the notes before anyone saw them? *All* of them?

Beryl jabbed one claw at the night sky overhead, where a flash of phosphorescent green was circling. "Catch that dragon and lock her up."

"What?" Quokka gasped. She scrambled over Sora to crouch next to Umber. "But Your Majesty — she's just a ghost, she can't —"

"She has annoyed me for the last time," snarled the queen. "MudWing, do your job."

Is this my job? Umber's heart was pounding. *When did I agree to do any of this?* Aurora was still singing, and so was Sora; his sister hadn't even noticed the queen in the aisle. All around them, dragons were singing while catching the notes and reading them or hiding them away.

"We'll do it, Your Majesty," Taipan said, strutting down from one of the higher benches with Royal and Dugong, as always, one step behind him. He sneered at Umber. "If this MudWing is too scared, we'll catch the ghost for you."

If I let them go after Platypus, they'll hurt her, Umber thought, and he could tell from Quokka's panicked face that she was thinking the same.

"No, I'll go," he said. He spread his wings and met Quokka's eyes, and then he leaped into the sky.

"Go after him," he heard the queen growl. "Make sure she doesn't get away."

The three dragons were right behind him, snorting and riling one another up. How was he going to do this? How could he keep Platypus safe without making it obvious he was trying to help her? Taipan would go straight back to Beryl with that information, if he saw Umber let Platypus go.

Please just fly away, he prayed. *See us coming and escape.*

But he saw her glowing wings circle around and come

sailing back, still flinging handfuls of notes down onto the crowd. He wasn't sure she had even spotted him and the three dangerous dragons soaring toward her.

"Hey, GHOST!" he shouted. He hoped the music and the crowd singing along would drown out his voice for any listeners below, but he had to sound convincing, just in case. "By order of the queen, you're under arrest!"

Her shadowy figure wheeled around and saw him.

"You can't arrest a ghost!" she shouted back.

"Those are my orders! Surrender yourself!"

"Ha ha YESS," she yelled. "MAKE ME!"

She swooped away around one of the castle roofs and Umber soared after her. She was fast, but he could hear Taipan's wingbeats close behind him.

"Go that way and we'll cut her off!" he called to Taipan, pointing to the other side of the castle.

"Nice try!" Taipan called back. "We're catching her without you and taking the credit!"

So that confirmed Umber's theory that Taipan would do the opposite of whatever Umber said. He wheeled around a tower and saw Platypus flinging purple fruits through an open window, until she saw him and took off again.

They sped through the dips and whirls of the castle, startling bats out of the eaves in chaotic flurries. A couple of dragons doing an astronomy lesson on a high platform shrieked and dropped their papers when Platypus shot by. They had recovered enough to yell at Umber and the others about "irresponsible flying" as they zipped by a moment later.

"Sorry!" Umber called over his shoulder. He glanced back and saw Royal deliberately kick over their telescope.

Suddenly Platypus dove through an open skylight into a section of the palace that Umber didn't know. He spiraled after her, skidding across the polished wood floor as he landed. Platypus was already whisking around the corner up ahead. He ran to catch up.

Thump thump thud came the sound of the three dragons landing behind him, and then a crash as one of them knocked over a statue.

"DUGONG!" shouted the other two angrily.

There were sculptures and paintings and tapestries all along this corridor, like some kind of museum or art gallery. Galloping around the corner, Umber ran headfirst into a mirror, which turned out to be the entrance to an entire maze of mirrors.

What in the world . . .

Maybe they could lose Taipan here, but Umber thought they could just as easily lose themselves, get turned around, and walk straight into his claws. He ran into the maze anyway.

Three turns later, a voice whispered, "This way," and a mirrored panel swung open. A pair of claws reached out to grab him and he let himself get yanked through into the dark.

But not entirely dark: familiar green scales glowed as Platypus grinned at him. She put one claw to her mouth and slipped away.

They were in the walls.

Umber listened for a minute against the back of the mirror, to be sure nobody had seen him disappear from the maze.

"Which way did he go?" Taipan demanded.

"Dugong lost him," Royal said.

"Uh — that way, I think?" Dugong suggested.

"So definitely not that way," Royal countered.

"Split up. Find him! And the ghost!" Taipan snarled.

Their footsteps faded away.

Umber tiptoed quietly after Platypus. At the end of the hidden passage was a kind of staircase where the stairs were haphazard sizes made of leftover construction materials. Umber had to hop from one to another, sometimes using his wings to help him climb.

Finally, at the top, a secret door stood ajar into a room full of candlelight.

Umber slipped through and froze in place, blinking.

He'd never seen such an enormous bedroom. He guessed forty MudWing siblings (if some poor mother ever carried that many) could have lived in here comfortably, with room to roll around and share wandering feasts of hippos.

One corner was dedicated to a fake tree as tall as he was, carved from black wood and polished to a shine, with jewelry hanging from every branch in a glittering rainbow. In front of one of the windows was a sprawling desk covered in unrolled scrolls, with more scrolls scattered all around it. Blotches of ink on the scrolls and an old spill of blue on the corner of the desk told Umber that someone here had been writing, apparently on multiple scrolls at once.

The secret door behind him was a mirror as tall as the wall and twice as wide as his wingspan. Opposite that was a magnificent balcony, and even from across the room Umber could see that they must be in one of the tallest towers of the castle. The lights of the concert twinkled far below them, and a cold wind blew from the mountains straight into the room.

In the center of the room was a bed large enough for eight dragons, and sprawled out in the middle of it, among the pink sparkly cushions and fluffy white blankets and gossamer silk hangings, was Platypus.

"Hieee," she said cheerfully. "That was fun."

"Where are we?" Umber asked. His heart was pounding. Who could afford a tree full of that much jewelry? "Please, *please* tell me this isn't the queen's room."

Platypus laughed. "It isn't." She pointed at the real door to the room just as it swung open. "It's hers."

Aurora stepped inside and closed the door behind her.

"Platypus," she said. "You are so dead."

CHAPTER 14

"Nice to see you, too," Platypus said, throwing one of the pillows at Aurora.

"Aren't you in the middle of a concert?" Umber asked.

"Not anymore," Aurora said. "The queen canceled it because *somebody* decided to stage one of her quirky protests all over *my* audience."

"It's not QUIRKY!" Platypus yelled. "It's RIGHTEOUS and IMPORTANT!"

"Shhhhh," Umber pleaded. He'd accomplished step one — evade Taipan — but he still hadn't figured out what to do next. Probably go back to the queen and say he'd lost the trail of the ghost? That didn't sound like a terribly fun prospect.

"All you're doing is making Beryl angry!" Aurora snapped at Platypus.

"Hooray! Good for me!" Platypus snapped back. "That's GREAT news! I want her to be angry every day! I want her to wake up annoyed and never feel happy for one minute! I want her to know somebody remembers what she did and she can't just have the throne and do whatever she wants! I want *everyone* to know *someone* is fighting her, even if it's ONLY ME!" The little dragon buried her face in Aurora's blankets and screamed into them.

"But you have to convince everyone else, too!" Aurora picked up the pillow and threw it back at her. "You need other dragons on your side if you want anything to change!"

Platypus sat up again, her eyes glittering with furious tears. "No! You don't get to lecture me! I don't want to hear about how I'm 'doing it wrong' from someone who is doing NOTHING!"

Aurora let out a little gasp. "Are you serious? Weren't you even listening?"

"To your songs?" Platypus said. "Is that your idea of fighting back? You wrote a *song* vaguely conveying some *feelings* and everyone's supposed to guess that it's really about the king and queen?"

"Yes! I think my songs *can* make a difference!" Aurora cried. "That's what music is for! The whole point is for dragons to hear it and feel braver or understood or more sympathetic to someone else. That way they can be strong enough to stand up when they have to!"

"They have to stand up *right now*!" Platypus said. "Why *not* now?! Tell yourself whatever you need to, but you *know* what would make a real difference is you landing on that stage and saying: 'Beryl is a terrible queen who stole the throne from good dragons and now we're all terrified of her!'"

"But they know that, Platypus! Everyone *knows* that, but

no one knows what to do about it! I don't think it's wrong to try and make dragons happy, or to give them all something that brings them together when everything is terrible. At least my music can make them feel less alone! I mean, that's what I'm *trying* to do — I don't know if it's working, but I'm not doing nothing!"

"I think you're both right," Umber said, and immediately regretted it as they swung around to look at him. "Um. Not that I know what I'm talking about."

"Who are you?" Aurora asked. The candlelight reflected off the gold scales along her snout, turned her wing scales a warmer shade of pink, and made the spikes along her tail look even sharper.

"He's going to help," Platypus said. "He's going to fight with us."

Ack, Umber thought. *Am I?* "I'm Umber," he said. "I'm kind of new here. My sister really loves you."

"Oh," Aurora said with a practiced smile. She looked down and started taking off her rings. "Thanks. That's so nice. Do you want to explain what you mean, that we're both right?"

"Um — I mean, I guess I think what you're both doing is important," he said. "Like, you've made a really big difference to my sister," he said to Aurora. "She was — she was really sad, and your music helps, exactly how you said. And watching everyone tonight, singing together . . . I think it does change things. Even if they don't all understand what your song was saying, some of them must have."

"It's not enough," Platypus said stubbornly. "Aurora is the most popular dragon in the court. Everyone adores her. She could change everything if she spoke up."

"Until I was also arrested, or turned into a ghost, or not allowed to do concerts anymore," Aurora said, sliding her rings onto a branch of the jewelry tree. "And then I'd be useless. Some of us just fight differently. You *know* that." She crossed the room and threw herself onto the bed beside Platypus. "I miss you, noisy chaos dragon."

"I miss you, too." Platypus buried her head in Aurora's neck and Aurora curled one wing over her.

"The queen told me to arrest you, Platypus," Umber said awkwardly. "I'm not sure if it was the song or your notes or something else, but she was really mad. I don't think she's going to keep treating you like a ghost anymore."

"I don't care," Platypus mumbled.

"You should care," Aurora said. "If she gets her talons on you, you'll disappear like the dragons who wrote that pamphlet about her. Or the one who asked about her succession plans in front of the whole court. Remember? No one ever saw him again? Or even if she just puts you in the dungeon, I'll be so sad."

"Wait, what do you mean?" Umber asked. "Dragons have disappeared?"

"What do you think the King's Teeth have been doing for the last two years?" Platypus asked. "That's why everyone's so afraid — if they say anything to make the king or queen mad, they could just vanish into the night."

"The King's Teeth do that?" Umber said.

"Only when Mulberry's not here," Aurora pointed out.

No one had told Umber he was training dragons who secretly . . . what, murdered other dragons? Kidnapped anyone who questioned the king and queen?

Or maybe they did tell me, and I just didn't listen, Umber thought. *When the queen said "fight our enemies," I should have asked more questions. I thought she meant enemies out there, not "anyone we don't like" in here.* He felt sick all the way from his stomach through his claws.

"Luckily they're slow and bad at hunting," Platypus said, pulling away from Aurora and flopping onto her back, "or the Triumvirate would already be dead."

"If it weren't for *you,* they'd definitely be dead," Aurora said.

Platypus gave a little shrug.

Umber tilted his head. Had he heard — was that a noise outside Aurora's door?

Like someone's there . . . listening.

He waved to catch Aurora's attention and put one claw to his mouth, nodding at the door. She sat up with a frown. Platypus looked from her to Umber to the door, and then rolled quietly off the bed and vanished over the edge of the balcony.

Umber peeked after her and saw a flash of green swarming down the wall. As she ducked into another window, he nodded at Aurora again.

Aurora slipped across the room and threw her door open.

A dragon stood there, talon raised as if he were about to

knock. He blinked innocently at Aurora, but Umber had the strongest feeling he'd been standing there for longer than he wanted them to know.

"Oh, hey," Aurora said, lowering her shimmering pink-and-gold wings. "Come on in. Borealis, this is Umber; Umber, this is my brother." She went back to her bed and flung herself onto it again.

"The drummer!" Umber said, hoping he sounded normal. "You're amazing!"

Borealis turned light pink all across his pale white cheeks.

"Thank you," he said shyly. "You're the new MudWing, right? The one running the training drills? Queen Beryl wanted me to go to those, but I haven't had time yet, sorry."

"He practices drums a lot," Aurora said fondly. "And then he also has to practice with me."

Borealis glanced around the room. "What are you doing here?"

"The queen sent me to catch the ghost," Umber said. "I thought I'd check in here, just in case."

"Huh." Borealis looked around the room again. Umber wondered if he knew Platypus had been here, and if he thought Aurora was hiding her. "Why in here?"

"I thought the ghost would expect it to be empty while the concert was on," Umber said. "But there's no sign of her."

Aurora didn't say anything. She stayed curled on the bed, watching them both with her cool blue eyes.

"OK," Borealis said slowly. "I haven't seen her either. But good luck finding her."

Umber dipped his head. "I'll go keep looking. Nice to meet you both."

"Bye," Aurora said, waving.

Umber went out the door instead of over the balcony, taking the spiral stairs down from the tower.

Was that strange? Am I being paranoid about Borealis?

What do I do with this information about the King's Teeth?

How much danger is Platypus in?

And . . . is there anything I can do to save her?

He found Queen Beryl with King Snakeroot in the throne room, glowering down at Taipan, Dugong, and Royal.

"You failed me, too?" she snapped as Umber came in. "She's *one* small dragon! How did you let her escape?"

"I'm not sure, Your Majesty," Umber said. He had to pretend he knew less about all of this than he did. "Sorry, just so I understand, she's . . . not really a ghost?"

"She's a ghost to everyone else," said Beryl, her scales like smoldering rubies in the torchlight. "To you she is a threat to me and the king, and you will *find* her and ensure that I *never have to hear from her again*."

"I see," Umber said.

"I think you mean 'Yes, Your Majesty,'" Taipan hissed.

Umber bowed his head. "Yes, Your Majesty."

"Blood," King Snakeroot muttered. "Secrets. Lies."

"Get back to training tomorrow," Beryl said to Umber. "As soon as the King's Teeth are ready, I have a few other dragons I want you to hunt down."

Umber felt sick to his stomach. *Tuatara, Horizon, and Monarch,* he thought. *And then what happens to them?*

"There must be blood," Snakeroot added, unfolding the dark green leaves of his wings.

"Yes, dear. You are all dismissed," said Beryl. "But I'm not going to forget how you displeased me."

Taipan whacked Umber with his spiky tail on the way past and Royal sneered down his nose at him, but Umber was too tired and worried to care.

He didn't think the dragons of the court were likely to stand up to Beryl and Snakeroot anytime soon. Maybe they just wanted to survive, or they were too scared, or they didn't think they could change anything.

The only thing he could think to do was to break the enchantment so Platypus and the dragons in hiding could leave the island. It wouldn't get them the throne back, but at least they could go somewhere safe, far away from Beryl and Snakeroot. *Maybe even Jade Mountain Academy,* he thought wistfully. He wondered how Platypus would feel about history classes and assemblies.

He stood outside the throne room, thinking.

I have to find the object the original animus dragon enchanted to build this place.

But how? I could search this castle from top to bottom, but I wouldn't know if I found it. I have no idea what I'm looking for.

Maybe he should start with what he knew about the first dragons here. This castle was built much later, and so were the orchards. But when it was first created, he knew the prison must have had: (1) the Barrier, (2) the Memory Room, (3) the entrance gate — *oh,* Umber suddenly realized, remembering the inscription over the entrance.

For the Safety and Protection of All. That didn't mean "this place will be a safe place for everyone." It meant "we're putting you here to protect everyone else from *you." That's . . . kind of mean, I think.*

And there was one other thing that came with the original prisoners: the little metal dragons. The guards of this prison.

Maybe *they* knew what the enchanted object was. Maybe Umber could figure out a way to communicate with them.

Which means first I have to find them.

CHAPTER 15

Umber searched the castle for half the night with no success. He hoped the castle wasn't growing extra hallways and staircases just for him to get lost in, because it certainly felt like it might be.

I wish Mulberry were here. He wondered how long the prince would be gone. Umber didn't even want to ask him questions. He just wanted to look at Mulberry's face and listen to him talk and surprise him into laughing one of his real laughs. He'd be happy to wander the endless halls for months if Mulberry was next to him.

Eventually he had to go to sleep, knowing he'd be up early for training. He went back to his room with Sora and told her his theory about the metal dragons. She wasn't fond of it.

"I think you should stay away from those creepy little things," she said.

"Don't you wonder about them?" he asked. "Like, can they think? What do they do when they're not greeting new prisoners or yelling at dragons who hit the Barrier?"

"They *lurk*," Sora said. "They pop out of shadows and *hiss* and are *weird*."

"Have you seen them do that?" he asked.

"All the time," she said. "They're obsessed with me."

OK, new plan, he thought, curling up on his bed. *Find one who's following Sora, and then follow it until it returns to its lair, or wherever they hide.*

First he had to get through the morning with the King's Teeth. There seemed to be more of them than before he'd gone into the infirmary. More faces to learn and details to memorize. He paced around them, standing in neat rows in an inner courtyard, greeted each newcomer, and ran each name through his head.

There was one face he recognized that surprised him.

"Dugong?" he said, pausing next to the hulking hybrid MudWing. "What are you doing here?"

Dugong hunched his shoulders and refused to meet Umber's eyes. "Gotta get better at fighting," he muttered.

"OK," Umber said, feeling a flicker of despair. He didn't want to be like Taipan and Royal, forcing Dugong to "toughen up." He didn't want to make any of these dragons more violent or better at hurting one another — and he definitely didn't want to help them make other dragons disappear.

It doesn't have to be like this. He thought of Platypus's note, and then, like an echo, he remembered something Reed had said the night before they went to join the MudWing army.

Umber had been jumping around their campfire yelling

"pow!" and kicking trees. "Take that, SeaWing!" he'd shouted. "Bam bam! Got you, IceWing!"

"Umber, stoooooop," Crane said wearily.

"Yeah, don't make them mad," Marsh said, flicking pine cones into the fire.

"The trees?" Pheasant said. "What? Are you afraid they're going to hit him back?"

"I'm going to find all our enemies first thing tomorrow and punch them in the face!" Umber announced.

"Umber," Reed said. He held out a roasted lizard on a stick and Umber happily sat down to gnaw on it. "It's not like that. We're not going looking for dragons to punch in the face."

"We're not?"

"No. We fight if we're attacked. We train so we can defend ourselves. We want to become strong and powerful in order to protect the weak and powerless."

All of Reed's siblings stopped eating to gawk at him. Reed rubbed his snout, looking embarrassed. "I read that in a scroll."

"I like it," Sora said softly.

"Yeah, OK," Umber had said. "I think I get it. I'll find dragons who are being mean to someone else, and punch *them* in the face!"

"I suppose that's one option," Reed said with a chuckle.

Maybe I can make them think differently about what they're here for, Umber thought, looking around at the assembled hybrids and WildWings. *I mean, imagine if Dugong could defend himself from the Toughen Up Stick.* "Let's start with some defensive techniques," he announced.

At midday he let them go and went to find Sora in the library. She was at the checkout desk, frowning at a list in her talons.

"Everything all right?" Umber asked.

"We've been ordered to remove these scrolls from the library," she said, handing him the list. "This is the third time they've sent over a list like this."

"Why? What happens when you remove them?" Umber asked.

"The king takes them away, and then I don't know," Sora said. "I'm horribly afraid he's burning them. Burning *scrolls*, Umber! Who would do that? And we have no way to replace them! Most of the scrolls in this library were written over the last centuries by dragons who were trapped here. There are no copies anywhere else in the *world*." She brushed away a tear, her voice trembling.

Umber read the list of scrolls, wondering why the king and queen wanted to get rid of them. He couldn't see any immediate reason — there were scrolls for dragonets, scrolls by MudWings and SandWings and RainWings and hybrids, adventure stories, love stories, history scrolls, memoirs. He guessed the only unifying factor was that Beryl and Snakeroot didn't like them.

"Can you save any of them?" he whispered. "Say you can't find them? Or make copies of them?"

"I'm going to try," she whispered back. "Shhh." She slipped the list into a box as another librarian went by.

"Have you seen any of the little guards today?" Umber asked.

Sora's eyes flicked up and to the right, and he followed her gaze to one of the library lanterns overhead. A tiny copper-and-silver dragon perched on the edge of it, glaring at Sora.

"Oh, hello," Umber said to it. "How are you?"

It fluttered its wings in a busy, rattly way and shifted its glare to him.

"Have you been here from the very beginning? Since the first prisoners arrived?" Umber asked. "Do you remember how the prison was made?"

No response. Unless *glare intensifying* counted as a response.

"Hmmm. If you leave the library, will it follow you?" Umber asked Sora.

"Usually," she said. "They sometimes change shifts while I'm sleeping."

"Let's try that!" he said. He lowered his voice to a whisper. "Could you go back to our room and pretend like you're going to sleep? So if it leaves, I can follow it?"

Sora rolled her eyes. "You're lucky it's not busy in here today. Also, why are you whispering? It can't listen or think for itself."

"I feel like we don't *know* that," Umber said. He trailed Sora back to their room and waited across the hall as the metal dragon settled on the ledge over their door. It reminded him of the owls that could sit in trees for hours without moving, only to suddenly swoop down and stab their claws into unsuspecting prey.

Moments ticked by. A few dragons came out of their

rooms and gave him strange looks as they passed him. Umber started to worry that the queen would find him here, apparently just sitting in a corridor staring into space. It was alarmingly easy to picture her saying: *"If you have time to lounge around, you have time to go wipe out my enemies."*

He nearly yelped aloud when someone sat down next to him, but it was only Quokka.

"Sorry!" she said. "I didn't mean to startle you. Have you seen Sora?"

Umber found that interesting and reassuring, that Sora couldn't disappear without someone coming to check on her. He wondered if that was an official assignment, or if Quokka had decided on her own to keep an eye on Sora. Or had Mulberry asked her to? It seemed like something Mulberry might do.

"She's helping me with something," he answered Quokka. He nodded at their door. "I want to follow one of the little metal guards to see where they go."

"Oh, I've always wanted to know that!" Quokka said. "But I didn't want to bother them. I mean, I wasn't sure they would like it if I busted into their secret space." She rubbed one of her palms absentmindedly.

"I'm sure they'll let me know if they don't like it," Umber said with a rueful smile.

"Um . . . Umber," Quokka said. "Did you . . . last night, did you, um . . ."

"Catch the ghost?" Umber finished for her. She nodded. "No. I've met her now, Quokka. I know she's your sister. I don't want to do anything to hurt Platypus, I promise."

"She's a really good dragon," Quokka said in a rush, keeping her voice low. "She saved Tuatara and Monarch and Horizon. I know she causes a lot of trouble, but I get why she does it. I wish I could be as brave as her."

Umber heard a metallic hum approaching along the hall. "I think more guards are coming," he whispered.

Two new little dragons came swooping around the bend. They circled the first, and Umber got the distinct impression they were all very put out about Sora changing her routine. It was like listening to bees muttering "very suspicious, yes, very suspicious, what do you think, Buzz? Oh, that it's suspicious, agreed, yes, hmmm."

The new ones landed and the copper-and-silver one zipped up and headed off down the hall. Umber bounded to his feet and Quokka hopped up to join him.

"Can I come, too?" she asked. "I won't get in the way."

"Of course." He smiled at her as they hurried after the metal dragon. "Have you ever wondered if they have names?"

"All the time!" she said. "I've named some of the ones I see most often. I call this one Clink, at least until I can find out what it calls itself."

Clink led them on such a long and winding trek that Umber began to suspect the little dragon was playing a prank on them. He knew Sora would say that wasn't possible, but he couldn't help thinking of them as real and alive, with personalities. In his mind, Clink was only pretending to ignore Umber, but really was hoping they'd become friends just as much as Umber was.

Eventually Clink flew into the great entrance hall of the castle and paused, hovering in midair. Umber tugged Quokka behind a curve of the stairwell. Maybe Clink was waiting to make sure no one was watching.

Between the posts of the banister, Umber watched the dragon fly to the far wall, land, walk in a small circle, and disappear.

"Did you see that?" he whispered to Quokka. They crossed to the wall and studied it.

Please don't be magic, Umber thought to himself. If the little metal dragons could magically phase through walls, too, then there was no way he'd ever find them.

Quokka rested her front talons on the wall and tapped it. It looked like the rest of the room: wood the color of Reed's scales in the sunlight. Umber ran his claws lightly around the section where Clink had disappeared, and one of them caught on something.

A crack in the wood. A hole hidden in one of the knots, large enough for a small metal dragon to slip through. He slid his claws around it: a thin line extended from the knot sideways and down, disguised by the grain of the wood.

A door.

At eye level, his claws came to another knot. When he pushed on it, the door slid gently back and then sideways, revealing a staircase going down. A faraway smell of the sea wafted up from below.

"Wild stars," Quokka whispered. "I had no idea this was here. I don't think *anyone* knows."

Umber wondered if it *had* been there, before he went looking for it. He still wasn't sure if the castle's magic worked like that.

They started down the stairs cautiously. There were torches embedded in the wall, which he lit with a small burst of flame as he reached each one. They were spaced far enough apart that most of the stairwell was shadows. The steps were made of a strange petrified wood that felt like stone underfoot. At the bottom, they stepped into a vast, cold room where the floor was a huge pool of water, with columns rising out of it in neat lines all the way across. Firelight flickered in the still reflections, creating a strange upside-down world that blended right into the real one.

A marble walkway led between the columns toward two exits on the far side. Umber saw a flash of copper dart through the archway on the left; he pointed to it and Quokka nodded. They hurried across the walkway to follow it.

As they approached, he thought he heard a sound from the archway on the right. There were no torches in that direction; only darkness that rolled like a fog. But it sounded as though something was breathing raspingly, in the distance far below. There was a smell, too . . . a wet, poisonous smell.

Umber shuddered, glad the metal dragon had gone the other way.

To the left, beyond the archway: a long blank hall, and then, at the end, finally, a room.

A room full of metal dragons.

Umber had been picturing miniature sleephouses, one for

each metal dragon, but there was nothing like that. To the left and right, the walls were lined with shelves, and about twenty dragons perched all along the shelves in eerily even lines. The ceiling was dotted with holes. Umber guessed those led outside, so they could all swarm out to the Barrier or the entrance quickly whenever they needed to.

But the weirdest part was what filled the middle of the room. It looked like a sort of tower built from thousands of small random things. Chips of rubies and sapphires glimmered in between sunflower seeds, twigs, gray pebbles, snail shells, dark purple feathers, peach pits, dragon scales of every color, tiny rodent skulls, spoons, scraps of paper, needles, and more. It was like a magpie's stash of stolen treasures: each item small enough for one of the dragons to carry, but all arranged into one giant . . . something.

"What *is* it?" Quokka breathed from beside him.

"They must have built it," Umber said. "Maybe they're trying to build their own castle inside the castle? Or could it be a kind of nest?"

Clink poked its head out from a gap in the tower and spotted them.

"Intruders!" it barked. Every dragon on the shelves turned their head toward the door in exact unison.

"Wait, wait," Umber said, holding up his front talons. "I just want to talk to you!"

"This space is off-limits!" Clink snapped. It flew over and jabbed one of its claws into Umber's palm. "No prisoners allowed!"

"*Ow*, yikes," Umber yelped. The pain was more than a pinprick; there had to be something in Clink's claws that was intended to hurt extra. "I'm not a prisoner!"

"Everyone is a prisoner," Clink said — a bit smugly, if Umber was honest.

"Are you enchanted not to talk to us?" Umber asked, clutching his talon to his chest. "Is that a rule?"

Clink hovered in front of his face. Umber wished he could meet the dragon who had crafted each of them; he could see that someone had put care into making them each a little different and all a little beautiful. Precise miniature copper scales overlapped all along Clink's back and sides, and the membrane of its wings was the thinnest beaten silver. Its face was like a tiny SkyWing's, slender and elegant.

"We don't answer questions," Clink said, and the haughty tone also reminded Umber of SkyWings.

"But maybe you *can* talk to us, as long as we don't ask any," Umber guessed.

Clink flicked its tail and glanced at the other guards. They all stared back like judgmental sparrows, twitching their wings but not offering any advice.

"Like, for instance," Umber said, "I'm really curious about this amazing thing you've built in here, which I assume you all built together, but I wouldn't dare ask you any questions about it."

"You better not," Clink said. "This belongs to the SharpWings. It's for our eyes only."

SharpWings, Umber thought. *They gave themselves a tribe name.*

"It's really cool," Quokka said. "I didn't know they could make things."

"If I were stuck in this room for thousands of years without much to do, I'd want to build something, too," Umber said.

"I bet it would get very boring," Quokka agreed.

Clink made a small scoffing noise and flew over to the tower like it was planning to ignore them.

"Unless the animus who enchanted you added a never-get-bored element to the spell," Umber said. "But I'm sure you all don't remember that dragon."

All the SharpWings in the room clattered their wings, stamped their feet, and looked annoyed.

"You started this conversation with the squishy ones," one of them said to Clink from the top shelf. "*You* set them straight."

"Of course we remember Precipice," Clink snapped at Umber.

"Precipice," Umber echoed. "Wait, so the animus was a — *I* mean, that's so interesting, because Precipice sure sounds like a SkyWing name, but SkyWings don't have animus dragons. Hm!"

"Probably an IceWing," Quokka agreed. "They have animus magic the furthest back."

"Precipice was a SkyWing," Clink growled. "And a genius."

Umber wondered if any of his Jade Mountain teachers knew that SkyWings used to have animus dragons. "So

Precipice probably cast the spell to create the whole prison, too," he said casually. "I *wonder* what object they enchanted to do that. I mean, not that anyone here would know."

"We wouldn't," Clink said. "The prison was created first, then us."

"Oh," Umber said, deflating. So much for *that* clever plan. He thought for a moment. "I guess you probably don't know the spell Precipice used to make you either."

"Grrrr," said Clink, and then recited in a toneless voice: " 'I enchant these twenty-five dragons to come to life. I enchant them to guard the Dungeon Isle, so that as long as there are prisoners here, they shall record their names and categories, and they shall prevent them from trying to cross the Barrier. I enchant them to have a paralyzing toxin they can inject at will from their claws and to know instantly whenever a prisoner arrives or one attempts to escape.' "

That was interesting. Umber wondered what would happen to the SharpWings if he broke the Barrier — or if there ever weren't any prisoners here. "It seems to me," he said cautiously, "that you are all trapped here just as much as the prisoners are."

"Shut up," Clink snapped. "*We* have a purpose."

The other little dragons hissed and shifted in their spots, claws digging into the wood.

Umber glanced around the room again, hoping maybe there was another clue here. Or maybe the animus-touched object itself — it would make sense to put the guards in the same room with it, right? He really hoped it wasn't inside their miscellaneous tower . . . or, worse, one of the hundreds of bits and pieces that made up the tower.

For the first time, he noticed that one of the metal dragons near him wasn't glaring and stamping in sync with all the others. Instead it was curled up like a roly-poly bug, still and unmoving.

"Is this one — um." He stopped himself and tried again. "This SharpWing looks a little sick."

"It is broken," said the dragon next to it in a flat voice. "A hawk tried to take it."

"Oh, poor dragon," Quokka said.

Umber hesitantly reached out, and then, when no one attacked him for it, he scooped the limp dragon off the shelf into his talons. This one was dark blue and iridescent purple, with perfect little silver claws. Once he was holding it, he could see that one of its wings had been snapped at the shoulder. There was no way it could fly.

The dragon opened its eyes for a moment and regarded him expressionlessly. Umber tried to imagine what it must feel like to have magic instructions calling you and be unable to respond. To have one purpose you were built for, but no longer be able to fulfill it. He wondered if the SharpWings could feel pain, or despair, or grief.

"I'd like to try to fix your wing," he told the injured dragon.

It blinked at him, then nodded once.

Umber knew a little bit about metalworking from hanging around the blacksmiths in the Diamond Spray Delta.

There were two sibling groups in charge of smithing: one for weapons, one for armor. None of them made anything nearly as small and delicate as the SharpWings, but Umber thought the principles must be the same. If he could line up the broken edges and apply fire to them in exactly the right way, they should melt together. He thought. He was pretty sure. "In exactly the right way" was doing a lot of work in that sentence.

"I need something to narrow my flame to a point," he said to Quokka. "Like a funnel, but for fire."

She glanced at the tower, clearly wondering, as he was, whether the SharpWings would put up with anything being removed from it. But Clink was already hopping toward them, holding out a flat rock with a small hole in the center of it.

"It won't work," Clink said gruffly. "But try this."

"Thank you," Umber said. "I wish I knew this wounded dragon's name."

Clink frowned at the little shape in Umber's talons. "That is Nineteen," it said. It turned and hopped back to its perch, pretending to ignore them again.

Umber set Nineteen on the stone floor, trying to make it as comfortable as he could. He carefully moved the broken wing back into alignment with the dragon's shoulder, positioned the rock with the hole right over the break, and breathed a small burst of flame onto it.

The edges of the break bubbled slightly. Encouraged,

Umber tried a bit more fire, and then a bit more, until the bits of metal had melted together and the break was gone, replaced by a small misshapen blob.

"It's not super beautiful," he said apologetically, setting it back on its shelf, "but once it cools, I think maybe you'll be able to fly again."

Nineteen regarded him for a moment, then closed its eyes.

"If any other SharpWings needed help," Quokka said, "I hope they know they can come to one of us."

"Go away now," Clink said, edging back into a hole in the tower.

Umber turned with a sigh, and as he did, he saw a metal plaque next to the door, etched with writing. At the top it said **CATEGORIES** and below that was a list.

1 — FAMILY OF CRIMINAL

2 — UNWITTING ACCOMPLICE

3 — INTENTIONAL ACCOMPLICE

4 — PETTY THIEVERY, NONVIOLENT

5 — GRAND THIEVERY, NONVIOLENT

6 — HARBORING DANGEROUS CRIMINALS, CONSPIRACY TO PLAN VIOLENCE

7 — ASSAULT, NON-DEADLY ATTACKS ON OTHER DRAGONS

8 — CONSPIRACY TO COMMIT MURDER, TREASON

9 — MURDER, NON-ROYAL

10 — **MOST DANGEROUS CRIMINALS; MURDER, ASSASSINATION, TREASON; EXTREMELY VIOLENT**

Oh no, Umber thought, his heart falling. He touched the list with one of his claws. *The categories* do *mean something. What did I say when they asked for Sora's? Didn't I say ten? The scariest prisoners . . .* that's *why they follow her around. They think she's the worst kind of dangerous, and it's all my fault.*

"Is there any way to change a prisoner's category?" he asked desperately.

"OUT!" Clink roared, rocketing back out of the tower. "Questions! Intruders! Out!"

All the dragons except Nineteen let out small metal shrieks and leaped off their shelves. They swarmed at Umber and Quokka like furious wasps.

Umber shoved Quokka ahead of him and they ran with the SharpWings at their heels, down the long corridor, through the watery room, up the stairs, and all the way back to the entrance hall.

CHAPTER 16

"So I wouldn't say it was the *most* successful expedition," Umber said to Sora. They were up on one of the highest ledges of the castle with Quokka, sharing a large bird Quokka had caught and a bowl of fruit from the orchards. The night sky was clear and full of stars upon endless stars, like a mirror maze that went on forever and had no exit.

"What are you talking about?" Quokka said. "We learned so many things! For one, that they were created by a SkyWing animus — maybe we can find something about Precipice in the library."

"If the scrolls about her haven't all been taken away," Sora said gloomily.

"And for another," Quokka said, giving Sora a sympathetic look, "they definitely want more out of their lives than the loops they're stuck in now."

"Hang on, that's a stretch," Sora argued. "They don't *want* things. They're just little cogs in a big wheel, going around and around. Like gears in a clock, but scary and pointy."

Umber felt a little wave of warmth through his scales. He loved seeing Sora so comfortable with Quokka; normally she was too shy to argue or say much to dragons outside their sibling group, at least since the war.

"Clock gears don't build themselves towers out of hoarded treasure," Quokka pointed out. "That's a dragon thing."

"And the spell said 'come to life,'" Umber added. "Not just 'do this job,' although they are also stuck doing that job over and over. But *life* is different from clockwork."

"Well, *I'm* not going to make friends with them," Sora said. Umber hadn't worked up the courage to tell her about the categories yet. He would, he told himself. Whenever she was less scared of the SharpWings.

"They didn't tell us anything about what Precipice used to make the prison," Umber said. "I'm not sure where to look next."

"Maybe the Memory Room?" Quokka suggested.

"Have you been there?" Umber asked her.

She nodded. "Platypus and I found it together, the first time." She lowered her voice to a whisper. "And I use the tunnels sometimes to bring food to the exiles. I could go with you, tomorrow."

"After training?" Umber said. "That would be great." He didn't have a lot of hope — he remembered the emptiness of the Memory Room and the domed cave outside it — but it wouldn't hurt to check them again. And maybe he could find Tuatara and the others and warn them about Beryl's escalating plans.

To his alarm, Queen Beryl herself showed up at his training in the morning. She prowled into the courtyard, climbed onto one of the windowsills, and glared at him while he ran drills. Halfway through the lesson, Snakeroot slithered in and joined her, folding his leaf-shaped wings close to his sides.

When they finished and all the other dragons left, Beryl beckoned him over.

"Yes, Your Majesty?" he asked.

"That didn't look very impressive," she said. "When will they be ready to hunt the dragons I mentioned?"

"I'm not sure," Umber said. "Everyone's working very hard."

"Work harder," she said, leaping down to the ground. "Snakeroot thinks something is about to happen."

"Coming for the queens," the king muttered.

"Queen," she snapped at him. *"Singular."*

She swept out of the courtyard grumpily and Snakeroot frowned at Umber. "She's always like this when Mulberry is away," he said in a startlingly lucid voice. "It makes her very anxious."

"I understand," Umber said. He so wished he could have gone with Mulberry out to the islands, to look for dragons who needed help and to keep Mulberry from being alone. It was maybe a bit ridiculous how much he missed a dragon he'd known for such a short time.

As soon as the king was gone, Quokka popped out from behind a pillar and beckoned to him. She had two sling bags full of food and other supplies. Umber caught a glimpse of scrolls and ink in the bag she slipped over his head. He wondered if she was smuggling out some of the endangered scrolls from Sora's library list.

"Quickly," she whispered, and they hurried into a nearby room, where she lifted a tapestry, slid aside a secret door, and led the way into the walls.

The journey felt a little different from the one he'd taken with Platypus, but just as long. Instead of glow-in-the-dark scales, Quokka had a lantern hooked on one of her wings, casting a shadowy, swaying light as she walked.

"Have you been bringing food to the Triumvirate this whole time?" Umber asked her.

"Whenever I can," she said. "That's one of the reasons I stayed in the court instead of running away with Wollemi and the others. I thought maybe I could help them from there." She shook her head. "I don't know if I made the right choice. I haven't done anything helpful at all."

Umber paused and glanced behind him. Had he heard something? Like . . . a quiet scratching sound?

The tunnel was dark and silent. He waited a moment, but didn't hear it again. He didn't smell anyone following them either.

I'm imagining things. Easy to do, when everything is mysterious and creepy.

He scurried to catch up to Quokka. "Is it only you and Platypus, or do you have any other siblings?" he asked.

"Just us," she said. "What about you?"

"I have another sister, and three brothers, and one sister who died in the war," he said. He told her about Marsh's hilarious fear of cats and Crane's habit of saving caterpillars and protecting them until they became butterflies. He talked about the time Pheasant had to help heal an outraged SandWing soldier who'd been bitten by a snake, and the way Reed always said "Good night, best siblings in the Mud Kingdom" no matter how many mistakes they'd made that day or how much they'd complained about training. He explained how Clay had grown up with other siblings and saved the world with them, but how he felt like Umber's brother from the moment Umber saw him across the swamp.

"You get to see and do so much over there," Quokka said wistfully. "I mean, I wouldn't want to be in the war like you were. But the Dungeon Isle feels so small when I know we can't ever leave. I wish I could see the MudWing palace or the rainforest or your school."

"Maybe you will," Umber said. "If I can't figure out what the animus-touched object is, I'll just go ahead and break everything on the island. That should work, right?"

Quokka laughed. "Platypus is way ahead of you there," she said.

"I VOLUNTEER!" Platypus cried, springing out of a niche in the wall ahead of them.

Quokka shrieked and dropped the lantern. Umber managed to catch it before it smashed on the tunnel floor.

"Hello, boring," Platypus said affectionately to Quokka.

"Hello, walking heart attack," Quokka said, clutching her chest. "Why are you lurking in a dark tunnel?"

"Because scaring dragons is fun," Platypus said. "Also a

few jerks upstairs are, like, *really* determined to catch me right now, so the castle is feeling a bit more stressful than usual."

"Taipan?" Quokka said with a worried face.

"And some other no-necks he's recruited." Platypus shrugged. "It's fine. I filled his bed with every venomous spider and giant weta I could find, which brought me enormous joy."

"What's a weta?" Umber asked.

"Ooo, they're these absolutely ENORMOUS grasshopper-y bugs," Platypus said, waving her wings. "They're actually very cool, but huge, and Taipan once found one in his oatmeal and has never recovered. Heh heh heh."

Quokka sighed. "Always causing trouble," she said. "You're going to get caught one day, Platypus."

"But not TODAY!" Platypus said cheerfully. "Where are we going?"

"The Memory Room," Umber said. "I want to see if there are any clues about what animus-touched object is holding the prison in place."

"Amazing," Platypus said, bounding off at a brisk pace. "I love impossible quests!"

"We found out the name of the animus dragon who cast the spell," Quokka said. "It was a SkyWing named Precipice, apparently."

"Oh, she's in the Memory Room scene," Platypus said offhandedly.

"She is?" Umber said.

"Yeah, she's the dragon at the beginning with the

SkyWing queen — the queen says her name. Oof, if she was an animus, those assassins *really* made a big mistake killing *her* queen."

"Beryl would love an animus pet," Quokka said. "She was so mad that Paua didn't inherit any power — and she's even more mad that Paua doesn't want to have dragonets."

"Bleh, dragonets," Platypus said. "No, thank you."

Umber thought it would be really cute to have a dragonet to take care of, actually, but he'd never told anyone that. That wasn't how MudWing families worked. *Maybe* if a dragonet hatched alone or lost its sibs when it was still little, then another sibling group would take care of it. But the rest of Umber's siblings had never seemed very interested in that idea.

"It's not fair to Paua," Quokka said. "None of Waterfall's descendants have been animus dragons, so why would she be? Or her dragonets?"

They emerged into the domed antechamber of the Memory Room. Platypus hopped up on one of the benches and tucked her tail around her back talons.

"I've seen this grisly murder enough times, but have fun!" she said. "Let me in when the vision is over."

"It won't keep repeating?" Umber asked.

"I don't think so," Platypus said. "I slept in there once and it only happened the first time; after that it was just an empty room all night."

"That's a terrible place to sleep," Quokka said sternly. "Apart from how it is *super creepy* and probably haunted, it only has one exit and you could have been caught in there."

Platypus rolled her eyes. "I can sleep wherever I want! You're not the boss of me!"

Umber opened the door of the Memory Room, hoping to forestall an argument. He was grateful when Quokka followed him inside. He'd been dreading watching the scene by himself.

It unfolded exactly the same way as it had the first time. Umber studied Precipice closely as she came through. Nothing about her gave away that she was an animus dragon, although now he realized the little dragons on her wristbands were prototypes of the SharpWings. She seemed like any other SkyWing. He wondered if her queen even knew she was an animus.

Finally the murdered queen faded away and the glass walls appeared around them.

"Three moons, that's horrible," Umber said as Quokka went to open the door for Platypus. "I wonder how they got prisoners to come down here to watch it." He ran his talons along the wall, feeling the smooth, flat surface. No bumps, no cracks, no clues. Nothing on the walls or the floor.

Platypus lodged a rock in the doorway to keep it open. "My guess is it involved some angry little metal goblins."

"There was nothing about the Memory Room in their spell, though," Umber said. "If Clink told us all of it." He circled the pedestal in the middle of the room.

"Did you hear something?" Quokka asked. She stared out at the waiting cave, her blue-dappled yellow wings flickering nervously. "I thought I heard a noise."

"Me too," Platypus said. "Uh-oh . . . brace yourselves . . . I think it was . . . YOUR BUTT."

"You are such a brat," Quokka said as Platypus fell over laughing.

Umber crouched and looked under the curve of the basin. There were words carved around the edge, hidden by the shape of the bowl. He traced them with his claw as he scooted around to read them.

FOR THE TRUTH SEEKERS

I mean, Umber thought. *That's me, isn't it? But now what? Couldn't there be more detailed instructions?*

He tried tapping his claws along the inside of the bowl and up and down the pedestal. He pressed each of the letters in the message. Nothing happened.

"I don't know," he said with a sigh. "This seems important, but how?" He looked up and froze.

There was a SharpWing spying through the crack in the door.

He could see its small face peering at them, silver eyes bright.

That must be what I heard behind us, and why I didn't smell anyone, he thought. *It followed us here. What if it tells Queen Beryl? Or are there SharpWing punishments for prisoners who sneak through the walls and poke around the Memory Room?*

"Nobody move," he said quietly. He held out his front talons toward the door, palms up. "We're not doing anything wrong," he said. "I promise. Please don't tell the queen we're here."

Quokka let out a little gasp as the metal dragon climbed through the gap. It clung to the wall like a panther in a tree, wings spread wide, studying each of them in turn.

"Oh — Quokka, look," Umber said. "It's Nineteen." He recognized the blue and purple scales — and the blobby bit on its wing where he'd melted the metal together. "It worked? You can fly?" he asked.

The dragon shook out its wings and flew over to perch on the basin. It paced around the edge for a moment, watching him, and then it sat down and pointed at Platypus.

"Ahaha, what," Platypus said. "No, thanks. Please go back to ignoring me."

Nineteen flared its wings and pointed at Platypus more demandingly.

"Why her?" Umber asked the SharpWing. "What do you want?"

"Can I do it instead?" Quokka asked. She took a step toward the pedestal and Nineteen held out one of its talons. Quokka cautiously did the same, extending her palm across the bowl toward it.

Nineteen's tail whipped around and stabbed into her skin.

"Ow!" Quokka yelped. She yanked her talon back, and as she did, a drop of her blood fell into the basin.

Instantly the room went dark. Behind Umber, the door slammed shut, and the green glow of Platypus's phosphorescent scales flared up.

"How dare you!" Platypus cried. "You little clockwork

monster! I'm going to dismantle you and feed all your gears to crocodiles!"

"Quokka, are you OK?" Umber called. He reached out, trying to feel anyone else in the dark.

And then, all at once, they were standing in the throne room of the Court of Refuge.

CHAPTER 17

Umber flinched back instinctively, thinking it would be Beryl and Snakeroot on the dais — but there were three chairs instead of two, and they were occupied by different familiar faces: Tuatara, Horizon, and Monarch.

Next to Umber, Platypus growled softly in her throat. Quokka reached out and twined her tail with her sister's.

The throne room was humming with dragons, including a line of about ten waiting to speak to the Triumvirate. Glowworm stood by Monarch's side, holding a scroll open for her to study. A dragon Umber didn't know was at the front of the line with two dragonets clinging to his legs.

"Of course we can find you bigger quarters," Tuatara said to him kindly. "Those two are growing so fast. Horizon, what do you think?"

"Maybe in this wing," Horizon agreed, leaning over to point at Glowworm's scroll.

"That's what I was thinking," Monarch said. "There are other families with dragonets in these rooms nearby, here and here. You can all help each other."

A WildWing, a hybrid SkyWing-SeaWing, and a SilkWing, ruling together. Seeing them up there made Umber feel hopeful, the way Jade Mountain Academy did. They felt like proof that dragons could coexist without endless war.

"Thank you," said the dragon in line. "We can be ready to move tomorrow."

"We'll send a couple of dragons to help," Tuatara offered. She glanced to her right and Umber realized that he knew the three dragons gathered at a table near the dais. It was Wollemi, another Quokka, and another Platypus, all smaller and younger than they were now. They were sorting tangerines, root vegetables, rolls of bandages, and small loaves of bread into bags, then handing them out to the petitioners in line.

"Sure!" younger Quokka said.

"I can move things!" small Platypus added beside her. "Throw me a couch! I can carry twice as much as these two combined!"

"Wonderful," Tuatara said, cutting Wollemi off before what was clearly going to be an argument, or possibly a fight involving citrus fruit shoved up somebody's snout.

Present-day Quokka turned and touched Umber's shoulder. "Umber. You don't have to watch this."

"Why?" he asked. "What —"

The grand doors crashed open, banging back against the walls.

Dragons swarmed into the throne room. At the forefront were Beryl and Snakeroot. Mulberry's LeafWing father looked imposing and powerful, not like the haunted shadow of a dragon Umber had met, but terrifying in a different way. Beryl's face was gleeful.

Umber recognized most of the dragons with Beryl — they were the ones she was having him train now.

"What is this?" Tuatara asked, rising to her feet.

"It's good-bye," Beryl said. "You three have been in charge long enough."

"Beryl, you had your chance," Horizon said. "There weren't enough votes for you. You lost, but you can try again next time."

"No," she snapped. "This weird court ritual of *voting* and taking turns is over. It's not the dragon way. *I'm* the queen now — and I'm taking my throne the way dragons have always taken them!"

She charged down the length of the room and leaped on Tuatara. Snakeroot was a moment behind, catching Horizon and flinging him off the dais. Glowworm and Monarch jumped away from them, each trying to shield the other.

Umber wanted so badly to wade in and help — but he knew he couldn't. He wasn't really here. He was just seeing Quokka's memory of this terrible day.

He wished he *had* been here, though. He could see why Beryl wanted her followers trained; the King's Teeth fought haphazardly and were easily distracted. His troop of siblings could have taken down all twenty of them on their own. But in this throne room they were attacking small dragons, peaceful dragons, and dragons who'd come here to escape violence; there wasn't anyone, really, who could fight back.

"Royal!" Monarch called frantically, searching the crowd for her dragonet. All around them, dragons were attacking, slashing with their claws or breathing fire. A bolt of frost-breath seared the ground by Monarch's feet and she jumped back again. *"Royal!"*

"Quokka," Umber said softly. "You don't have to watch this either."

It was true: There wasn't an enchantment compelling him, like there was for the SkyWing queen's murder. He could close his eyes and turn away if he wanted to. But there was no way to leave; he had no idea where the Memory Room door might be.

Nineteen is showing us another part of the Memory Room's magic. But why? Umber wondered as Beryl and Tuatara fought. *"For the truth seekers" — does it show you your worst memory? Who would want that?* He knew he wouldn't want to see the moment Crane died again.

Beryl's dragons outnumbered the ones in here, and most of the dragons in line had given up without fighting. They crouched with their wings over their heads, each with a dragon looming over them. The father had folded himself around his dragonets and was trying to quiet their crying.

Two dragons cornered Monarch and Glowworm, holding long spears to keep Glowworm's claws at a distance. Everyone was watching the fights that mattered: Horizon and Snakeroot in the center of the room, Beryl and Tuatara up by the thrones.

"Beryl, stop!" Tuatara cried as they crashed into the back wall. "Mulberry wouldn't want you to do this!"

"Maybe not," Beryl said, raking her claws across Tuatara's neck. "But when he gets back, he'll be a prince, and you'll be dead, and there will be nothing he can do."

A turnip flew across the dais and clonked Beryl in the head. She whipped around, hissing.

"YOU WILL NEVER BE MY QUEEN!" Platypus bellowed at her from atop the table. She wound up and flung a potato that clipped Beryl's ear. Below her, Quokka and Wollemi were under the table, huddled together.

Beryl signaled one of her dragons to attack Platypus, but before he could get to her, Platypus leaped off the table, darted around the father and his dragonets, and threw herself at Snakeroot. A spray of black venom shot from her fangs, splattering across Snakeroot's green scales. He shrieked and staggered back from Horizon.

Platypus whirled and flew at Beryl. The SkyWing slashed at her face as Platypus dove toward her; Platypus ducked and rammed herself into Beryl's chest. They grappled across the dais as Tuatara struggled to her feet. Platypus was barely a third of Beryl's size, but her claws glistened with venom and she fought relentlessly.

"Platypus!" Quokka screamed from under the table. "Behind you!"

Three of Beryl's dragons swarmed the dais, and some of

their claws were venom-tipped as well. Platypus rolled under their outstretched talons and vaulted over the chairs to kick one of Monarch's guards in the back. The two guards tumbled into each other with startled grunts, and Glowworm jumped forward to stab them each in the neck. Both dragons collapsed, alive but temporarily paralyzed.

"FIGHT WITH US!" Platypus yelled to the rest of the room. She turned and held out a talon to Quokka. "We can stop them!"

Beryl reared up behind her and slammed Platypus into the wall with her tail. Platypus scrambled to her feet, bleeding, and leaped at her again. The rest of Beryl's guards were converging on their fight.

"I've got this one," Beryl said, seizing Platypus around the throat. "Kill the other three."

"No!" Platypus shouted. She slashed her claws across Beryl's arm and kicked her in the face with her back talons. Beryl dropped her with a roar of fury.

Umber realized that Glowworm had fought through the crowd of dragons to reach one of the large windows with Monarch. "But Royal —" Monarch said pleadingly.

"If we stay, you'll die," Glowworm said to her, clasping her talons in his. "If we run, we survive — that's what Royal needs. Living parents. Remember our escape from Wasp Hive? We have to fly so we can *live*."

Monarch turned with a sob and leaped out the window. Glowworm stabbed another attacker with his paralyzing claws and then hurtled after her.

Platypus was fighting five dragons now, spraying venom in an arc as they closed in warily. Horizon had fought his way to Tuatara's side. The old WildWing leaned against him, blood dripping from a wound on her head and smeared across her scales.

Snakeroot stumbled across the room, kicked over the table, and dragged Quokka out. "The antidote," he growled, hunched in pain over the spots where Platypus's venom had struck him. "Now, or I kill him." He knocked Wollemi to the ground and pinned him under one huge talon.

Quokka cast an anguished look at her sister, who was fighting too hard to notice. She looked down at Wollemi, who was gasping for breath as Snakeroot's talon pressed harder and harder. And then she grabbed one of the rolls of bandages, shot a tiny spray of venom from her own fangs onto a strip of fabric, and pressed it to Snakeroot's wounds.

He let out a long hiss of pain and relief, and then he shoved them aside and headed straight for Horizon. Wollemi scrambled up and threw himself on Snakeroot's tail, trying to slow him down.

"Follow Monarch," Tuatara said to Horizon. "Don't let them kill you."

"I'm not letting them kill you either!" he protested.

Snakeroot kicked Wollemi off him and leaped onto the platform. Beryl seized one of the spears the guards had dropped and ran toward Tuatara from the other side.

Platypus vaulted over the dragons she was fighting and

threw herself at Snakeroot. She tucked into a roll under his feet, tripping him and sending him sprawling into Beryl's spear. He roared as it pierced one of his wings.

Beryl's followers froze for a horrified moment — just long enough for Horizon and Tuatara to make a run for the window.

"Snakeroot!" Beryl shrieked, yanking her spear back. He collapsed at her feet. There was blood everywhere.

Platypus shoved Wollemi and Quokka toward the window; they caught up as Tuatara leaped out.

"You don't have to come with us," Horizon said, turning back toward them for a moment.

"Um, I think I do!" Platypus objected.

"Yes, *you* definitely do — I mean them," Horizon said, indicating the other two. "It might be safer for you two to stay here."

This, Umber noticed, was when real-life Quokka closed her eyes and buried her face in her talons.

"Shut UP with your TERRIBLE IDEAS and let's GO!" Platypus shouted.

"We'll fix this — we'll figure it out," Horizon promised. He spread his wings and leaped into the sky.

Wollemi scrambled up right behind him and took off. Platypus reached to help Quokka up to the windowsill.

"I — I think I might — stay," Quokka said.

"What?" Platypus cried.

"I can help from here," Quokka whispered. "Can't I?"

Platypus clearly wanted to argue, but there wasn't time. Beryl was getting to her feet with Snakeroot's blood on her talons and a murderous look in her eyes.

"I'll be back," Platypus said, squeezing Quokka's talon. She threw herself out the window and soared after the others. Quokka ran up and leaned out to watch as they winged away toward the yellow plains.

Umber realized that both Quokkas — past and present — were crying.

Beryl slid up behind the other Quokka and put one bloodstained talon on her shoulder.

"You made the right choice," she said. Her claws dug into Quokka's scales. "It's no use fighting or running or hiding. There's nowhere they can go that we won't find them." She pressed down until Quokka folded into a bow at her feet. "All of those dragons are dead. And I'm the queen now. Say it."

"You're the queen now," Quokka whispered.

"Yes," Beryl hissed. "Finally."

The scene faded away there and slowly the greenish-glass walls of the Memory Room appeared around them again. Platypus came over to Quokka and put her wings around her sister.

"I'm sorry," Quokka said.

"It's all right," Platypus said. "It happened really fast. And you *have* been helping, I'll admit it, even if I would rather have you smashing things and punching bad guys with me."

Platypus wrinkled her snout at Umber as if she wanted him to say something. Something distracting, maybe?

"Um," he said. "So, wow, I had no idea you both have magical death spit."

Platypus's eyes lit up. "YESSS," she said. "That IS what I have! MAGICAL DEATH SPIT!"

Quokka half laughed and wiped her eyes. "It's just RainWing venom," she said.

"I know — that's what my brother calls it," Umber said.

"But only Platypus has the venom in her claws, too," Quokka said. "Like some HiveWings."

"So why did we have to relive all that?" Platypus asked. "What was the point?"

They all turned toward the basin, where the SharpWing was still sitting. Nineteen clattered its wings together and looked very pleased with itself.

"Thank you?" Umber said to it. "I think? Can you tell us anything else?"

He didn't know why Clink could talk and Nineteen apparently couldn't. He wondered if the hawk attack had damaged more than Nineteen's wing. Did they have tiny voice boxes that could break?

"Blood magic in the Memory Room," Platypus said. "Who knew! I mean, literally, did anyone know? Did the prisoners come down here and drip blood around and watch their own pasts? But, again . . . why?"

Umber suddenly remembered Snakeroot murmuring,

"There must be blood." He shuddered. Had the king known they'd come here? Did *he* know about the basin?

Nineteen pointed at Platypus.

"No, thanks," Platypus said to the little dragon. "I remember all my memories just fine."

Nineteen curled its claws and pointed at Platypus again.

"I said no!" Platypus frowned at it. "Stop trying to boss me around!"

The SharpWing hissed at her and Platypus hissed right back.

"Are you scared of it?" Quokka asked. She displayed the palm that Nineteen had stabbed. The wound was just a small red dot now. "It's not that bad."

"I'm not scared! I just don't feel like being experimented on by an enchanted metal gremlin," Platypus said. "Besides, most of my memories are the same as yours. If it's looking for our worst day, it's going to end up in the same one, and I *personally* don't need to see it again."

Umber was worried about the same thing — he didn't want to relive his worst day either — but he felt as though Nineteen was trying really hard to show them something important. "Do you want mine?" he asked the SharpWing.

Nineteen waved at his talon dismissively and pointed at Platypus again.

"ARGH, FINE," Platypus huffed. "But if we end up back in the same memory, I'm going to sing REALLY LOUD to drown it out and THEN you will ALL BE SORRY."

She held out her talon over the basin and scrunched her eyes closed.

Nineteen inspected Platypus's claws for a moment, then climbed straight onto her talon. Platypus shivered a little, but held it still.

The SharpWing flared its wings, pacing back and forth. Umber suppressed the urge to laugh. It felt as if the small creature was deliberately trying to build suspense — like a presenter onstage, about to bring out a troupe of traveling dragons and their trained tigers. (Marsh had *really* not enjoyed that show.)

Finally Nineteen stopped, squinted up at Platypus, and held up its front talons like *Don't move.*

"I KNOW," Platypus growled at it. "Just do it already!"

Nineteen swung its tail around and stabbed it into Platypus's palm — but instead of stopping, it stabbed again: twice, three times, and then slashed a tiny X in her skin as if signing its work.

"OWWWWW!" Platypus yelled with outrage. A cascade of blood droplets rained from her talon into the basin as she shook Nineteen off and clenched her fist. "What the —"

This time the dark rolled up from their feet like a dense fog in a terrible hurry. It swallowed them entirely, so within a heartbeat Umber felt as though he was drifting in an endless silent sea; he couldn't even hear Platypus shouting anymore.

When something touched his side he almost screamed, until he realized it was Quokka.

"Where are we?" she whispered.

"Inside a tiny metal goblin's nightmares," Platypus said,

appearing on her other side. She clenched her wounded fist. "I'm going to crush that thing. Slowly. One teeny bolt at a time."

"I think we're in a forest," Umber said. "At night." He was starting to make out the dark shapes of trees all around them. An indecisive rain was falling, half drizzle, half splatters. He couldn't tell how many moons were up because what he could see of the sky was stuffed with heavy clouds.

"What!" Platypus barked. "Hey, clockwork monster, where are you? Your stabby magic is broken! I've never been here!"

There was no response.

"I mean, this can't be my memory," Platypus said to Umber. "There's nothing like this forest inside the Barrier."

"There's light over there," Quokka said, pointing. "Let's go see what it is."

They wove through the trees, brushing through wet foliage. Umber stumbled into a bush and startled a couple of very tall, grouchy birds with bright blue heads, who clacked their beaks angrily as they stalked away.

The light came from filaments of glowing silk, warm and golden orange, woven around and through the branches of a willow tree. The branches hung all the way to the ground, creating a hidden space inside.

"That's flamesilk," Quokka whispered to Umber. "Only a few SilkWings and BeetleWings have it."

"Why isn't it setting the tree on fire?" he asked.

"They have different kinds," she said. "They can make a silk that burns or a silk that just gives off light."

"Yeah, I definitely haven't been here," Platypus said. "And I've never seen *those* dragons in my life." She pointed at the two dragons inside the arms of the willow tree.

One was an emerald-green LeafWing, wearing a crown of white magnolias on her head. The other looked a bit like the BeetleWing assassin in the first Memory Room scene. But instead of dark purple, her insect-like wings were iridescent teal, and she held a shining ball of flamesilk in her talons.

"We should tell the other queens," said the LeafWing. She leaned against the teal dragon's side and they twined their tails together. "I think it's time, Euphoria. We can show them how beautiful Harmony is."

"I'm not sure they'll think it's beautiful," Euphoria said. "In fact, I'm *pretty* sure they'll be scared of the whole idea of it."

"Happy dragons? Peaceful families?" the LeafWing said. "They'd have to be missing hearts to find that scary. Besides, *they* don't have to live there. They can just leave them alone."

"Leaving dragons alone is not how most of the other queens operate," Euphoria pointed out. She curled one of her wings around the LeafWing and brushed a wayward magnolia out of the green dragon's eyes. "And they really aren't going to like our plan to merge our kingdoms."

"Rrrgh," the LeafWing growled, burying her head in Euphoria's shoulder. "Whyyyyyy."

"Because we're so terrifying," Euphoria said affectionately. "Imagine a vast forest kingdom full of dragons who take care of one another. BeetleWings and LeafWings living together instead of fighting over every acorn like our ancestors did. Everybody PANIC."

"Hey, Platypus," Umber whispered. "That BeetleWing kind of looks like you."

"Yeah, right," Platypus said.

"No, she does," Quokka agreed. "Her eyes — and something about the shape of her face."

"She looks more like *you*," Platypus objected. "Like, all . . . *friendly*. Blergh."

"Maybe we should wait a little bit longer, Magnolia," Euphoria said.

"Can we tell Queen Hibiscus, at least?" Magnolia asked. "Then she can tell everyone that our merged kingdom is no threat to *her* rainforest right next door, so it shouldn't bother anyone else either."

Euphoria sighed. "I just — I like that we're only the two of us right now. When everybody else knows, they'll be *looking* at us all the time."

"Darkling and Sorrel know, and they don't look at us a weird amount," Magnolia said.

"Shhh." Euphoria lifted her head, peering out into the dripping trees. Both dragons stepped away from each other at the same time.

"Someone's coming," Platypus said.

Umber realized he was holding his breath as two dragons came racing through the trees. Based on what the Memory Room had shown him so far, he was horribly sure whatever came next would involve blood and murder, and he didn't want to see anything awful happen to the sweet couple under the willow.

As they came closer, he realized the new dragons were also a LeafWing and a BeetleWing. They pushed through the willow branches and threw themselves to the ground at the queens' feet.

"Sorrel?" said Magnolia. "Darkling? What's wrong?"

Umber poked Quokka at the same time as she was poking him. "That's Darkling!" she whispered.

"I know!" he whispered back. "The one who kills the SkyWing queen! This must be from the same time period as the other Memory Room scene!"

"Some of the other Queens' Claws found the village of Harmony," Sorrel gasped. He climbed to his feet and Darkling did the same, panting slightly. Umber noticed they were both wearing necklaces similar to the one Precipice was wearing in the SkyWing palace, with nine different claws strung on each. "We saw two of them spying on it — Precipice and Bloodshed. They've gone to tell their queens."

"Right now?" Euphoria said, flaring her wings.

"We have to get to them first," Magnolia said in a rush. "We have to explain."

"That's not going to work," Darkling said. "They're going to come for Harmony and they're going to come after you."

"I think we have to evacuate the village," Sorrel said.

"*I* think we have to attack them," Darkling said. "The

only way to stop them is to show we're stronger than they are. Kill their queens and then no one will mess with us and the village will be safe."

"No," Euphoria said with horror threaded through her voice. "Darkling, *no*. We're not going to break the peace and we're definitely not killing any queens!"

"But *they're* going to break the peace!" Darkling protested. "We heard them say it: they're going to wipe out Harmony!"

"Not if we talk to them," Magnolia said firmly.

"That's the whole point of the Accords," Euphoria said. "We talk instead of fighting."

"We have been talking!" Darkling said. "We talk to the other Claws at every council. They want everything to stay the way it is. Separate kingdoms, no hybrids ever. They won't let you change things. They definitely won't let you merge your kingdoms."

"Bloodshed knows your plan," Sorrel said quietly. "I'm worried that if you go try to talk to his queen, she'll kill you right there."

Magnolia took Euphoria's talon, her face resolute. "We'll bring other queens with us. They won't kill us in front of Hibiscus and Dolphin."

"That's true; they don't want to start a war," Euphoria said. "And neither do we." She looked down at Darkling, suddenly fiercer and more commanding, and Umber saw the queen in her for the first time. "Darkling. If you attack any of the other tribes, they will retaliate. I forbid it — do you understand? I forbid you to try to kill anyone."

Darkling lowered her head and folded her wings close to her back. "Yes, Your Majesty."

"Promise me," Euphoria said.

"I promise, Your Majesty," said Darkling. "I won't kill anyone until you tell me to."

She sounded sincere. Umber studied her, puzzled. What had happened in between this scene and the one the Memory Room normally showed? Whose "orders" was she talking about when she killed the SkyWing, if not her queen's?

"Thank you, Darkling," said the BeetleWing queen. "I want you to go to Queen Hibiscus to ask for help. We need protection for Harmony, and we need some queens on our side."

"Sorrel, you go to the SeaWings," Magnolia said. "See if Queen Dolphin will support us."

Sorrel and Darkling bowed again and turned to leave the warm circle of the willow. As they did, the scene faded slowly back into the walls of the Memory Room.

BeetleWings and LeafWings reaching out to RainWings and SeaWings. This must be when it started — those are the four tribes that were punished for the death of the SkyWing queen.

"What in the three moons?" Platypus exploded. She turned to glare at Nineteen. "WHAT WAS THAT."

The SharpWing hissed at her again.

"Wait, I — I have a guess," Umber said before Platypus could storm over and throw it against the wall. He crouched so he was eye level with Nineteen. "So, clearly one drop of our blood shows us one of our memories."

The SharpWing nodded, eyeing him narrowly.

"But Nineteen wanted us to see what happens when you use more drops," Umber went on. "That wasn't supposed to be a glimpse of your own past, Platypus. I think more blood shows you a memory from one of your ancestors — and the dragons we just saw are the ones who ended up imprisoned in the Dungeon Isle."

CHAPTER 18

Nineteen sat up on its back legs and applauded, clattering its wings together at the same time.

"Oh, wow," Umber said, grinning. "I'm right?"

"That's so weird!" Platypus cried. "I don't like that! Ancient ancestor memories, YEEERRGH."

"Platypus prefers to imagine that we sprang fully formed from, like, one of the moons or something," Quokka said to Umber. "Our parents died when we were too young to remember them, so it's an avoidance mechanism."

"YOU'RE AN AVOIDANCE MECHANISM!" Platypus yelled at her.

Quokka rolled her eyes. "Well, *I* think seeing our ancestors is cool, and I bet we are descended from that BeetleWing queen. But I don't really understand what we just saw or how it's all connected. Do you?" she asked Umber.

"I mean . . . it must be related to the other Memory Room scene, right?" he said. "Now we kind of know why Darkling wanted to kill the SkyWing queen. But did she disobey her queen to do it? Or did Euphoria change her mind, and why?"

"THIS IS THE WORST," Platypus announced. "In case you were wondering, hmmm, how can I drive Platypus into a murderous rage today? The answer is: trap her in a tiny room, show her awful things, stab her multiple times, and then stand around asking questions with no answers for a thousand years."

"We've been asking questions for *two minutes*, tops," Quokka pointed out.

"AND IT'S TORTURE." Platypus bounded over to the door. "I'm going outside! Gremlin, you are not invited!"

"Its name is Nineteen!" Quokka called, but Platypus was already halfway across the outer cave. "I'm sorry about her," she said to the SharpWing. "The part of a dragon's brain that's reserved for manners is just EMPTY SPACE IN HER HEAD!"

"I can't heeeeeeeeeeeeeeeeear you," Platypus called back. "Because I'm going to the suuuuuunshine where things aren't creeeeeeeeeeeepy!"

"I think this can help us," Umber said to Quokka. "I'm just not sure how yet. Maybe if we bring other dragons down here to watch their ancestors' memories, we'll find out more?"

"Maybe," she said. "We have to be careful who we tell, though. It's hard to know who's on Beryl's side and who is just pretending to be." She picked up the two sling bags and handed him one.

"Thank you for showing us that," Umber said to Nineteen. The SharpWing made a little shrugging motion with its wings and flew past them into the domed cave. As Umber and Quokka headed for the surface, it zipped away into the dark tunnels that led to the castle.

"Maybe somebody's ancestor knows what object Precipice enchanted to make this prison," Umber speculated, following Quokka into the bright midday sun. He squinted up at the cloudless sky and the rock face looming over them. The ground was scorching beneath his feet and all the plants looked like they wanted to crawl back into the dirt. In the distance, Platypus was leaping over clumps of withered grass and cracks in the earth as she bounded away.

"I wish she would be more careful," Quokka fretted. She looked back at the castle, where a few dragon shapes were winging around the towers. "She can camouflage her scales if she concentrates really hard, but she almost never does." She started picking her way through the yellow grass, wincing at the heat on her soles.

Umber guessed they were walking instead of flying in order to stay inconspicuous. "Is that where we're going?" he asked, pointing to a rock formation in Platypus's path. The rocks looked disturbingly like five huge claws thrusting up from the ground, as though a rust-red dragon deep below them were trying to scratch its way to freedom.

"Yeah, that's where we usually meet," Quokka said. "I don't know exactly where everyone is hiding, just . . . in case."

Three dragons were waiting in the shade of the claw rocks with Platypus. Wollemi galloped out toward Quokka and tackled her into a hug.

"Eeee!" she yelped, falling over. "You big galumpher!"

"Did you bring us oranges?" he said breathlessly. "Or raisin buns or sweet potatoes or ICE CREAM?"

"You know I can't bring you ice cream!" she said, rolling him off her. "It would melt all over me as soon as I stepped out here. I did bring you the other things but you probably squished them!"

"I would take melted ice cream," he said, bouncing around as she shook herself. "I would take ice cream in any form. I miss ice cream almost as much as I miss — uuuuuuuuumm." His runaway words crashed to a stop and he clapped his talons over his snout, looking mortified.

"SHE MISSES YOU, TOO, WOLLEMI!" Platypus called cheerfully.

"You talk SO MUCH!" Quokka yelled back. "Hi, Wollemi. Ignore her."

"She's right, though," Crescent observed, sliding around them and sticking her nose in the bags to see what they'd brought. "Quokka and Wollemi think about each other constantly and it is absolutely boring."

"Umber, please take everything out of this bag so I can put it on my head forever," Quokka said. "Wollemi! Stop grinning like that! You'll only encourage them!"

He bumped her side and she bumped him back. Crescent rolled her eyes and took Umber's bag from him. "OK, now all their thoughts are mushy and cute and I hate it," she said. "Thanks for this. Please don't come back with an army to kill us."

Umber jumped. "I — I'm not planning to!"

"But Beryl *wants* you to," Crescent said shrewdly.

"She does? How soon?" Tuatara asked from the shade.

"When she thinks we're ready," he said. "I don't know."

"You're going to do it if she tells you to," Crescent said. "You always follow orders."

I mean . . . I always have, Umber thought uncomfortably. He remembered the night Clay and Sunny had saved the MudWings by visiting Queen Moorhen in her dreams. Sometimes he still woke up in terror, thinking he was back in that camp and the war was still going and they were marching off to slaughter in the morning.

The whole army had been gathered, preparing to invade and destroy the Ice Kingdom. Those were their orders: a massive offensive to overwhelm them, kill as many IceWings as they could, and hope that it ended the war.

He'd hated it — they all had. Reed and Pheasant hadn't been able to sleep, they were so worried about the attack. They were all terrified about losing another sibling, and Umber also felt sick at the thought of trying to wipe out the IceWings. He was sure the others did, too, but they tried not to talk about it.

Because what could they do? Orders were orders. Umber was loyal to Reed, and they were all loyal to their queen. They had to do as they were told.

That was before they'd known about the IceWing cliff that killed any other kind of dragon who crossed their border. Most dragons would never try to enter the Ice Kingdom, where it was too cold for them to survive, so the cliff had faded from memory for the tribes who once knew about it.

Or, Umber sometimes suspected, *maybe Burn did know about it, but she didn't tell Queen Moorhen or Queen Ruby.* He had this awful fear that her plan had been to throw the MudWings at it first and hope their corpses overwhelmed the wall, so her army could sweep in after them, unscathed.

If it wasn't for Clay and Sunny — if the army had attacked as planned — so many dragons would have died instantly. Including, most likely, Umber and all his siblings.

Should we have said no to our orders? Could *we have said no?*

And that was a situation where I trusted my queen. What about when I don't?

But it's not as easy as saying no. If I try, what will Beryl and Snakeroot do to me — or Sora — or to these dragons?

"I'm hoping it won't come to that," he said to Crescent, who looked profoundly disturbed by everything that had just gone through his head. "I'm trying to find you a way off this island before it happens."

"Oh," Tuatara said with a chuckle. "You're one of those. The great escapers, we say. Well, I wish you more luck than all the others."

"If Mulberry can cross the barrier, there must be a way you can, too," Umber said.

"Hmmm, I don't know. He's very special," Tuatara said.

He is, but why? Umber wondered. *What makes him different from everyone else here?*

"I should go," Quokka said regretfully. "I've already been gone too long, and I promised I'd help set up for the concert tonight."

"WHAT CONCERT?" Platypus demanded.

Quokka winced. "The rescheduled Northern Lights concert — Platypus, *please* don't sabotage this one. Beryl is *so* mad and I think she thinks you and Aurora might be working together. You could get her in *huge* trouble."

"Everyone's in huge trouble RIGHT NOW," Platypus cried, lashing her tail. "Evil dragons have stolen the throne and rule the court! We should all be sabotaging everything until we get it back!"

Quokka sighed. "I know, but *you* know they're trying to catch you right now. Can you just stay away? For this one concert?"

Platypus huffed, spun around, and took off into the sky. Umber watched her soar away south until she was a tiny dot in the endless blue.

Isn't that what happens when you try to fight the dragons with all the power? You end up alone, throwing yourself against an outstretched spear over and over again.

He admired her, but he couldn't imagine being her — waking up every day and hurling herself against a wall of spikes. Always trying to change things, but with no one to tell you how or what to do. It sounded enormously stressful.

"Please convince her," Quokka said to Tuatara. "It's so dangerous right now."

"I'll try," Tuatara said.

Wollemi hugged Quokka again, and then she and Umber flew back toward the castle. As they got closer, Umber felt a fluttering tug in his chest, like his heart had tripped over something.

What was that?

He did a roll in the air, doing a quick check in all directions the way Reed had taught them to do. The flutter happened again when his eyes traveled over the mountains northwest of the castle.

"If we catch a few rabbits for the Gathering, we can say we were out hunting for the court," Quokka suggested. "That's what I normally do."

"Sure," Umber said. "Can you show me where the Barrier is around here?"

"It runs through the foothills of the mountains on either side of the palace," Quokka said. She swooped over the boulder-strewn landscape behind the concert pavilion and pointed out the charred line that trailed up into the hills.

Umber felt it again — *tug, tug.*

"I'm going to follow the Barrier for a bit," Umber said. "See you at the concert tonight?"

"Be careful," Quokka said. "Don't let any part of you cross that line. The consequences get worse every time you try."

Umber rubbed his arms, remembering the sharp lightning-strike pain. "I'll be careful."

He wondered if the Barrier itself was luring him in — but

that didn't make any sense; it had the biggest GO AWAY energy of any landmark he'd ever met. The tugging feeling was friendlier and more hopeful than that.

He stayed on the ground and well away from the Barrier as he trekked uphill. It was still hot here, but there were more shrubs and even a few hardy trees stubbornly clinging to life. Little hopping furry things darted away from his claws. At one point a scaly rock turned to look at him, and he realized it was a lizard with the same spikes many of the WildWings had.

It started to feel kind of peaceful, walking away from the Court of Refuge. He remembered the forest they'd flown over, on the far side of the mountains, way beyond the Barrier. He wished he could get there. It probably had mud, and mist, and water, and shade, and new interesting things to eat.

It sure was a choice that the animus dragon who made this prison had trapped everyone on the dry, sunbaked part of the island, when there were other available areas teeming with life and resources. Had Precipice been hoping they would all die here? The scorched dark line of the Barrier radiated even more menace when he thought of her like that.

He climbed over a pile of rocks that looked as though they had all tumbled down together, like MudWing dragonets play-wrestling, and found something that looked like a trail heading through a grove of olive trees. Umber followed it for a while, until he heard the sound of running water up ahead.

It was a waterfall. An actual, cascading waterfall leaping

down the rocks from higher up the mountain, droplets sparkling in the sunlight. It arced right over the Barrier and into a deep pool five times as wide as Umber's wingspan.

On one of the sunbaked rocks around the pool, Mulberry was curled up with his leaf-shaped wings spread out to catch the light.

The prince opened his eyes and saw Umber.

"Oh, wow," Mulberry said. "It worked."

CHAPTER 19

"Mulberry!" Umber felt as if the whole sun had melted into his scales and was beaming out through his face. "You're back!" He bounded down the hill toward the pool.

Mulberry leaped off the rock and met him halfway. Their wings tangled as they tried to hug, and a wave of affection and worry rolled through Umber. He wasn't entirely sure how much of it was his and how much was Mulberry's. He didn't care; he was so happy to see him. The sparkle of gold scales danced in his vision as they stepped back and smiled at each other.

"Could you hear me?" Mulberry asked. "I've been trying to call you here all morning, but my dragonspeak doesn't usually work over distances. So maybe it was less like calling and more like . . . hoping really hard." He made a "yeah, I just admitted that and I feel silly about it" face.

"I didn't realize it was you," Umber said. "I just had a feeling like I should come this way. What is this place?"

"Come see!" Mulberry galloped down the slope and leaped into the water. A cluster of frogs on lily pads started warbling indignantly as the wave splashed over them. Mulberry surfaced, grinning, and spread his wings to float. "I come here sometimes after patrolling, before I go back to the castle."

"Why?" Umber asked, slipping into the cool water. He buried his talons in the soft mud at the bottom of the pool and dreamy contentment radiated through his scales.

"Oh, um," Mulberry said. "For a little bit of quiet, I guess."

A place he can go where he isn't followed around by a thousand dragons competing for his attention. Somewhere to rest before facing his parents again.

But he wanted me *here.*

Umber ducked under the surface to hide the definitely ridiculous smile on his face. Maybe Umber wasn't just another of the prince's hundreds of admirers. Maybe Mulberry did like him, and maybe it was all right that Umber was starting to really, really like him, too.

Out of the corner of his eye, he noticed something swimming by. He came up again to watch as it reached the opposite side. A small, furry brown creature wiggled out of the pool and settled on the bank, watching Mulberry and Umber with grave suspicion.

"I've never seen one of those before," he said, pointing to it.

"That's a platypus," Mulberry said. "I think they're so cute. Don't make them mad, though."

"So, just like Platypus the dragon; that's funny," Umber

said. He winced, realizing what he'd said as Mulberry blinked at him.

"You've met Platypus?" Mulberry asked.

Well done, Umber. Was that one nanosecond or two you lasted before spilling a secret?

"Yes," Umber said awkwardly. He badly wanted to tell Mulberry everything — about the Memory Room, the SharpWings, the blood magic, Beryl's orders, and meeting the exiled Triumvirate. But he couldn't, could he? Mulberry was Beryl and Snakeroot's son. He was the prince of the Court of Refuge; presumably he thought everything was fine the way it was. If Umber said anything, Mulberry might feel obligated to go back and tell his parents.

"Oh no, something is upsetting you," Mulberry said. He paddled closer and brushed Umber's wing with his, sending *don't worry, don't worry* through his scales. "Are you all right? What did Platypus say?"

"She told me your mom and dad stole the throne from three other dragons," Umber said. That wasn't a secret. Everybody knew that had happened and how Platypus felt about it.

Mulberry sighed, tracing ripples in the pond with his claws. "I know. She thinks I can do something about it, but I don't know what. I tried talking to my parents, but they really think they're the better leaders for the court. And if I make them mad, they might stop me from patrolling and helping dragons." He gave Umber an anxious look. "I think what I'm doing is important, maybe? So I should keep doing it the best way I can, and hope everything with my parents works out somehow."

"It is important," Umber agreed. "They wouldn't really stop you, would they? Don't they need the things you bring back?"

"The community does, but my parents care more about being in charge," Mulberry said. He shifted his shoulders. "What else happened while I was gone?"

"I've been trying to figure out if there's a way to break the prison spell," Umber said. "No, no, don't look so sad!"

"Sorry, sorry," Mulberry said, covering his face with his talons. "Keep talking, ignore my face!"

"It's not for me," Umber said. "I'm totally fine." He wondered if he could carefully talk around some of what he wanted to know. "It's — I was hoping there might be a way for Platypus to get out, so she can go somewhere safe. Are you *sure* you're the only one who can cross the Barrier?"

Mulberry's expression shuttered suddenly, like all the doors of every sleephouse in the village flapping shut. "Yes," he said. "I'm sure."

"Do you have any idea why?" Umber asked.

"Luck?" Mulberry said. "Or maybe there's something wrong with me. Maybe the Barrier doesn't recognize me as a dragon."

Umber flicked water at him with his tail. "Or *maybe* it thinks you're the *perfect* dragon and it's decided your perfection cannot be contained."

"What?!" Mulberry cried. He splashed water back in Umber's face. "If it worked like that, it would let *you* across!"

"No, it loves me too much," Umber said dramatically. "It told me it can't live without me. I'm afraid I have to marry the Barrier."

Mulberry tackled Umber and they chased each other through the shallows, laughing. The platypus and the frogs wandered off to mind their own business.

At length Umber climbed up onto one of the flat boulders and lay down in the sunshine. "What if we just lived here forever?" he asked. "Do you think anyone would notice?"

"Probably not," Mulberry said, lying down beside him. "I bet everyone would be very chill about it. Zero consequences, no freaking out whatsoever." He rested his head on his talons and closed his eyes.

"Mulberry . . . are you scared of your parents?" Umber asked.

"Isn't everyone scared of their parents?" Mulberry answered.

I don't think so, Umber thought. *That doesn't seem right*. "I didn't know mine. MudWings grow up with their siblings instead. The closest thing I had was my brother Reed, our bigwings. But I was never scared of him."

"Even when he was mad at you?" Mulberry asked, opening his eyes to meet Umber's.

"No," Umber said. "I always knew we'd work it out."

"I just feel sick inside when they're mad at me," Mulberry

said. "Like an enormous stone dragon is sitting on my shoulders, making everything I do feel small and pointless. Waiting for me to apologize. And even if they say they forgive me, I know they don't really, and that sick awful feeling is still there, crawling under my scales."

"Mulberry." Umber reached over and traced the gold scales along the prince's face. "You shouldn't feel that way. No one should make you feel that way."

"Sorry," Mulberry said, dropping his gaze. He sat up, shaking water off his wings. "I'm being melodramatic. It's only sometimes. Hey, did I miss any Northern Lights concerts while I was gone?"

"There was one, but it had to be rescheduled," Umber said. "So it's actually tonight. Do you . . . want to go together?"

Mulberry smiled, radiating *yes absolutely yes*. "I'll meet you there."

They returned to the palace separately and Umber went looking for Sora in the library to tell her what he'd learned about the Memory Room. Once again, she was significantly less excited than he was.

"I think those little stabby menaces were just looking for an excuse to stab you," she said. "They don't care what memories you see."

"But if we can find a memory of the animus dragon enchanting the prison," Umber said, "we'll know what she enchanted."

"She was a SkyWing, wasn't she?" Sora said. "What if

Mulberry is related to her? Could that be why he can cross the Barrier?"

Umber thought for a moment. "No," he said slowly. "That can't be it, because then Beryl would be related to her, too, and *she* can't cross the Barrier."

"Oh, right." Sora shrugged. "Ah, well. I found one interesting thing." She pulled out a scroll and spread it across the low table beside them. "It's a record of the early days of the prison, and it talks about the dragons who sentenced them here — which is most of the queens. Queen Summit (I assume that's a SkyWing) and Queen Retribution — that must be the NightWing — were in charge of the trial. Then five others signed the sentencing document . . . see, Queen Icicle, Queen Dolphin, Queen Hibiscus —"

"Wait, Queen Hibiscus?" Umber interrupted her. He remembered that name from the memory of the queens under the willow tree. "So that must mean the RainWings and SeaWings didn't side with Queen Magnolia and Queen Euphoria, after all. But there was a RainWing assassin in the murder scene!"

"OK," Sora said. "And?"

"And didn't Quokka say the first prisoners included RainWings and SeaWings, too?" Umber asked. "So Queen Hibiscus and Queen Dolphin sent some of their own dragons here?"

Sora lifted her wings expressively. "This is really old history, Umber! Who knows what's true! Also the queens of other tribes are strange and unpredictable; it's pointless to try to understand them."

Umber puzzled over this information as they headed to the concert, trying to move the pieces around so they fit.

Darkling was told not to kill any of the queens, but she did.

With the help of a RainWing.

But the BeetleWing queen said not to . . . and the RainWing queen punished them for it.

And Darkling said she was following orders. So . . . whose orders?

A tapestry on the wall next to him billowed and Mulberry appeared from behind it. "Hey," he said, smoothing the tapestry back into place and shaking out his wings with a smile. "Found you."

"Hey," Umber said, smiling back.

"Mulberry!" cried the three dragons coming up behind Umber. "Come sit with us!"

"Oh, sorry," Mulberry said, "I already promised Umber I'd sit with him. I'll look for you later, though?"

Two of the dragons made exaggerated sad faces and the third one openly glared at Umber. Apologizing again, Mulberry arched one of his wings over Umber and gently steered him away.

"Sorry about that," the prince said quietly.

"There's nothing to be sorry for," Umber said. "You're allowed to choose who you sit with."

The ripples of guilt ebbed and Mulberry let out a soft exhale. "Do what *I* want?" he said, mocking himself. "Surely you jest."

"Only for a little while," Umber said. "You can get back to

the endless list of what everyone else wants tomorrow." He couldn't bear how solemnly Mulberry nodded, as if yes, of course that was what he had to do.

Umber pointed at the sky as they went into the arena. "Look," he said, "the smallest moon is passing through the Capybara constellation. That means we each get a wish." He bopped Mulberry's face with his snout. "I wish that Mulberry had something that made him happy every day."

Mulberry's true smile escaped, blossoming across his face as he bopped Umber back. "I was *going* to say I'm pretty sure there's no such thing as a Capybara constellation," he said, "but your wish came true, so who am I to question the Great Capybara in the Sky?"

"Oh," Umber said, flustered for a moment. *Did Mulberry mean me? Is that what he meant?* "Right. Yes. Don't ever question it, or it will make a classic 'who allowed you to speak?' capybara face at you."

Mulberry laughed. "I'm familiar with that face." He paused, then added, so quietly Umber almost didn't hear him, "I missed you."

"I missed you, too," Umber whispered back.

Once again, Borealis had started onstage alone, playing what sounded like ten drums at once. Sora waved to Umber from a row of seats she'd saved on one of the aisles. As they scooted in next to her, there was a muted scuffle in the row behind them — dragons trying to sit as close to Mulberry as possible.

"How are you, Sora?" Mulberry asked, leaning over Umber.

"I'm great," she said. "You don't have to worry about me; Umber does that enough for everyone." She grabbed Umber's talon suddenly, her wings whacking him in the face. "Here she comes, here she comes!"

But the dragon climbing onto the stage wasn't Aurora. Instead of her shimmering white and pink scales, his were dark green, and he wore a gold crown woven with thorny vines.

A hush fell over the audience.

Why is the king onstage?

King Snakeroot paced across the stage to Borealis, whose drumming faltered as the king stared down at him. In the eerie silence, Snakeroot whipped around and glided to the front of the stage. The moons overhead reflected in his eyes as he began to speak.

"Dragons lost and long forgotten
Abandoned in the sunlit isle
Ruled by power and betrayal
Haunted by an ancient trial.

Lines of blood will hold the key
As danger threatens from the past
And when the claws are at his throat
The hybrid prince will rise at last.

Who springs the trap, who saves the queens,
And which of them is friend or foe?

The smallest claws must choose the path
To right a wrong from long ago."

The king stopped and swayed on his feet. The stillness in the audience felt like an indrawn breath that everyone was too scared to release.

Umber saw the look on Mulberry's face and reached out one of his talons. Mulberry took it and held on as if he were sinking.

"But is it wise and is it safe," Snakeroot hissed. *"To break the curse, unleash the tide."*

Suddenly, motion: Queen Beryl, striding through the crowd toward the stage. The movement ricocheted outward as WildWings scrambled over one another to get out of her way.

"What happens when the walls come down," Snakeroot cried. *"If something else was trapped inside.* It's coming! We have to stop them — it's not safe — I see it broken, I see everything broken!" He backed away from Beryl, lashing his tail, as she swept onto the stage.

"That was beautiful, dear," she announced, her voice ringing across the frozen arena. "A lovely poem. I can't wait to hear Aurora set it to music. Thank you for that enchanting preview." She held out one talon to him.

"Yes," he said, shaking his head. "No. There must be blood. It's too late. The end has begun."

Beryl flicked her tail at Borealis, who began to play again, the drumbeats cautious and a little ominous now. She curled one claw at Snakeroot.

The king went to her side. She took one of his talons and patted it briskly. "Yes, so talented. Enjoy the concert, my dears!" With a gracious wave, she steered King Snakeroot off the stage and out of the arena completely.

Sora's eyes were as wide as full moons. "What was *that*?" she said in a hushed voice.

"Are you all right?" Umber asked Mulberry.

"Are *they*?" Mulberry said softly. "Umber . . ." He trailed off.

Voices murmured all across the arena, dragons turning to one another and echoing the king's words. Many of them were pointing to Mulberry as they whispered. *The hybrid prince, the hybrid prince* rippled around them.

"Maybe he wasn't talking about you," Umber said. "There are other hybrid princes." He couldn't think of any in Pyrrhia, but he didn't know everything. There had to be others. Surely?

"That was impossible, wasn't it?" Sora said. "What we just saw?"

"He's gotten so much worse," Mulberry mumbled. He pressed his talons to his face. "I didn't know."

"But he wasn't just talking nonsense," Sora said. "That was a *prophecy*. Right? We all saw that? A real actual prophecy?"

"Was it?" Umber asked. "I thought Tsunami said there wouldn't be any more prophecies."

"I mean, if she could boss them out of existence, I'm sure she would," Sora said, "but guess what, she can't actually stop dragons from seeing the future, no matter how fierce she is."

"You think my father can see the future?" Mulberry said in a low voice, glancing at the gossiping dragons all around them.

"How?" Umber asked. "He's a LeafWing. That's something only NightWings can do."

"Are we sure he's all LeafWing?" Sora asked. "Didn't his mother die before his father brought him here? Maybe she was a NightWing."

The puzzle started falling into place in Umber's mind.

"Sora, that's it," he said. "I think you're right — and I think I know why Mulberry can cross the Barrier."

PART THREE

INTO THE PAST

CHAPTER 20

A wave of feelings rippled from Mulberry's scales into Umber through their connected wings: *disbelief, fear, curiosity, alarm, despair, worry.*

"It's all right," Umber said. "Mulberry, it'll be OK."

"Sorry," Mulberry said, pulling his wings in close. "I can usually keep all that from crossing over."

"I don't mind," Umber said. "Can we go somewhere quiet?"

Mulberry looked around — *eyes everywhere, everyone looking, everyone wondering, what is he doing, what will he do* — and stood up to leave, which set off another round of murmurs and stares.

"But the concert," Sora said wistfully to Umber.

"You can stay," he said. "I'll find you later."

He trailed after Mulberry, trying to stay close. Dragons reached for the prince as he passed, like they always did, but there was a new strangeness to their smiles and questions, as though they were talking to him through a sheet of thin silk. He didn't know how Mulberry could do this all the time, but especially when it felt this weird. Even though the prince kept smiling, Umber could see his wings trembling with the effort.

Finally they made it out of the arena and into the halls of the palace, where there were fewer dragons out and about, although all of those wanted to say hello to Mulberry as well. Umber felt their hope and hopelessness as it eddied through Mulberry.

What did you bring us what did you see what is the world like tell us everything

why are you like this why are you special

am I real can you see me

can you set me free

He could see why Mulberry cared about them; their emotions were as real and present to Mulberry as the prince's own, maybe more so. They weren't simply a crowd of clamoring faces to the prince. They were Kea and Cypress and Raspberry and Algae and every individual dragon in the palace, and all of them were real and all of them mattered. It was so much, to worry about every single one, but Mulberry couldn't help it.

There's hope, Umber tried to send to Mulberry as they climbed the central staircase. *We can help them.*

He hoped they could — if his theory was correct.

"In here," Mulberry said, waving Umber into the infirmary. It was quiet and dark, with only one candle glowing by a window. They padded down the long room, checking that all the beds were empty. At the far end, Umber spotted

Blob, Paua's animus-touched octopus, draped over one of the pillows. Blob perked up and waved all his tentacles as they approached.

"Aww," Umber said, picking him up and letting the octopus climb onto his shoulder. "I guess Paua went to the concert without you."

Mulberry patted Blob on the head and climbed onto one of the cushions by the window. The candlelight cast a warm glow over his autumn-colored scales. "So what do you think?" he asked. "What did you figure out?"

"I think Sora is right that your dad is half NightWing," Umber said. He collapsed onto one of the other cushions. "Which means you're not just a SkyWing-LeafWing — you have NightWing blood in you, too. My guess is that you're descended from the SkyWing and NightWing queens who ordered this place made."

The prince shook his head. "But if that was all, then my parents would be able to cross the Barrier, too."

"Not necessarily," Umber said. "Not if the spell specified that only someone descended from *both* the queens could go through."

"Oh," Mulberry breathed. "They must have done that because they were sure their bloodlines would never cross, right? They figured there would never be a dragon who could trace his ancestry back to both of them."

"That makes sense," Umber said. "They weren't big on leaving a lot of loopholes, is the impression I've gotten so far."

Mulberry sighed and leaned forward to bury his face in

his talons. "But if that's what it is — that doesn't help *anybody* else. I can't make everyone related to me. Oh, unless you think marrying them would work? Maybe I could marry everyone one at a time and get them across?"

"I feel like even the dimmest magic would catch on to that plan after about spouse number three," Umber said. "But there's something else we can try, I think, except . . . I'm sorry, Mulberry. I'm kind of worried you might tell your parents."

"Yeah, I would be, too," Mulberry said. "I mean, I won't, but I understand why you'd worry about that." He tugged on a feather sticking out of the cushion under him, avoiding Umber's eyes. "My dad has been so angry lately. More unpredictable, more frantic about something. Maybe because of this prophecy. He could be having visions and not realize that's what's happening. And my mom . . . I don't believe either of them really *are* the right rulers for the Court of Refuge. But I can't say anything to them."

Blob meandered down Umber's arm and across the cushions to wrap his tentacles around Mulberry's head. Mulberry laughed softly and patted the octopus again.

"I promise, whatever you're doing," he said to Umber, "I won't stop you. And I swear on this octopus that I won't tell my parents."

He held out his talon, palm up, and Umber rested his own talon on top, palm down. Mulberry closed his eyes, and a kind of skylight seemed to open in Umber's mind, letting him into Mulberry's heart. It wasn't much different from what Umber already knew of him: kindness and worry, the pressure of Mulberry's ability, his fear of his parents. There was no deception. No plans to run and tell the king and queen everything. Only a fierce trust in Umber that ran like a thread through everything else.

"All right," Umber said. Mulberry opened his eyes. "Let's go to the Memory Room."

It was eerie to visit the Memory Room at night. The long underground path from the castle felt somehow unnaturally quiet . . . a feeling like someone in the next room had woken up and was holding very still, listening.

Umber would have been thrilled to have Platypus jump scare him from the shadows and light up the dark, but there was no sign of her.

"Have you been here before?" Umber asked Mulberry as they reached the dome-shaped outer cave and the door to the Memory Room.

Mulberry shook his head. "Dragons in the court know about it, but most of them avoid it. My parents said what's in there would scare me."

Umber stepped closer and brushed his wing. "I'll be with you," he said. "And remember, it happened a long time ago."

He stayed close to Mulberry as they went inside. As the Sky Palace scene unfolded, he watched it intently. Darkling looked the same as she had in the forest memory — determined and furious. Umber wished he could talk to her.

"You're sure about this, Darkling?" whispered the RainWing.

"Yes," she said. "We have our orders. No mercy, Lemur. This is the only way."

And then she killed the SkyWing queen.

And then she said, "One down. Now we go after the NightWing queen."

Whose orders? Umber wondered again. *Why did Darkling think this would keep her tribe safe?*

The glass walls and floor appeared around them. Mulberry blinked, looking shaken.

"Sorry — I know it's awful," Umber said.

"I can't understand what they did," Mulberry said. "But I guess it's exactly what my own parents tried to do to the Triumvirate." He sighed and walked over to the basin.

Nineteen was sitting on the edge, preening its tiny metal scales.

"Oh, hello. How did you get in here?" Umber asked it. "Or have you been waiting for us?"

The SharpWing gave him a look, and even on a tiny metal face the message was clear: *Don't ask silly questions you know I can't answer.*

Mulberry studied the inside of the basin, which was as pristine and clear as if no one had ever spilled a drop of anything on it. He read the inscription Umber had found, and then he looked at Nineteen.

"All right," he said. "Please help us. We want to see all the way back to the dragons who made this prison."

Mulberry held out his talon over the basin.

"We think two of them were his ancestors," Umber said. "So we'd like to see the moment they cast the spell, if possible."

Now Nineteen's face conveyed: *And? What do you want me to do about it?*

"So . . . we probably need as much blood as Platypus gave last time," Umber said. "But don't hurt him!"

Nineteen did the tiny metal equivalent of rolling its eyes, buzzed up into the air, and stabbed Mulberry's palm. A drop of blood fell into the basin . . .

. . . and the dark fog rolled in.

The first thing Umber heard was crying. More than one dragonet crying, and the buzzing of angry SharpWings.

"Next," said Snakeroot's voice, and it was so loud and cold and close by that Umber's claws curled with fear.

From one blink to the next, he found himself standing outside on the windswept yellow plain not far from the castle. Beryl and Snakeroot, each wearing a crown, sat atop a wide, flat rock, looking down over a crowd of dragons. They were steps from the Barrier, its scorched grass glistening in the heat. A cloud of SharpWings hovered overhead, humming furiously, like indignant hornets.

Umber turned to look for Mulberry and saw that he still had his talon outstretched, although they could no longer see the basin.

"Wait," Mulberry said. "No, don't show us this! This isn't what we're looking for."

Below the rock, two of Beryl's guards wrestled a dragonet out of her father's arms. They carried her over to the Barrier as two others held her father back.

"Please don't," the father cried. "She's not like your son, I'm sure she isn't!"

Snakeroot flicked his tail, and the guards tossed the dragonet at the Barrier. She hit the invisible wall with a shriek and fell back, clutching her scales and crying. Her father ran forward and scooped her up.

"Next," Snakeroot said with a bored expression.

The guards grabbed another dragonet. But as they lifted her to throw into the Barrier, a dragon came over the ridge on the far side. He had a silk bag slung across his chest with purple and blue fruits poking out, and his red-gold scales shone warmly. It was a smaller, less worried-looking Mulberry, peacefully collecting berries from bushes no one else could get to.

Small Mulberry stopped short at the sight below him. His wings flared, and then he came running down the hill, leaping from rock to rock.

"Father! Stop! What are you doing?"

Mulberry tumbled over the Barrier and halted in front of the guards, his wings spread wide and his front talons outstretched.

"Now, Mulberry, don't cause trouble," Beryl said.

"We need to know if anyone else can do what you can," Snakeroot said. "You found out by accident — so perhaps there are others. It would be *useful* for the whole community for us to know."

"But you're scaring them," Mulberry protested. He lifted the dragonet out of the guards' talons. They glanced at the king and queen for permission, then let her go. Mulberry tucked her into his side and she latched on to his leg, tears rolling down her snout.

"No, no, no," the present-day Mulberry whispered, closing his eyes.

"Can't we let dragons volunteer to test the Barrier?" past Mulberry said. "Why do we have to force them?"

"This is the most efficient way," Snakeroot said. He narrowed his eyes. "Perhaps you can take them across. We all want to know if that will work."

"Show us something else," said the present Mulberry. He pressed one of his own claws into the wound Nineteen had left. "Anything but this."

Another drop of blood fell from his palm. It seemed to vanish in midair as the scene went hazy in front of Umber's eyes. Then, with a jolt, Umber stumbled sideways into a new, unfamiliar, terrifying place.

It looked like a banquet hall — a SkyWing banquet hall, Umber guessed, open to the air and surrounded by mountains, with long stone tables covered in food. It did not smell like a banquet hall, however; it smelled like a battlefield, which was probably because of all the corpses scattered across the floor.

The sun was rising in the distance, casting cold beams of light through the jagged peaks. Peach-colored clouds dotted a calm sky, but whatever birds would normally greet the sunrise had wisely shut their beaks and fled for safer perches.

At one end of the hall were two giant gold statues of dragons, and at the other end were the two dragons themselves. One of them was bent over, trying not to be sick.

The other, Umber recognized.

It was Queen Scarlet. Queen Scarlet before the venom scars Glory had given her. Queen Scarlet, wreathed in rubies, smiling with all her teeth at the carnage below her.

A dragon came up the stairs from the kitchen below and paused at the edge of the hall.

"I thought," she said to Queen Scarlet, surveying the bodies, "that you were going to use it to poison *one* dragon."

"Mother?" Mulberry whispered. Umber realized he was right; the newcomer was Beryl, wearing old-fashioned tourmaline earrings and sheaths of many-colored vials under her wings. Umber edged his way through the destruction to stand next to Mulberry, twining their tails together.

Scarlet waved one talon carelessly. "I didn't know which goblet she would take, so I poisoned all of them."

"I see," Beryl said. "How . . . efficient." There was a hint of a skeptical question mark at the end of the word, and Scarlet tilted her head sharply.

"*You* agreed to betray my mother and sister," she snapped. "*I* agreed not to murder your son, even if he annoys me, which frankly he is already. Canyon! Canyon, stop making that disgusting horking noise. It makes me want to rip out your tongue." She smirked at Beryl. "And I never promised I wouldn't do *that*."

The dragon beside her clutched his snout closed and crouched lower, trying to be as quiet as possible.

"Better," Scarlet said. "Beryl, I'm going to need more of that poison."

"For whom?" Beryl asked.

"That's not *your* business," Scarlet said. "*Your* business is *making* the poison and *giving* it to me. I know my mother used you as a secret advisor, but *I* don't need any advice. I'm going to be a *thrilling* queen and have a *thrilling* time making all my enemies pay."

"Yes," Beryl said. "Your Majesty," she added, after just a half second too long.

"Off you go," Scarlet said with a flick of her tail. "Canyon, beloved husband, all muscle and no brain, say good night to your mother."

"Good night, Mother," he mumbled.

Beryl bowed and headed back down the steps. From his vantage point, Umber saw her stop, just out of sight of Queen Scarlet, and tip her head.

"She doesn't seem very enthusiastic about all this, does she?" Scarlet asked, throwing a hawk leg at Canyon's head. "I don't appreciate her attitude."

"I'm sure she's just tired," Canyon offered. "She adores you a-almost as much as I do."

"Well, who doesn't," Scarlet said. "And how fortunate,

because otherwise it would be quite unwise to keep a skilled poisoner around the palace, wouldn't it?" She tapped one of her claws against her chin.

"Sh-she's really more of an herbalist," Canyon said. "With only a few poisons she can make for the queen in, um, emergencies."

"Every day's an emergency when you hate as many dragons as I do!" Scarlet said airily. "For instance, I might urgently need to punish the current royal painter for that last hideous portrait of me."

"I thought it was beautiful," Canyon said, then quickly stammered, "b-b-but not as beautiful as you, of course," when Scarlet frowned at him.

Just out of sight, Beryl rolled her eyes.

"Well, let's keep an eye on your mother," Scarlet said. "She's useful now, but that could change! Ha! And we should be prepared for betrayal at all times. Oh, it *is* going to be fun to be queen." She poked Canyon with one foot and patted the chain of jewels around her horns.

Below them, Beryl stood looking thoughtful for a long moment. Finally she shook her head and slipped quietly away down the stairs.

Scarlet and Canyon sat frozen, their images wavering and starting to blur.

"Wow," Umber said. "Your mom had another son before she came here? Did you know that?"

Mulberry shook his head. His gaze was fixed in wonder

on Canyon, who was profoundly the opposite of Mulberry, as far as Umber could tell.

"So your half brother was married to Queen Scarlet — which means you're basically Queen Scarlet's brother-in-law! That is . . . a lot to process."

"But not what we're looking for," Mulberry said, nudging his side. "We need to go back further." He closed his fist over the wound, then opened it again and slashed a claw across his palm. Blood poured into the invisible basin — at least, Umber hoped they were still standing over the basin.

"That was too much," he said anxiously, reaching for Mulberry's injured talon. "Mulberry, you're really hurt."

"It's all right," the prince said, although his face was tight with pain. He nodded at something behind Umber. "Look. I think it worked."

CHAPTER 21

They were in another castle, but not one Umber recognized.

More mountains loomed just outside, but he was sure they weren't the Claws of the Clouds. Umber had never seen these mountains before. The pale claws of two crescent moons hung in a star-filled sky, with the third moon huddled low on the horizon.

Scrolls in labeled niches covered two entire walls and huge tables took up most of the center of the space. Another wall held a large door and two tapestry portraits of a diamond-bedecked NightWing. The fourth wall opened onto a balcony, which overlooked a view of construction far below. Umber could see torches flickering and dragons moving over the foundations of stone buildings.

The ancient Night Kingdom, he guessed. *Where they lived centuries ago, before they moved to the volcano island.*

Three dragons were gathered around a scroll, which was rolled all the way open on a portable metal contraption. Two of the dragons were SkyWings and one was a NightWing.

Two of the dragons wore crowns; the third, Umber realized as she leaned forward to put something on top of the scroll, was Precipice, the SkyWing animus from the vision. Her claw necklace clattered as she moved and she slung it back over her shoulder with an annoyed *tsk* sound.

The object she set on the table was a SharpWing — but it hadn't been brought to life yet. This one was dark shimmery green with a few silver scales here and there. It was strange to see one so inert. Nothing glinted in its little eyes; its wings were perfectly motionless.

"That's it?" said the NightWing queen. "I didn't picture them so . . . small."

"But there will be a whole swarm of them," Precipice said. She regarded her creation with a faintly fond smile. "And they will be so fierce."

"Hmmm. Won't this prison need *real* guards, Summit?" the NightWing queen asked the other SkyWing.

"The prison spell will do most of the work," said the SkyWing queen with a shrug. "I mean, the guards are barely necessary when there's a Barrier no one can cross anyway." This was not Queen Falcon, from the original Memory Room vision; Umber guessed this must be her successor. He remembered her mentioning a sister named Summit.

The NightWing squinted at the scroll. "You're sure your 'animus magic' can do this? My impression from the IceWings was that the power is quite limited."

"It's not," Precipice said.

"IceWings have no imagination," added Summit. "Really the power is only limited by what you can think of to do with it."

"Indeed," said the NightWing queen. "Sounds useful. And, to be frank, extremely dangerous."

Precipice gave her a sideways look. "I'd only use my magic in the service of my queen."

"Didn't do the last one much good, though, did it?"

Precipice scooped up the SharpWing, her tail lashing. "Queen Falcon preferred me to hide my magic," she growled. "I would have given her magical protection if she had let me."

The SkyWing queen interrupted them, pointing to a paragraph in the scroll. "You can leave this out of the spell, Precipice."

"The lake?" Precipice said, tilting her head. "But they're going to need it if we keep the prison inside the mountains as you requested. There's not a lot of reliable fresh water on that side of the island."

"They'll be fine," Summit said. "They'll learn to manage their resources carefully."

"It just . . . seems especially cruel to the SeaWing prisoners," Precipice said.

"Then they shouldn't have murdered my sister, should they?" Summit said, unruffled.

"Well, *they* didn't, technically —" Precipice started.

"Fine, shouldn't have *conspired to murder my sister*, are you happy now?"

"Besides, this is what these dragons wanted," the NightWing

queen interjected. "A place where their tribes could mix together. Yuck." She gave a performative little shudder. "Now they can have that, far away from the rest of us."

"I wish I knew where the ones who escaped went," Summit murmured, flexing her claws as she stared down at the scroll. "If they tried to cross the ocean to the lost continent, they *must* all be dead. Don't you think, Retribution?"

"Indeed," agreed the NightWing queen. "But I'm more worried about the ones currently crowding both of our dungeons. The sooner we can get rid of them, the better. How long will this spell take to set up?" She tapped the scroll.

"If my queen approves the details in this scroll, I can cast it tomorrow," Precipice said.

"Take out the lake," said Queen Summit. "And this last section, from here to here."

Precipice leaned over to see what she was pointing at. "Wait — all of it?"

"That's what I said. Are you questioning me?"

"I — no, but —"

"We don't want the prisoners' grandchildren turning up in a hundred years looking for vengeance, do we? Even if you and I are gone by then, think of our dragonets. Would you really leave a mess like that for them to deal with?"

"But then what should the time limit be?" Precipice asked. "If a hundred years is too short — I could make it two hundred?"

"I said *take it out,*" Queen Summit growled. "Entirely. We're making a prison that will never fall. The prisoners will never leave, and neither will their dragonets or any of the dragonets who come after them."

"But dragons could end up there by accident and get trapped forever," Precipice said. "And generations from now, there will be dragons stuck on the island who never did anything wrong."

"Yes, and that way all of Pyrrhia will remember what happens when you kill a queen," the NightWing snapped. "That is the point. This prison will keep us safe. No one will dare come near us, knowing this is what awaits their families if they do."

Precipice looked down at the tiny dragon in her talons. "So . . . the guards will be stuck there forever, too?"

"The *guards*?" Queen Summit echoed. "You mean your little toys? Who cares what happens to them?"

Precipice closed her talons gently around the SharpWing. "I just wonder if there should be *some* way for dragons in the future to leave. I mean, what if one of your great-grandchildren got blown off course in a storm and ended up inside the Barrier?"

"Oh, that's a fun idea," the NightWing queen said. "Summit, what if we add a clause saying the only dragons who can leave the prison are ones descended from both of us!"

Summit snorted. "A future SkyWing-NightWing hybrid? Sounds monstrous. And utterly impossible, so, sure, Precipice, go ahead and add that if you'd like to."

"But what about everyone else?" Precipice protested.

"Shut up, shut up now," Summit said. "I've told you what

I want. Go rewrite this." She ripped the scroll off the metal scrollholder and threw it at Precipice.

"Yes, Your Majesty," Precipice said. She gathered the pieces, bowed, and hurried out the door.

Queen Retribution waited until her footsteps died away, and then she raised a skeptical eyebrow at Queen Summit. "I'm not sure your pet animus is as agreeable as you think she is."

"She will be," Summit said. "My sister didn't know how to use her magic properly, but Precipice will get used to doing what I say. Especially once she realizes that driving out the BeetleWings and LeafWings means almost doubling the size of the Sky Kingdom. All those useful forests! I'm the smartest queen we've ever had."

"Indeed," Retribution said. Umber kind of wanted to throw something at her head if she said "indeed" one more time. "You and Hibiscus split their land and we get their treasure. But you don't think Precipice is suspicious about how much of this you planned?"

Summit looked at her sharply. "No."

"Hmmm." Retribution tapped her claws along the table. "You don't think she might suspect Hibiscus was working with you?"

"Why would she?" Summit snorted. "Why would anyone think I'd have a secret plan with the RainWing queen?"

"Well," Retribution said, "it's quite convenient that *someone's* top assassin helped Darkling murder your sister and make you queen."

"Lemur and Darkling were following Euphoria's orders," Summit said.

"Sure," said the NightWing queen. "Although that's not what they said before they escaped."

"Who is everyone going to believe?" Summit asked. "A pair of murderers, or the RainWing queen who says she had nothing to do with it?"

"Mm-hmm," Retribution said, sliding her claws along the table.

"Queen Hibiscus is *so* uninvolved that she's willing to punish all the RainWings related to Lemur," Summit pointed out. "She's absolutely heartbroken about my sister's death and shocked, *shocked* that the assassins would try to blame her."

"Somehow I think all that new territory will cheer her up," Retribution said drily. "Which is about when a certain SkyWing animus might start to put some pieces together."

"Nonsense," Summit said. "Precipice isn't suspicious. I assure you."

"*I* would be," Retribution said. "If *I* were a clever little animus. And then I might be tempted to *do* something about it with alllll my lovely magic. Something like . . . take the throne for myself."

Summit hissed out a plume of smoke. "Fine. I will keep an eye on my 'clever little animus,' and if she seems like she might be a threat to me, I'll kill her first."

Retribution paced away from her and lifted a goblet of

wine off the sideboard. With her back turned to Summit, only Umber and Mulberry could see the secret little triumphant smile that flitted across her face.

At the same time, Umber felt the slight wobbling that indicated the scene was about to come to an end. "Wait," he said to the air. "We need to see what's enchanted. Or at least where it is. Don't stop here!"

"Umber," Mulberry said, and his voice was so shaky that Umber immediately turned to wrap his wings around him.

"Are you all right?" Mulberry felt colder than normal, and he leaned heavily against Umber's side.

"Over there," Mulberry said, pointing with a trembling claw. "Quick. Is that —?"

Umber saw what he meant. A square of parchment had fallen from the papers in Precipice's talons as she left, and even from across the room, Umber could see that it was a map. A spray of small islands around one large one — it had to be the Dungeon Isle.

"Go see." Mulberry shoved Umber gently. "Hurry."

Umber stepped back, making sure Mulberry could stay upright, and then hurried across the floor, which was feeling more insubstantial by the moment.

The map said THE DUNGEON at the top and a dark line was drawn all around the inside of the mountains on the large island. That had to be the Barrier.

Umber leaned closer, searching for any other marks — and he found one.

A small oval, barely visible between two peaks of the southern mountain range, but inside the Barrier.

Could that be it?

Is that where Precipice is going to hide the animus-touched object to enchant the prison?

If we go there — can we find it and break it?

The map was turning into smoke below his talons. Umber frantically tried to memorize where the oval was — how far from the west coast, the shape of the mountains around it, the nearest river —

Suddenly it was gone and Umber was crouching over a random empty space in the Memory Room. He whirled around and ran back to Mulberry.

The prince was lying on the floor, pressing his uninjured front talon against his other palm to stanch the blood flow.

"It'll be all right," Umber said. Pheasant was their healer; he tried to remember everything she'd taught them about battle wounds. "Let's get you somewhere with bandages and water. If you can't make it back to the infirmary, I'll go bring Paua here." He slung Mulberry's wing over his and supported the prince to his feet. "Here, if I take over pressure on the wound, and we lean against each other, it'll be like we have two working front talons between us."

Mulberry relinquished his bleeding palm and Umber clasped it firmly. Waves of *worry* and *feeling stupid* were coming through Mulberry's scales.

"You didn't do anything stupid," Umber said. "This is easily fixed, trust me."

"I know," Mulberry said with a wan smile.

"And we know more now," Umber said as they limped toward the door. "We know that Queen Summit worked with Queen Hibiscus to plan the murder of the SkyWing queen. Then they blamed it on the BeetleWings and LeafWings in order to steal their land."

"We also might know that the NightWing queen convinced Summit to kill her animus, which could be why SkyWings don't have animus dragons anymore," Mulberry said. "What lovable ancestors I have."

"And," Umber said, "we know that Precipice marked a spot on the map of the Dungeon Isle. If we can find it, maybe we'll find what she enchanted."

They nudged open the door of the Memory Room and emerged into the outer cave, talon in talon, smiling at each other.

But the cave was no longer empty.

"Well, hello," said Queen Beryl. "I must say I hate *everything* about this."

CHAPTER 22

"Mother!" Mulberry cried. He instinctively flinched away from Umber and then stumbled without the support. As he pulled away, blood dripped from his talon.

"You're hurt," Beryl said, hurrying to his side. Behind her, a force of dragons pointed spears at Umber, herding him back against the stone wall. "I *knew* it. I *knew* this common MudWing was bad for you."

"He's not," Mulberry said faintly.

"Getting you in trouble," Beryl growled. "Dragging you down *here*, of all places. Subjecting you to the horrors of that room. *And* stealing your blood? What was he trying to do — give himself the power to cross the Barrier, too?" She glared at Umber. "That doesn't work! We already tried it!"

Umber remembered the little dragon in Mulberry's memory, trying to protect the other prisoners from his parents' experiments. Had he volunteered himself in their place? What had they "tried" doing to him?

"He didn't do this to me," Mulberry said. "I did. It was just an accident."

"It's all right, dear," Beryl said, stroking his face and putting one wing around him. "You're safe now. I'm here." She snapped her claws at one of the King's Teeth and he passed her a sling bag of first aid supplies. Mulberry closed his eyes as she poured something from a vial over his cut and then started wrapping it in bandages.

"Your Majesty, we just wanted to know more about —" Umber started.

"Don't talk," Beryl said. "The sound of your voice makes me very inclined to kill you."

"Mother, *no*," Mulberry said, opening his eyes again. He repeated himself more forcefully. "No. Do *not* hurt Umber. Promise me."

"One of my spies thinks he's working with the exiles," Beryl said to him. "Did you know that? He could have brought you down here to hand you over to them. Imagine my poor sweet Mulberry as a hostage, trapped in the grasping claws of those *snakes*."

The King's Teeth around Umber all nodded, murmuring *how awful* and *imagine* and *our prince!*

"I would never do that," Umber said.

"How can we trust you?" Beryl asked. "Go back to shutting up."

"*I* trust him," Mulberry said woozily.

"No, dear," Beryl said. "He's a bad influence on you. Look at you: you're avoiding your responsibilities, spending time with him instead of us, and risking your life following him to dangerous places. *No one* is good enough for *my* son — *especially* this distracting, disobedient upstart."

Mulberry swayed and blinked down at the bandage on his talon. "Oh no . . . Mother, did you use sleep powder on me?"

"Of course I did, dear," she said as he slumped to the ground, unconscious.

Eyes glinting, Beryl turned to Umber. "All right, MudWing. You seem a bit slow, which I should have expected for a dragon from your tribe, so I'm going to be *very* clear. Here are your orders: kill the exiled dragons who are hiding from me. Tonight. I know you know who they are. It should be easy for a seasoned soldier like you. One who is *good at following orders*."

"But —" Umber started.

"Shh, shh, shh," she said. "These are very simple orders. Kill them, bring me proof that they're dead. And until you do, Mulberry is staying locked up where I can keep an eye on him." She patted the prince's head with an expression like she'd just stolen all the treasure from every other dragon in the world.

Umber's heart sank. "You'd make your own son a prisoner?"

"It's to keep him *safe*," she said in a tone of oily sweetness. "From *you*."

"Yeah," said one of the King's Teeth, and she shot him a quelling look.

"Take my son to my chambers," she commanded. A group

of five gathered around Mulberry, lifted him like a precious, delicate carpet, and carted him away up the tunnel to the outside. Umber listened to their wingbeats depart and felt as though half his soul was going with them. He imagined fighting all the King's Teeth at once to get Mulberry back — but he knew there were too many and he didn't stand a chance.

And that word, *orders*, hung around his shoulders like a boa constrictor.

"Now give this one a spear," Beryl said, flicking a claw at Umber. "And off you go, MudWing. Remember, this is your one chance to prove your loyalty and set Mulberry free. Chop, chop. We'll have some murder by morning, if you please."

She smirked as someone pressed a spear into Umber's arms *(should I use it? should I fight back now? what if I went for Beryl — I can't attack Beryl; that's Mulberry's mom)* and then she swept after her son with all the other guards, and it was too late.

For a moment, Umber stood there and considered what she'd said. His "orders."

Kill six dragons. That was basically what he'd been sent out to do during the war, although he'd never actually struck a killing blow himself, as far as he knew. He thought he could, if he had to . . . but he *knew* he couldn't if those dragons were Tuatara or Wollemi or any of the other exiles.

Umber's talons closed around the spear.

No.

No to Queen Beryl, no to these orders.

I won't hurt the dragons who should *be ruling the Court of Refuge, and who have been nothing but kind to me.*

I'm going to set Mulberry free. And then we're going to find a way to leave this prison, all of us together.

Umber was running through the dark tunnels back to the castle when he heard a sound — a distant, small scraping sound. He skidded to a stop and pricked his ears, listening intently.

scrrrp

scrrrtch

scrrrape

"Platypus?" Umber whispered. If it was her, he didn't think she'd hear him — the sound was too far away for a whisper to reach. But if it *wasn't* her, he didn't *particularly* want to attract the attention of something else down here.

A buzz zipped by his face in the dark and he stumbled back a step. It zipped toward him again, and he realized it was Nineteen. The SharpWing circled his head for a moment before landing on his shoulder. Umber knew Sora would roll her eyes at him for the thought, but he could swear the little metal dragon seemed nervous. It kept making jittery, sudden moves, and its wings flickered oddly against his neck.

"That wasn't *you* making that noise. Do you know what it was?" he asked. "All right, I know, you can't tell me and I should stop asking questions."

He kept going, carrying Nineteen with him. The sound settled back into silence, and Umber tried to think about Mulberry instead. Where would he be? He said he slept in one of the towers near his parents — and Beryl said to take him to her chambers.

Umber had a flash of memory: Platypus, the night of the first Aurora concert, pausing to throw smelly fruit through a tower window even while she was being chased.

Could that be Beryl's window?

It gave him a place to start, at least. He reached the other side of the secret door to the infirmary and hesitated, listening.

Silence from the other side.

He slipped through quietly and scanned the room — still empty, apart from Blob waving happily from his pillow again. Umber wondered how long he'd been gone and whether the concert was over. He tiptoed over to Blob and patted the octopus's head, thinking.

Maybe there was something in here he could use.

Sleep powder, said the voice of Platypus in his head. *They use that stuff LIBERALLY around here.*

Umber gently disentangled himself from Blob's curious tentacles and ventured around the room, opening cabinets. In the third one he checked, he found a shaker with little holes in the top, labeled REST in neat handwriting. When he pried it open, it was full of the yellow powder he'd seen on his food the day he met Platypus. He put the top back on and packed it into a bag with more bandages, in case Mulberry needed them, plus two other REST shakers he found in the next cabinet.

Next question: How could he get through the castle without being spotted by Beryl or one of the King's Teeth? He'd have to use Platypus's secret passageways, although he didn't know all the ways in and out of them, and it was already hard to map the castle and the towers in his head.

He went back into the wall, turned left, and squeezed through the narrow space between the walls. Tiny beams of light crisscrossed the hidden spaces from holes that peeked into various rooms. A common room lined with cushions where three WildWings were chatting. A kitchen where a mother and her dragonet were sharing roasted peaches. An art studio where two dragons were arguing over who had drawn the best picture of Aurora.

Soon he was hopelessly lost. None of the rooms he saw looked even remotely familiar, and safe places with exit doors were few and far between. Twice he saw one of the King's Teeth hulking grimly along a hall, as if they were patrolling, which made him afraid to pop out anywhere even to orient himself.

It had to be past midnight, Umber guessed. He wanted to get Mulberry out before dawn — it would be easier for them to escape across the plain in the darkness. And he hoped that moving quickly would take Beryl by surprise, especially if she truly thought he'd be out hunting down the exiles right now.

Finally he saw someone he recognized through one of the spyholes, in a room with a secret door.

Unfortunately, it was Dugong.

On the plus side, he was alone. Dugong was flumped woefully across the floor of a small, empty room, filling almost the whole space. His head rested on his front talons, and he appeared to be just . . . staring at the regular door.

Is he waiting for something? Hiding? Meditating? Forming a deep spiritual relationship with the door?

Umber rubbed his forehead. He couldn't risk trusting Dugong, could he?

But did he have much choice? He had no idea where he was in the castle, and time was running short.

Worst case scenario, if he tries to capture me or yells for help, I can throw sleep powder up his nose and run away.

Taking a deep breath, Umber slid aside the secret panel in the wall and stepped gingerly into the small corner of space Dugong wasn't already filling.

"Hey, Dugong," he said.

Dugong turned his head in a slow, ponderous way and his eyes went wide.

"WHAAAAAT?" he said.

"Which part what?" Umber asked.

"There's a secret door in here?" Dugong asked. "Has it been there this whole time?"

"I assume so?" Umber said. "At least since Platypus went into hiding."

Dugong sighed. "She was loud," he said. "And talked too fast. But she would fight with Taipan. That was pretty great." He looked mournfully back at the normal door.

"Dugong," Umber said, his intuition nudging him. "Are you . . . locked in here?"

"Yes." Dugong heaved himself to his feet and hung his head.

"By Taipan and Royal?" Umber guessed.

"They think it's funny," Dugong said. "So I can't go to the concert. Because I was too annoying today, they said."

"Does this happen a lot?"

"Yeah," Dugong admitted. "I almost never get to see the concerts." He looked close to tears. Umber felt so sorry for him.

"Don't you have any brothers or sisters?" he asked. "Who can take care of you?"

Dugong shook his head. "Just me."

A MudWing with no siblings. That's one of the saddest things I've ever heard. I wonder if his MudWing instincts led him to Taipan and Royal — if part of him is so loyal to them because he's looking for a sibling group, like MudWings are supposed to have.

"You deserve better friends, you know," Umber said. "I wish I could take you to the Mud Kingdom and find you a group who would treat you better than those two do."

Dugong shrugged. "If I *could* ever get to the Mud Kingdom, Taipan says I'd have to try and take the throne."

"That's a terrible idea," Umber said. "You don't even want

a throne. You just want friends and safety, right?"

"But it's *my* throne," Dugong said. "That's what they say. My ancestor ran away instead of taking it when her sister died. If she had stayed, our family would still have it."

"But *you* still wouldn't be queen," Umber pointed out. "You wouldn't even exist. Besides, we have a good queen now. You would like her, I'm sure of it."

"Huh," Dugong said. He looked contemplative for a moment. "*Not* take the throne. Interesting. Huh."

This train of thought seemed as if it might take the rest of the night. "Do you know the way to Beryl's tower from here?" Umber asked.

"Yeah," Dugong said. "I'd show you. But I can't leave."

"What in the isles — of *course* you can leave," Umber said. "Come through the secret door with me."

"Uhhh." Dugong looked back at the regular door. "But. Won't they be mad."

"I have a wild guess," Umber said. "How often do they forget and leave you here all night?"

Dugong sighed again. "Once they forgot for four days."

"Three moons, Dugong," Umber said. "You definitely do not need to sit here and wait for them. Besides, imagine the looks on their faces when they open the door and you're gone! And they have no idea how! Wouldn't that be great?"

"Huh," Dugong said. "I guess that could be funny." He scrunched his face and thought about that.

"I *am* in a bit of a hurry, though," Umber said. "Sorry to rush you."

"OK," Dugong said agreeably, lumbering to Umber's side. "Hey, do you know you have a pointy little dragon on your shoulder?"

Nineteen rattled its wings and buzzed at him.

"Yeah," Umber said. "This is Nineteen."

"Huh," Dugong said again. "All right. Let's go."

The passageway was even more of a tight squeeze with Dugong leading the way, but after a moment it seemed to ease out a little bit, as if giving them more space. Umber wondered whether he was imagining it, or if it was Waterfall's magic at work.

Dugong muttered as they walked, apparently giving himself directions and counting off steps between rooms. At length he stopped, peeked through a spyhole in the wall, and grunted, "Here."

They emerged into something that was clearly not Beryl's chambers, or even the foot of the tower leading to her chambers. It was, instead, a pantry, full of barrels and jars and long shelves of stored food.

Dugong beelined for the shelves, opened a bag, and began stuffing dried fruit in his mouth.

"Er," Umber said. "Dugong?"

"Hungry," Dugong said.

"Sure, me too," Umber said. "Always. But, um, remember the part where I'm in a hurry?"

Dugong flung an apricot at him. "This will help."

"This apricot?" Umber asked, catching it.

"Being here." Dugong waved a talon at the rest of the pantry. "She comes here a lot."

"She who?" Umber said. "Please don't say Beryl."

"The ghost," Dugong said. "I know because whenever *I* come to . . . uh, borrow food, there's always more missing than I took. Pretty sure this is her favorite room to nibble from. Because they don't check it often." He waved his talon again.

"You're saying you think Platypus will come here? Tonight?" Umber asked.

"OK FINE I'M ALREADY HERE!" Platypus burst out of a barrel, sending potatoes rolling in all directions. Dugong yelped and fell over, throwing his wings over his head.

"Platypus!" Umber cried, delighted. "OK, Dugong, I owe you an apology — this *is* really helpful."

"It is?" Dugong said. Umber wondered whether anyone ever said anything nice to him.

"I can't believe *you* of all dragons noticed this is my number one pantry to steal from," Platypus said to Dugong. "That is wild. But if you tell anyone, I will steal every single fig in this palace so there are none left for you."

Dugong made a woebegone face. "But . . . figs are my faaavorite."

"I KNOW," Platypus said. "So just think about that if your big jerk friends start asking nosy questions about me."

"Oh, they won't," Dugong said placidly. "They don't think I know anything."

"Platypus, I need your help," Umber said. "The queen has locked up Mulberry and ordered me to kill the exiles, or she'll keep him prisoner until I do."

Platypus growled, whacking a potato into the wall with her tail. "That is VERY BERYL," she said. "She'll use anyone to get what she wants."

"Can you help me set him free?" Umber asked. "We found a clue that I hope will help us bring down the Barrier, but I want to take him with me when I go after it. And I need to get Sora to come with us, too. I don't want to leave her here with Beryl and Snakeroot."

"Definitely, good call," Platypus said. "And Quokka."

"Sora?" Dugong said, looking much more awake all of a sudden. "Uh . . . I can go get Sora."

There was something funny in his voice. Umber squinted at him.

"Are you friends with my sister?" he asked.

"I mean, whatever, kinda, I just, uh, think she's really interesting," Dugong mumbled.

Platypus gave Umber a "who saw THAT coming?" face and clapped her front talons together. "That will work," she said. "No one will suspect Dugong is helping us. He can get Sora and Quokka and tell them to meet us outside the Memory Room rock formation."

"Can I come with you, too?" Dugong asked wistfully. "I don't mind where we're going."

"Um . . . sure," Umber said. "But we have to move fast to get as far away as we can before dawn."

"Yup," Dugong said, taking one last apricot and closing the bag again. "Got it. I'll go now."

"Be careful," Umber said.

"And don't you DARE say anything to Taipan or Royal!" Platypus said. "FIGS, Dugong! I swear I'll throw them ALL over the Barrier!"

"OK, OK," Dugong said affably. He peeked through the door, then slipped out and closed it behind him.

"All right," Platypus said to Umber. "Let's go rescue a prince."

CHAPTER 23

Umber and Platypus crouched on a rooftop just below Beryl's tower window. Wind tugged at their wings and tails, hotter and drier than Umber thought a nighttime wind should be. The moons were hidden behind clouds, and only a few stars were visible here and there.

Two dragons were flying a patrol circle around the tower, around and around in maddening loops. Umber recognized them from his training sessions; one was a WildWing named Quoll, and the other was a SkyWing named Ravine. He suspected Ravine had arrived with Beryl. There were a few other SkyWings among the King's Teeth, and his guess was that they had all fled from Queen Scarlet together.

There was no clear way past them, but two guards was still better odds than the five who were pacing the halls below them and blocking the staircase at the foot of the tower.

"Any ideas?" Umber asked Nineteen, who had crawled along to one of his talons and was hunkered down, holding on to one of his claws. The SharpWing narrowed its eyes at him like, *No, this was* your *stupid plan,* you *figure it out*.

"I bet we can take these two," Platypus said. "How about *I* magical death spit Quoll and *you* go punch that SkyWing really hard, and then boom, we're done, grab Mulberry, fly for the hills."

"It'll be too loud," Umber said. "We need to get in and out quietly, without any other guards noticing. And someone will definitely notice a dragon shrieking his head off because you melted his scales."

Platypus let out a frustrated snort. "Fine. But I can't think of a way to give them sleep powder other than, like, flying up and throwing it in their faces. Which is also not the MOST stealthy plan."

Umber regarded the jar of pickles he'd brought from the pantry. "I guess we can't just . . . sprinkle this with sleep powder and leave it somewhere they'll find it?"

"And rely on them being observant? No, we need someone to bring it to them," Platypus said. "Too bad they don't like either of our faces. Those grumblebutts probably don't like any —" She stopped midsentence with a gasp.

"What?" Umber whispered.

"I have an idea," she said. "Wait here."

She grabbed the pickles and a sleep powder shaker from him, scuttled away across the roof, dropped down into a garden, and vanished into the shadows.

Umber didn't super love being left alone while guards

were everywhere. He huddled closer to the roof, hoping his scales blended into the dark well enough to avoid notice. Nineteen clambered back up to his shoulder and tucked itself into the spot on Umber's neck that was most sheltered from the wind.

What felt like a long time later, a tiny scrabble of claws on the roof announced Platypus's return.

"I'm back," whispered the empty space beside him. Umber realized she was using her RainWing camouflage, like Quokka said she could. "This will totally work."

After a few moments, a dragon came gliding from one of the other towers, silvery in the faint starlight. Jewels winked from her claws, ankles, and neck. She smiled at the guards as she drew closer, and they nearly crashed into each other in midair.

"Aurora!" Ravine cried.

"You were amazing tonight!" Quoll said, clasping his front talons together.

"*So* great," the SkyWing agreed.

"Oh, thank you so much," Aurora said. She tilted her wings to hover in the air beside them for a moment. "Is Queen Beryl in?"

"No, sorry," Quoll said. "She's with the king in the library."

"I see. Can I leave these for her, then?" Aurora held up a platter of something that smelled like chocolate and coconut even from where Umber was hiding. "Someone made them for me and I can't possibly eat this many."

"What happened to the pickles?" Umber mouthed to Platypus.

She whispered, "Aurora said nobody would want those."

"Why?" he whispered, ruffled. "Pickles are the best!"

"Uh, no one's allowed in her chambers tonight, I'm afraid," Ravine said. "Orders."

"Oh . . . that's too bad," Aurora said. "But I understand. I guess I'll go leave them at the Gathering."

"Can I have one?" Quoll asked.

"Me too?" asked the other guard.

"Oh, sorry, of course!" Aurora said. "Have as many as you like!" Quoll had three of them in his mouth before she finished the sentence.

"Our friends are on guard duty tonight, too," said Ravine, taking three as well. "Maybe we could bring the rest to them? Save you a trip to the Gathering?"

"That's *so* sweet of you!" Aurora said, and Ravine looked delighted with herself. "Sure, if you really don't mind. Thank you so much." She passed over the plate, gave each of them a dazzling smile, and flew back to her tower.

"Genius," Umber whispered.

"Thank you, I know," Platypus said. "I mean, everybody likes *her* face."

"Won't she get in trouble, though?" he asked. "When the guards wake up and Mulberry is gone . . . won't they figure it out?"

"Hopefully not," Platypus said. "She can always say someone gave it to her and she didn't know it had sleep powder on it. I'm not worried. She's clever and, like, *too* beloved. No one is ever mad at her."

"I hope you're right," he said.

"There they go," Platypus whispered. The guards were both yawning; their wings drooped heavily as they flew.

"I'll take this in to the others and be right back," the SkyWing said sleepily, waving the plate around.

"'Kay," Quoll mumbled.

Ravine drifted away toward a balcony, leaving Quoll flying in slower and slower circles all alone.

"Is he going to fall out of the sky?" Umber worried. "Should we do something?"

"I have no objection to *that* bug-eating traitor falling out of the sky," Platypus growled.

Quoll shook his head blearily and tipped his wings to fly up onto the roof of Beryl's tower. He tucked himself onto a small balcony that jutted out above one of the windows and rested his head on his talons. Umber could hear him muttering, "Good idea, Quoll. Keep watch from here. Smart," as his eyes slid closed.

Umber and Platypus waited for a long moment to make sure no one was coming or ringing any alarms. Then Umber quietly crept to the edge of their roof and glided across to Beryl's tower. He caught on to talonholds in the stone and peeked in the window.

Mulberry was there and alone and awake.

And chained to one of the carved wooden columns in the room.

Umber swarmed through the window and galloped across the floor to the prince. He skidded to a halt next to Mulberry, wrapping his wings as far around him as he could.

"Umber!" Mulberry said. "You can't be here! Mother is so mad!"

"I can't believe she put *chains* on you," Umber said. He tugged at the chains, which felt too tight to him. They were wrapped around Mulberry's neck and tail and the column, with a large padlock on the far side holding them together.

"I kind of can't either," Mulberry said. "They're not usually like this, Umber. It must be the prophecy. It's making them both so agitated. Father is having some kind of recurring vision he can't stop. He keeps repeating what he said at the concert and Mother hates it."

All Umber could remember was the line *the hybrid prince will rise at last*. If that was Mulberry, maybe now was the time. Maybe this was what the prophecy meant — the moment Mulberry escaped his parents and chose something else.

"We're getting you out of here," Umber said.

"We?" Mulberry echoed.

"Oh, right," said the empty air behind Umber. Platypus slowly shimmered back into view. "Ta-da!"

"Hey, Platypus," Mulberry said with an affectionate smile. "Nice to actually see you. I'm glad you're all right."

"I will be *more* all right when we are off heroically fleeing across the desert to break an ancient spell," Platypus declared. "This chain situation is a bit of a problem, though."

"Go without me," Mulberry said. "My parents won't really hurt me, Umber. You don't have to worry about me. I wouldn't be much help anyway."

"I'm not going without you," Umber said, "and I'm not expecting you to help. You can be perfectly useless the whole time. I'd want to be with you even if you had no powers and couldn't cross the Barrier and couldn't talk to krakens and took twenty-hour naps a day and smelled like a corpse flower. I mean, we might have a chat about bathing if you did, but if you were like, 'no! I refuse to ever bathe again!' I wouldn't care."

"Wow," Platypus said. "That was *almost* romantic, until it veered wildly off course."

"I thought it was great," Mulberry said, smiling at Umber.

"Did Beryl take the key with her?" Platypus asked, circling the column to peer at the padlock.

"Yes." Mulberry tried to twist around to look at it and stopped, wincing, as the chains cut off his movement.

"OK, what can we try?" Umber said. "Fire? Chopping down this column with an axe? Something to pick the lock?"

"I think we *probably* shouldn't set this column on fire while Mulberry is chained to it," Platypus said. "I am SUPER up for taking an axe to everything in Beryl's room, though! Do you have an axe?"

"No," Umber said.

Bzzzzt went little wings on his shoulder. *Zzzzztzzzzt*.

Umber reached up and offered his talon for Nineteen to

climb on. The SharpWing sat down in the center of his palm and met Umber's eyes. It looked as if it were trying to find a hidden treasure deep inside Umber's soul.

"Is there something you can do?" Umber asked it. "Please. He shouldn't be held prisoner like this."

The little metal dragon turned to study Mulberry.

"We want to set you free as well," Umber said. "All the SharpWings."

Nineteen's wings clicked together thoughtfully. Finally it rose up from Umber's talon and unfolded a long metal piece from under its wing, It flew over to the padlock and stuck it in the keyhole.

"A skeleton key?" Platypus asked as the lock went *click*. "Do you all have those? That would have been super helpful to know!"

Nineteen tossed its head at her and hopped off the padlock. Umber hurried over to unwind the chains and help Mulberry stand up. The prince rubbed his neck.

"Thank you," Mulberry said to the SharpWing. "So much."

"Let's get the others and go," Platypus said, herding them toward the window.

Sora and Quokka were clearly surprised to see Mulberry and Platypus together with Umber, but they didn't argue when Umber said, "We have to hurry. We'll explain as we fly."

He hoped the clouds covering the moons would also hide

them as they took off, heading south. Nineteen clung to his shoulder, Platypus and Quokka flew side by side, and Dugong brought up the rear.

"So *what* are we doing?" Sora asked, flapping up next to Umber. "Dugong said something about . . . figs?"

Umber explained what they'd seen in the Memory Room. "So now we're going to the spot that was marked on the map to see what's there," he said. "If I can find it." The island was feeling a lot bigger now that he was flying over it instead of looking at it on a charmingly small map. He was also starting to worry that the little oval he'd seen was actually a slip of the claw, a random scribble that meant nothing. What if he'd turned them all into exiles and there was no way out after all?

We'd be exiles anyway, he thought. *I would never do what Beryl asked, so we'd have to hide from her. This way at least there's a little bit of hope.*

They flew all the rest of the night and kept flying as the sun came up. There was nowhere to hide — the dusty plain stretched flat below them in every direction, and the Barrier blocked their way into the mountains. So they had to rely on speed and the hope that it would be a while before Beryl noticed Mulberry was gone and sent patrols after them. At that point, she'd have to guess which direction they'd gone in, and hopefully, Umber hoped, she'd guess wrong.

That was a lot of hoping. He tried to speed up, but his

wings were getting tired, which meant surely Sora's were as well. Of all his siblings, Umber usually had the most energy, which was something they always loved to grumble about.

He wished Reed or Pheasant were here now; he'd take any amount of grumbling in exchange for someone who could tell him what to do.

Wait. He pricked his ears. Had he heard a splash?

His eyes darted across the landscape below them. Yes — off to the west, he saw a small, rare pool of water.

"Let's rest for a moment," he called to the others.

They followed him down to the pond in an arcing spiral. The water was shallow and a bit too warm, but Umber drank from it gratefully anyway.

Quokka and Sora landed on the bank beside him and ducked their heads to drink as well. A moment later, Dugong touched down, waded straight into the pond, and collapsed with his head underwater, sending waves up all their noses.

Umber snorted and turned to Mulberry as the prince came up beside him. "To be fair," Umber said, gesturing to Dugong, "that was my first instinct, too."

"And mine," Mulberry agreed.

"Dugong's so funny," Quokka said. "And *so* much nicer without Taipan or Royal around."

Dugong hadn't complained once since leaving the palace; he hadn't even demanded to stop for food. Umber wondered if he was on his best behavior for Sora.

"SEAWING TAIL!" Platypus yelled, crashing into the

water at top speed and drenching all of them. She barely missed landing on Dugong, who sat up in a hurry, dripping and confused.

"Ack, Platypus!" Quokka yelped. "WHY! Just always WHY!"

"Because it's hilarious," Platypus said blithely, paddling from one end of the pool to the other.

Dugong looked at Sora. "Not under attack?"

"Not under attack," she reassured him.

He stuck his head under the water again and came back up with a fish. "Hungry?" he asked, offering it to Sora.

"Sure," she said shyly. "We could share it?"

"OK," he said. Dugong splashed back out of the pool and crouched beside Sora as she started a small fire. Platypus gave Umber the look again, like, "do you see this, can you believe it, what is happening here?!"

"How much farther, do you think?" Quokka asked him.

Umber sat up and shaded his eyes to squint toward the south. They could see the mountain range now, in the distance.

"That's where we're going," he said, pointing. "But I'm not sure how long it will take. Mulberry, have you been this way?"

"Yes, a few times," Mulberry said. "There's a snowplace far out that way, beyond the mountains and another stretch of ocean. I haven't spent much time inside the southern edge of the Barrier, though. I'd guess another day of flying before we reach the mountains?"

"Let's move on soon, then," Umber said. "Everyone keep

an eye out for a place where we can hide and sleep for a bit."

Flying in the intense sun was more exhausting than flying at night. Umber started to feel as if he were hallucinating, especially around midafternoon, when a whole section of the landscape below him suddenly got up and started leaping away in huge hops and bounds. He rubbed his eyes.

"They're kangaroos," Mulberry said, soaring up next to him. "Surprisingly hard to catch without getting kicked in the face; I don't recommend it."

Platypus went diving after them anyway, but with no success. Shortly after that, Umber spotted a cluster of rocks leaning together, and when they investigated, they found there was enough room for them to squeeze inside and lie down in the shade, hidden from view of anyone flying overhead.

Quokka, Sora, and Dugong fell asleep immediately. Platypus wiggled around, stepping on everyone's tails and adjusting her wings and going "ack!" under her breath and poking herself in the face by accident until she got fed up and went off to find them something to eat, and then it was much quieter.

Umber lay there listening to the others breathing, feeling their scales rise and fall, and it felt like being at home in his family's mud-walled sleephouse, side by side with all his siblings. Despite his terror about Beryl and Snakeroot coming after them, he felt his own heart start to calm down. He rested his head next to Mulberry's, their sides pressed together, and drifted into the ripples going back and forth between them: *safe, together, rest, peace, protect you.*

They woke as it was getting dark, or rather, they were woken by Platypus dropping a talonful of dead rodents on their heads.

"You're WELCOME," she declared. "Eat fast and let's go!"

"This dragon," Sora said to Umber, "is like an even louder, grouchier version of that RainWing Moon likes so much."

"Kinkajou?" Umber said.

"That one talks too much and this one talks too loud," Sora whispered.

Umber thought Kinkajou's talkativeness was meant to be a kindness to shy dragons like Moon. She seemed much less chaotic than Platypus to him. He couldn't imagine her fighting off guards or living in a ceiling or splattering fruit all over a queen's bedroom, but then, he hadn't had a chance to know her very well.

They flew all night again. A few times, Umber glanced back and worried that he might be seeing flickering lights behind them — was that SkyWing fire? Were Beryl and Snakeroot's dragons on their tails?

Sora seemed even quieter than usual, barely responding when he flew by and flicked her wing.

"Is everything all right?" he asked.

"I had a kind of terrible realization," she said. "I'm not sure I should tell you about it."

"Oh no," he said. "Now you have to! What is it?"

"I don't want to crush your hopes," she said. "I could be wrong. It would be mean to cast you into despair based on nothing."

"Sora, please tell me," he said. "It'll be better than me freaking out wondering what the terrible thing is."

She glanced around, but none of the others were close enough to hear them.

"Well," she said reluctantly, "I was thinking about the spell Precipice cast. And how we're looking for the object she enchanted for the spell. And then it occurred to me — why would the object be *inside* the Barrier? Surely Precipice cast the spell from outside, or else she'd be trapped here, too."

Umber's wings suddenly felt much heavier. "You mean — you think it's back in the Sky Kingdom?"

She nodded. "You said you saw that whole scroll she was using to design this place. I bet she could easily enchant something to create the prison from a distance."

Arrrrrrgh. Sora's logic made horrible sense. Precipice wouldn't have trapped herself here. She *must* have done the spell from outside the Barrier.

But maybe the object was still inside. Maybe she planted it here, flew to a safe distance, and then set off the enchantment? Umber wished he knew more about how animus magic worked and whether that was even possible.

"I think it's still worth checking out this map spot," Sora said hurriedly. "Maybe I'm wrong. I hope I'm wrong."

"Me too," he said. "But thank you for telling me."

They flew on, lost in their own spirals of worry.

Finally, soon after the sun began climbing the eastern peaks, they reached the foothills of the southern mountain range. The sky was pale orange overhead and golden rays of light slipped between the bushes and rocks below. Umber turned them west and began flying slower and closer to the ground.

"Look for anything unusual," he said. "The mark was inside the Barrier, between two peaks, near a small creek running down the slope."

"It wasn't labeled, was it?" Mulberry asked, swooping up to fly beside him.

Umber shook his head. "No, but it looked intentional to me. Like it was marking something." He tried to picture the map and lay it over the earth below them.

They landed a few times to investigate odd-looking outcroppings or funny-shaped rocks, but nothing seemed promising or quite matched the image in Umber's head.

Until he smelled running water . . . and spotted a small, half-dried-up riverbed running down from between two peaks.

He put on a burst of speed and soared down to land beside the creek. He could see the Barrier cutting across it halfway up the slope. Downhill, the creek jumped off a ridge and made a small waterfall, only about twice as tall as he was, which ended in a shallow, rock-filled pool. More rocks were tumbled all around it, as though a rockslide had come through here some time ago.

"Is this it?" Mulberry asked from the other side of the stream.

"Maybe?" Umber walked down to the waterfall, peered over, and hopped down onto one of the large rocks. "I think there's a space behind the waterfall, but it's blocked by rocks."

"Not for MEEEE," Platypus said, hurling herself at a gap between two boulders. She wiggled halfway in, got stuck, flailed around, wound up upside down, and finally extricated herself with a disgruntled snort.

"OK, never mind," she said. "Yes for me as well."

"Maybe I can help," Dugong said. He had immediately flopped into this pool, too, but he stood up as he spoke. "Moving rocks is, like . . . a thing I do OK." He demonstrated by picking up a rock the size of his head and depositing it gently on the bank. "See?"

"That would be great, Dugong," Umber said sincerely.

"If we move this one and this one," Quokka said, pointing, "I think we can make a space big enough to squeeze through."

The boulders were enormous, but the two Quokka had pointed out at least wobbled a little, so they weren't completely stuck in place. Umber, Dugong, and Platypus set their shoulders to the first one and managed to roll it away with a huge *thud*. The second one took all six of them, but at last they were able to shove it a dragon's length to the side, opening a shadowy gap into the space behind the waterfall.

"I'll go first," Umber said. "This was my idea, so if it's dangerous, let me find out before you follow me."

Mulberry brushed his wing — *be safe, be careful, come back* — and Sora clasped his talon, and then he left both of them and went forward into the cool darkness.

CHAPTER 24

First there was a tunnel, three dragons long, with smooth stone walls on either side and mossy rocks underfoot.

Then there was a cave, with a roof so perfectly formed into an oval that it must have been made with magic. Glowworms dotted the ceiling like stars, and an answering pale blue light radiated from the bottom of the pool that filled most of the space.

In the middle of the pool was a small island, the size of a table, with a hollow indent as though a scoop had been taken out of the top.

And nestled in the indentation were two dragon eggs.

Umber stood there for a long moment, awestruck and bewildered.

How long have these been here? Why haven't they hatched? Is this what Precipice enchanted to make the prison?

That felt strange — and a bit awful. Was he supposed to break the eggs in order to break the spell? He hated that idea. And from everything he'd seen of Precipice, he found it hard to believe she'd make a choice that cruel, when she could have enchanted anything.

On his shoulder, Nineteen stirred, as if it had heard his thoughts and agreed with him. A dragon who had crafted the SharpWings so carefully and given them life . . . would she have stolen someone's eggs and cursed them like this?

Mulberry slipped into the cave beside him and inhaled softly when he saw the nest.

"Whose are those?" he asked Umber. "I don't remember anything about eggs in the visions we saw."

"Me neither," Umber said. He stepped forward, his talons touching the pool and sending little ripples across its glassy surface.

Hello.

A translucent dragon shimmered into view behind the nest.

You found my secret, she said. *I knew you would one day.*

"Precipice," Mulberry breathed. He stepped into the water with Umber and twined their tails together.

"She looks like an actual ghost," Umber whispered. "Are you real?" he asked her. "Can we ask you questions?"

I'm leaving this here without telling my queen about it, the dragon said. *If she finds out, I may not live much longer, but I couldn't leave you trapped in this prison for all time, with no way to escape.*

"I think it's just a message," Mulberry said.

When you do escape, Precipice said, *please take my little dragons with you.* She opened her talons to show a pre-enchanted SharpWing cupped between her claws. *I'm so sorry to leave them here, trapped by my spell. I hope they'll be free one day.*

She set the little dragon off to the side, where it disappeared from the vision, and gestured toward the nest in front of her. *These eggs were taken by my queen from a settlement called Harmony. Sorry, I'm not sure why I said it that way — I know you remember Harmony. As I'm doing this spell, Summit hasn't found those dragons yet, so they may have made it to safety. I hope that's some good news for you. Maybe when you leave this place, you can find them and join them. I wouldn't recommend coming back to the Sky Kingdom. Once Summit and her daughters get their claws on the land they want, I don't think they'll give it back easily.*

Precipice took a deep breath and looked down at the nest again. *These eggs were left behind when the dragons who lived in Harmony all fled, knowing armies were coming to kill them. I don't know who they belonged to, whether they are siblings, or even which tribes they are, although I believe they are hybrids.*

Queen Summit ordered me to destroy them, but I couldn't.

Instead, I've suspended them in time. They will stay this way, on the cusp of hatching, for as long as it takes until the right dragons find them.

Are you the right dragons? She lifted her gaze, and Umber felt as if she could actually see him. *Are you kind? How long has it been, and what are you like now?*

Tonight, as I cast these prison spells, I find it hard to imagine what it will do to you all. I hope it's not as bad as the queens want it to be. Summit can't see it, but I think this island is astonishingly beautiful. Maybe you'll take care of one another, like Queen Euphoria and Queen Magnolia always wanted. I hope you find some happiness together here.

If you are kind, and patient, and gentle, these eggs are the key to unlocking your prison.

Whoever takes them and raises the dragons that hatch will be able to cross the Barrier and leave the Dungeon Isle. If these dragonets are loved and cared for, in three years they will be able to return and free everyone else.

But if they are not loved, the prison will summon you back forever.

I hope things are better in your time. I hope I'm not making a mistake, leaving you a way out. Please promise me you won't come looking for vengeance on our dragonets and granddragonets.

Good luck, and . . . I'm sorry.

Precipice faded away, leaving only the soft murmur of the water behind.

"She thought someone would find this much sooner," Mulberry said. "Don't you think? It sounded like she only thought it would be a generation or two — dragons who still remembered Harmony and might be dreaming of vengeance."

"She should have left better clues," Umber said. "Or told the SharpWings to guide dragons here."

"Maybe that is sort of what Nineteen was doing," Mulberry said.

Nineteen clicked its wings together, but its face was inscrutable.

"All right — so only the dragons who agree to care for these eggs can leave the island," Umber said. He waded over to the nest and gently touched each egg. One was pale yellow and warm, like sunbaked sand, and the other was gray and icy to the touch.

"At least, until the dragonets inside are older," Mulberry agreed, "when they'll come back and free everyone else."

Umber scooped up the yellow egg and cupped it in his talons, imagining the dragonet inside and how much pressure that would be for a small dragon.

"We have to give them to the Triumvirate and Platypus," he said. "Right? That's the solution. Then they can escape the island, and the rest of us just have to survive your parents for three years until they return."

Mulberry's wings dropped at the mention of his parents, but he nodded. "I think it's the only way for them to be safe."

"HORSEFEATHERS!" Platypus shouted from behind them, making them both jump. "I'm not running away! We can't just *let* Beryl and Snakeroot keep the throne they stole!"

"But if you run away now," Umber countered, "you could get help from the queens back in Pyrrhia. Or my brother! You could return with hundreds of dragons to overthrow Beryl and Snakeroot."

"In three years?" Platypus cried. "That's like a million years!"

"I mean, there's a *little* bit of a difference between three and a million," Mulberry said.

"Not to the dragons who'll be stuck here with them!" Platypus said furiously. "I'm not leaving, no matter what you or some ancient ghost dragon tells me to do!" She whirled and stormed out.

"I'll need some kind of sling to travel with these," Umber said to Mulberry. He was already so worried for the eggs; they seemed too fragile to hold an entire little dragon inside.

Mulberry took off the orange silk gathering bag he always wore, wrapping it carefully around the yellow egg. While he did that, Umber lifted the gray egg out of the nest. He shivered as its chill leached into his scales. He hoped this one was OK — it didn't seem natural for an egg to be this color or this cold. Mulberry wrapped the silk around the gray one as well and then tied the whole sling around Umber's neck.

"What!" Quokka said as they emerged from the cave into the dazzling sun. She came over to peek at the sling, her eyes shining. "I thought Platypus was messing with us! There were really dragon eggs in there?"

Platypus was flying in grumpy loops off in the distance, occasionally dive-bombing shrubs and kicking them.

"We have to take these to Tuatara and the other exiles," Umber said. "If they carry these eggs with them, they can cross the Barrier and get to safety."

Sora touched the shape of the eggs through the silk with a wondering look on her face.

"Aren't they hiding?" Dugong asked from his spot half-submerged in the pond. "How'll we find them?"

"Platypus will help us," Umber said. "Hopefully."

"Why WOULD I?" Platypus demanded when they caught up and asked her. "I don't believe in running away!"

"Fine, *you* don't have to," Quokka said. "*You* can stay trapped here with a king and queen who are determined to rip you scale from scale the moment they get their claws on you. But the Triumvirate and Wollemi deserve a chance to be safe. We should at least give them the choice!"

"ARRRGH FINE!" Platypus yelled, and spun around to fly north.

They trailed after her: Umber, Mulberry, and Quokka in the lead, with Sora and Dugong side by side behind them.

"So this means we can't all leave?" Quokka asked Umber. "With the eggs?"

"I don't know what the rules are," he said. "Precipice said 'whoever raises them' — that seems like it could be many dragons together, couldn't it?"

"If not . . . what do we do? Go back to the castle? Won't Beryl and Snakeroot be furious with us?"

"Maybe we can trick them into thinking the exiles are dead," Umber said, trying to picture the next steps. "Maybe I can say I took you and Sora and Dugong with me to help track them down."

"I'm the problem with that plan," Mulberry said ruefully. "They won't be happy that I escaped." He rubbed his temples. "I should have made you go without me."

"You couldn't have in any universe," Umber said. "So don't feel guilty about it. We'll figure it out once we find the Triumvirate."

They found another shaded, half-covered spot to rest during the hottest part of the day and flew on again once the sun went down. Platypus led them straight across the plain, away from the mountains, into what seemed to be the center of the island. Eventually they saw more rock formations shaped like claws, but instead of just five, there appeared to be over a hundred of them scattered across the dry earth.

By the light of the three moons, they soared down into the heart of the claw rocks. Umber landed as gently as he could, supporting the eggs with one of his talons.

Six figures stepped out of the pools of shadows around the rocks and approached.

"Oh, wow, this one is mad," Crescent announced, pointing at Platypus.

"Astonishing trick," Wollemi said to her. "Next see if you can guess whether I'm hungry."

"And this one is *not* here to kill us," Crescent said, waving one wing at Umber. "That's pleasantly surprising."

"What's happening?" Horizon asked. "There have been patrols of dragons flying everywhere for the last two days."

Umber explained, with Platypus jumping in periodically to yell about everything.

"And then we found these eggs," he finished. "With a message that whoever takes them and raises them can cross the Barrier, and in three years the dragonets will come back and break the prison spell for everyone."

"And he wants us to take them," Crescent said. "Wait, us? But if you take them, *you* could escape."

"You're in more danger than I am," he said. "This way you could get somewhere Beryl can't reach you."

Tuatara and Horizon looked at each other. Glowworm put his wing around Monarch and she leaned against him, her expression troubled in the moonlight.

"So we'd leave Snakeroot and Beryl here? In charge?" Wollemi asked.

"And we'd go raise two mystery dragonets," Crescent said. "Three moons, when I ran away from court to hide with you guys, I did not think I was signing up to be co-parents."

"We'd come back," Glowworm said. He rested his chin on Monarch's head. "We'd be safe."

"No," Monarch said. She looked up at him. "I'm sorry, Glowworm. I don't want to run away again." She turned to Tuatara and Horizon. "We were chosen by the dragons in that castle. They asked *us* to represent them and protect them. We can't leave them. We should be fighting for them."

"That's what I'VE been saying!" Platypus hissed in a loud whisper.

"I've run away from dragons I was supposed to protect before," Monarch said. "And then we got stuck here and I couldn't go back, even when refugees from Pantala started arriving and I realized how bad things have gotten under Queen Wasp." She shook her head. "And I'm not leaving Royal."

"I don't want to leave either," Tuatara said. "But I support anyone who does."

"I'm staying," Horizon said. "Wollemi, you and Quokka could go."

"Raise dragonets together?" Quokka cried. "Magic dragonets that the whole future of the Dungeon Isle depends on? I definitely should not be in charge of that!"

"Yeah, I don't want them either," Crescent said. "If anyone was about to suggest *I* take them, which I did not actually see in anyone's head, HMMM."

It was starting to occur to Umber that he should have run his "I'll set you free! I'll get you to safety!" plan past these dragons *before* he'd spent all that time trying to find them a way out.

"But what else are you going to do?" he asked. "You can't hide forever — the King's Teeth will catch you sooner or later."

"Storm the castle!" Platypus said promptly. "Venom them in the face! Take back the court!" She lashed her tail. "Together! Tonight!"

A sound caught Umber's attention . . . a breath, a scuff of claws on sand. He whirled and leaped into the dark outside the rocks.

His talons hit the dragon who had been lurking there, spying on them. Umber tackled the intruder to the ground.

"Wait!" the other dragon cried as they scuffled. "Stop!"

Horizon and Platypus came bounding over and helped subdue the strange dragon. Horizon dragged him into the circle and breathed a small flame to illuminate his face.

But to Umber's surprise, it wasn't one of the King's Teeth.

It was Aurora's brother, Borealis.

CHAPTER 25

"So you *were* spying on us before, outside your sister's door," Umber said. "Are you the one who told the queen I met with these dragons?"

"You've got it all wrong," Borealis said, holding up his front talons and trying to wiggle out of Platypus's grip. She bared her fangs at him and growled.

"You mean you're not a spy?" Tuatara asked.

"He's definitely a spy," Crescent said coolly.

"I am," he admitted. "But not for the king and queen! Look deeper!"

"I'm not a truth detector," Crescent said. "All I can tell you is that he's frantically thinking *I work for someone else I work for someone else.*"

"Who else?" Umber asked him.

"A group that wants you back," Borealis said, twisting to look at Tuatara. "We want the whole system back, with voting and a council we choose and a chance to elect new leaders with everyone a part of it. We didn't agree to be ruled by Snakeroot and Beryl."

Tuatara took a step toward him and Glowworm held out a wing to stop her. "Careful," he said. "Do we believe him?"

"How many dragons are in your group?" Umber asked Borealis.

"It's not safe to gather, so I don't know exactly," Borealis said. "But I've been talking to dragons quietly for the last two years, bringing them in. What I do know is that there's more of us now than there are of the King's Teeth."

Umber looked over at Platypus, who started bouncing on her talons as though she knew what he was thinking.

"If we *did* try to take back the throne tonight," Umber said, "would they help us?"

"Yes," Borealis said. "That's why I came out here looking for the Triumvirate. Half the King's Teeth are out sweeping the island for you and Mulberry. And the queen has arrested my sister."

Platypus gave a little gasp. *"Aurora?* She would never!"

"She did. Beryl's accusing her of helping to kidnap Mulberry."

"I'm not kidnapped!" Mulberry said.

"Sure, but I bet 'helped Umber release my son from the chains I put him in' isn't *quite* the story she wants everyone to hear," Quokka pointed out.

"So now is the perfect time," Borealis said. "There's fewer Teeth to stop us. And everyone is losing their minds about Aurora. Dragons who would have been too scared to stand up to Beryl before are mad enough to do it now."

"I'M MAD ENOUGH RIGHT NOW," Platypus growled.

"If she's hurt Aurora, I will spray her FULL OF VENOM HOLES!"

"Yes, we know you're terrifying," Quokka said. "This is the problem with living at full fury all the time, Platypus; there's no higher level of rage to go to."

"I ASSURE YOU THERE IS," Platypus yelled.

"OK, all right," Tuatara said calmly. "Are we all agreed? We do this tonight?" She searched each of their faces. "Even you, Prince Mulberry?"

"It's just Mulberry," he said. "And I'm with you." He took a step closer to Umber and Umber tried to radiate *thank you* in his direction.

"And Dugong?" Wollemi asked suspiciously.

The MudWing hybrid shrugged and glanced sideways at Sora. "Sure, if, uh, everyone else is."

Sora will say she is, Umber thought, watching her nod her head, *but I don't want her to have to fight. She's been so much better lately . . . if there's violence or bloodshed, it could set her back to how she was after Crane died.*

"Sora," he said, nudging her aside as the others talked. "Can you do something for me?"

"Is it 'sit here and do nothing'?" she asked, bristling. "That kind of something?"

"Not exactly. And you can say no," he said. "You're right, I'm not your bigwings. But someone should stay out of the fight to take care of the eggs. I can't put them in danger by bringing them into the castle."

"Oh," she said as he carefully untied the sling from around his neck.

"These are more important than anything," Umber said. He could feel the warmth of one egg and the chill of the other even through the silk. "They might be the only chance there is to break the prison spell."

"That's true," she said softly. She held out her talons and took them with an awestruck expression.

"If this doesn't go the way we want," he said, "if we lose . . . you have to take these and fly away from here. Take them somewhere safe."

"Back to Reed and Pheasant," she said.

"No," he said. "That's not —"

"It *is* the right thing," Sora said. "Whenever I leave here, I should turn myself in and accept whatever justice the queens choose for me. Like the dragon in Aurora's 'Mirrors' song — I need to face what I did."

He shook his head, fighting back tears. "That's not what I want."

"It's still right," she said. "But I promise I'll take care of the eggs first. If it's up to me, I'll make sure the dragonets are loved, like Precipice said." She took a deep breath. "Except I won't have to because you'll free Aurora and save the day and come right back to let me know."

"Right," Umber said. "So this is really all right? You don't mind staying with the eggs?"

"You mean, do I accept the most important mission of

the night?" she said. "Of course I do. I'll guard them with my life."

"Can I stay with her?" Dugong asked. "I'm a good guard, too."

"Dugong, I want you to go help my brother," Sora said, touching one of her wings to his. "And make sure our side wins, so you can make me those weird-sounding beet pancakes for breakfast tomorrow."

He grinned at her. "Yeah, OK."

Soon they were all lifting off to fly toward the castle, whose lights were visible in the near distance. Umber glanced back at Sora, who had curled herself around the eggs and was whispering a story to them. Within a few wingbeats, she had melted into the shadows and he couldn't see her anymore.

She'll be all right, he thought. *She's still Sora; she's always been Sora, inside. My sister, who is more than the bad things she's done. My sister, who I trust.*

They took one of Platypus's secret ways into the castle, although Umber didn't think it was terribly stealthy to have twelve of them bundling through a hidden door all together. Once inside the castle, Borealis peeled off.

"Give me ten minutes to spread the word," he said. "We'll meet you in the throne room."

"The council room," Tuatara corrected him. He smiled at her, nodded, and sprinted away.

"I could talk to my parents first?" Mulberry offered.

"Maybe they'll see reason and give the throne back?"

Quokka stopped Platypus before she smacked the prince with her tail. "I don't think you believe that will work any more than I do," she said to him.

He sighed. "I know."

Nineteen tugged on Umber's ear, went *clatter buzz buzz*, and zipped away without a backward glance. Umber wondered if the other SharpWings would wonder where it had been for so long, and whether they cared.

Despite the late hour, voices were coming from the throne room, echoing down the hall as Umber and his friends crept toward it. It sounded like a lot of voices — a rising and falling murmur like the sea at the mouth of the Diamond River.

Horizon held up one talon and they paused outside the golden doors. Tuatara looked the doors up and down and rolled her eyes.

"I told you they were hideous," Platypus whispered.

"EVERYONE SHUT UP!" roared the king from inside the room. The babble of voices quieted.

"You are all being unreasonable and heartless," the queen said. "I know Aurora is talented, but I thought you all *loved* Mulberry."

"We do!" someone called out.

"In that case, you should *applaud* us for arresting Aurora," said Beryl. "It's her fault he's missing! She stole him from you! What if we never see him again?"

There was a collective gasp from the crowd inside.

Mulberry rubbed his head, looking deeply embarrassed, and Umber leaned gently against his side to reassure him.

"You can do this," he said.

"I know," Mulberry said, touching his snout to Umber's. "I should have done something sooner. Thank you, Umber." He opened the doors and walked into the throne room.

"Mulberry!" cried a dragon near the entrance.

"The prince!"

"Look, it's him!"

"Mulberry!"

"I'm right here." Mulberry's voice rang out. "I wasn't kidnapped. Aurora did nothing wrong."

For a moment, a stunned silence rippled around the room. Umber wished he could see the looks on the king's and queen's faces.

"Oh," Beryl said. "Mulberry! Darling! I'm so glad you're all right! What an ordeal you've been through!"

"*Conspiring* to kidnap the prince," Snakeroot boomed. "That's Aurora's crime. Yes. Even if she failed. Or maybe you escaped your kidnappers in some heroic way, son?"

"No," Mulberry said. "The only dragons I had to escape were you."

"Mulberry, don't make a fuss," Beryl said as confused whispers skittered around the room. "Come here."

"No," Mulberry said. "I'm not going to do that." He turned and beckoned to the doors. Umber entered, weaving through the crowd to Mulberry and standing beside him, wings touching.

"I knew you were trouble," Snakeroot spat, glaring at Umber.

"Three nights ago, my parents chained me up," Mulberry announced to the muttering crowd. "This dragon set me free."

"Ha, what a wild story," Beryl said. She gave the dragons near her a pitying look. "Poor Mulberry hasn't been quite himself since that MudWing arrived. You know what I mean. No time for any of the rest of us, when we have loved him so much for years."

"Yeah, true, ours," murmured a few dragons. Umber scanned the room for threats and allies, trying to guess what each dragon felt from their expression. He noticed at least ten of the King's Teeth on guard close to the thrones — more than the royals normally had around them.

Think of them the way Mulberry does. They each have a name. They each have something they care about.

Several expressions in the crowd changed suddenly, and Umber saw dragons reaching to clutch one another's arms. The whispers changed, too.

"Is that them?"

"They're still alive!"

"I knew they'd come back!"

"Where have they been?"

Beryl and Snakeroot stood up, looking thunderous. "SILENCE!" Snakeroot yelled.

"Hello, Beryl," Tuatara said. She walked past Umber and stopped in the center of the room. Horizon and Monarch followed, pausing on either side of her. "I'm afraid your turn on the council is up now."

Beryl hissed. Smoke wreathed her horns, and her claws sank into the platform below her.

"I almost killed you before, Tuatara," she said. "Thank you for coming back so I can finish the job."

Umber could sense more dragons crowding into the room behind him, although everyone left a clear space around the Triumvirate. He hoped the new arrivals were the dragons with Borealis, not more of the King's Teeth.

"You will stand down," Horizon said.

"And face justice for what you've done," Monarch added.

"Someone seize them," Beryl said. She pointed to a WildWing near Monarch. "You! Throw that SilkWing to the floor before she runs away again."

Monarch turned to meet the WildWing's eyes. "Hello, Pademelon," she said affectionately. "Your little one must have mastered catching hawks by now."

"Oh, she has!" Pademelon said, beaming. "I can't believe you remember!"

"Enough!" Beryl roared. "Silence her!"

Pademelon glanced nervously at the dragons around her, then squared her shoulders. "No," she said. "I — I won't do that."

"Fine," Beryl said, vibrating with rage. "You'll regret it soon enough. *You* do it." She pointed at another dragon.

"I won't either," he said.

"I'll give you first access to the Gathering every morning," Beryl said shrewdly.

"No," he said, a little more slowly. He also kept checking

the faces of the dragons around him, Umber noticed.

"This isn't wise," Beryl hissed. "I am your *queen*."

"You shouldn't be," Horizon said. "This is not what these dragons chose."

"Kill them," Snakeroot snarled. He hit the closest member of the Teeth with his tail. "All three of them. Right now."

The guard obediently jumped forward and so did the other King's Teeth in the room.

"Stop!" Umber cried, throwing himself between their spears and the Triumvirate. "Listen," he said, addressing the King's Teeth directly. "*You can stop this*. They need you to keep their power. If you say no, they have none."

"But if we say yes," said one of the SkyWings, chuckling slightly as if Umber was daft, "then *we* have power, too."

"Maybe for a little while," Umber said. "But Ravine, why do you need it? You could be with your dragonets right now, playing that ball game you invented. Wouldn't you rather be doing that? Instead of arresting Aurora and knowing everyone hates what you're doing?"

Ravine hesitated.

"And Goana, what about your song?" Umber said, turning to the WildWing beside her. "You've been working on it for so long — didn't you want to share it with Aurora? Weren't you hoping she'd bring you onstage to sing it?"

"I could have my own concert," Goana said, but her talons were clenched around her spear. "I could make everyone listen to me."

"The king and queen don't care about you," Umber said

to all of them. "They are using you, but if you die following their orders, they will forget your names by tomorrow . . . if they even know them now."

The King's Teeth gave one another sidelong glances. From the dais, Snakeroot was shouting, "What's the holdup? KILL THEM ALREADY!" but his voice was muffled by the growing clamor of the crowd and the dragons moving to block the path between the king and his guards.

"Scorpionfish," Umber said, stepping closer to another dragon. "I know your leg still hurts from that old accident, but you've always worked harder, lifted more, and flown faster than I asked. We could end this here and you could rest. You could decide for yourself what you do tomorrow, instead of waking up to another day of training and fighting and treating fellow dragons like lizards."

Scorpionfish nodded with a thoughtful expression.

Umber knew it was easier to trust the dragons above you. He understood that so deeply. It was much easier to go along, to follow the group — easier to let someone else make the decisions.

He looked around at the guards he had trained every day, all the dragons he'd worked so hard to remember and understand. They weren't just a mass of obedient ants with sharp objects, stabbing whatever they were told to stab. They were each their own dragon. They could make a different choice.

Scorpionfish put her spear on the floor.

"I'm not killing anyone today," she said to Umber and

Snakeroot and all the dragons around her. "Probably not tomorrow either, unless you keep looking at me with those sappy cow eyes, Corella."

"I'll try not to, Mother," said a dragon in the crowd, beaming at her.

"If Scorpionfish is out, so am I," said another WildWing.

"Me too," said Ravine. They both set their spears down.

"COWARDS!" Snakeroot roared. "I'll do it myself!"

He leaped over the heads of the dragons pressing around the throne and came down right in front of Tuatara. Dragons scattered away from them, screaming. Snakeroot's tail slammed Umber aside and he raised his talons to strike.

Glowworm dropped from the ceiling onto Snakeroot's back.

"Not today, Snakeroot," said the HiveWing, stabbing his claws into the king's neck. As the paralytic toxin swept into him, the king's eyes rolled back in his head, and he collapsed to the ground.

"Not you either," said Platypus, shimmering into view perched on top of Beryl's throne. She hinged her mouth open to point her venomous fangs at the queen. "Nah ungleess oo ant a fayfoo o magicah ett itt!"

"That is much less intimidating when she tries to talk at the same time," Quokka observed. She bustled past Umber and started going down the line of King's Teeth, politely gathering their spears. Confused, most of them handed them over without question, like students turning in their tests to a very firm teacher.

"No!" Beryl shrieked. "This isn't fair!"

Mulberry climbed the dais to stand beside her. "I'm sorry, Mother."

"You are the *worst* son!" she screamed in his face. He flinched back, pulling in his wings. "I thought I already had the worst son, but you've managed to be even more disappointing!"

"Don't talk to him like that," Umber said.

"Yeah," said another dragon. "That's *Mulberry*."

"He takes care of us," said another.

"You idiots," said someone else, vaulting onto the stage. "He just betrayed you all." Taipan darted behind Mulberry, pinned his wings, and pressed a knife to the prince's throat. "And if you don't do as *I* say . . . well, I guess we won't have a beloved prince anymore."

CHAPTER 26

Umber had never felt his own terror magnified by everyone around him this way before. It was like all of Mulberry's ripples flooding in and out from every dragon at once: *not him, not Mulberry, this can't be happening.*

"How can you all still love him?" Taipan snarled, perhaps feeling the rising hostility in the room. "He's *not special.* Some magic lets him cross the Barrier, so what? He just betrayed your *king* and *queen.*" He shook Mulberry and a pinprick of blood appeared on the prince's throat. "I know what you're trying to do, so stop it," he growled in Mulberry's ear.

Mulberry's dragonspeak, Umber thought. *He's trying to calm Taipan down like he did with the kraken.*

"What do you want, Taipan?" Tuatara asked.

"We can talk about it," Horizon offered. "You don't need to threaten Mulberry. We'll listen."

"Yeah, right." Taipan glared around at everyone. "No one ever listens to me. I could be special, too, but no one pays attention."

"We could work together," Beryl said to him. "You, me, and Snakeroot. Three dragons in charge, if that's what all these lizards want." Platypus hissed at her, but Horizon made a "don't attack" gesture and she subsided.

"And this one goes into a real dungeon," Taipan said, shaking Mulberry again. "So I don't have to hear about him constantly anymore."

"You can't imprison Mulberry," said a WildWing near the dais.

"Or rule the Court of Refuge!" said another. "No one wants that!"

"I *can,*" Taipan insisted. "I'm the one with the knife and the precious prince. I'm the only one who's standing by our true rulers!"

Umber glanced around, thinking desperately. He wished they had more dragons in the rafters. No one was close enough to get to Taipan before he hurt Mulberry.

He saw a flash of black, orange, and purple scales nearby in the crowd. Was that . . . ? He edged closer, trying to move slowly to avoid catching Taipan's attention. The WildWing was explaining how everyone had wronged him and disrespected him, starting with Mulberry but including everyone in the room.

"Royal," Umber whispered.

The HiveWing-SilkWing hybrid looked down his long nose at Umber and narrowed his eyes. "What?"

"Can you stop him?" Umber asked. "Maybe talk to him? He'll listen to you, won't he?"

"Why would I bother?" Royal said. "He's doing a fine job of embarrassing himself. I do not need to get dragged into this."

"For your parents?" Umber tried.

Royal's eyes cut toward Monarch and Glowworm, still standing over Snakeroot. The antennae curling gracefully from his head trembled slightly, but his face was cool and haughty.

"The dragons who left me here?" he scoffed.

"That was to keep you safe," Umber said. "They didn't want to leave you. They talk about you all the time."

"Sure," Royal said dismissively. "Whatever."

"Imagine if they were back in charge instead of Beryl and Snakeroot," Umber said. "Then *you'd* basically be the prince here, wouldn't you? Instead of Mulberry?"

Royal's wings twitched. He stared at his parents for a long moment, then back down at Umber.

"Interesting," he said.

"Taipan's not going to succeed," Umber said. "There's too many dragons against him, and he can't hold a knife to Mulberry's throat forever. But he might hurt Mulberry before he's taken down. He clearly wants to."

"True," Royal agreed.

"So you could be the dragon who stands by while that happens," Umber said. "Or you could be the hero who stops him."

Royal snorted. "I don't care about being a hero. Nice try, MudWing."

"I'll do it," Dugong said from behind Umber, startling him. "I'll stop him!" He put his head down and started muscling his way through the crowd toward the dais.

"Oh, *now* look what you've done," Royal said in a bored voice, which Umber was beginning to suspect he put on whenever he was hiding a real emotion. "Here comes disaster. I guess I'd better clean this up." He swept away from Umber, following Dugong.

"Hey!" Dugong said to Taipan, marching up the steps toward him. "Let Mulberry go. Right, uh, now."

Taipan laughed. "Oh, are you here to stop me, you big manatee? *You?* Seriously?"

"Yeah," Dugong said. "Wanna fight me?"

"Go sit down," Taipan sneered. "This is out of your league."

Dugong puffed up his shoulders. "No, it isn't. I'm from the royal MudWing bloodline," he said. "*You* always tell me that."

"So?" Taipan said.

"So . . . uh . . ."

"So maybe *you* should listen to *us* for once," Royal said, gliding onto the stage. He nudged Dugong aside and gave Taipan a condescending face. "If 'royalty' is so important to you, technically Dugong and I are both princes and you're . . . not."

"Shut up!" Taipan yelled.

"The hybrid prince," a dragon near Umber whispered to her friend. "What if it's one of them instead?"

"You're *so boring*, Taipan," Royal said cuttingly. "You're so *petty* and small and proud of your own stupid cruelty. Imagine getting onstage to whine to the *entire court* about how no one pays attention to you."

A few dragons in the crowd laughed.

"Shut up, shut up!" Taipan shouted again. He swung Mulberry around to face Royal. "Nobody laughs at —"

As soon as his back was turned, Platypus whipped around and sprayed her venom at Taipan. It splattered across his wings and he shrieked, dropping the knife and Mulberry as he flailed backward.

Dugong jumped to catch Mulberry as Umber leaped toward the stage. Royal took out the Toughen Up Stick and stood over Taipan in a pose that said "I do have better things to do, but I suppose *someone* has to do this."

"Wait!" Beryl cried, holding out her front talons toward Dugong and Royal. "You're right, you are both of royal blood. You could rule with me instead! You could be my princes, instead of my disloyal son."

"Oh, no, thanks," Dugong said. "I don't actually care about that royal bloodline stuff."

Royal shrugged elegantly. "Seems like too much work."

Umber knelt beside Mulberry, their wings and tails tangled as he checked Mulberry's throat. There was a bleeding scratch, but nothing worse. Mulberry clasped his talon, and Umber could sense that he felt both relieved and ridiculous.

Dragons surged onto the stage around them. They stayed where they were, in a momentary bubble of peace.

Umber didn't see who ended up taking Beryl, Snakeroot, and Taipan off to the dungeons. He heard Platypus arguing with Quokka and Quokka ignoring her to tend to Taipan's venom wounds. He heard Monarch and Glowworm both crying as they threw their wings around Royal. It sounded as though a hundred dragons were asking the Triumvirate questions.

Dugong squirmed through the crowd to find Umber. "Can I go get Sora?" he asked. "Please please?"

"Of course," Umber said, smiling at him.

"DIBS I GET TO FREE AURORA!" Platypus shouted. This had the opposite of its intended effect as half the dragons in the room all bolted for the door, vying to be the first one to Aurora's cell. "WHAT ARE YOU ALL DOING?" Platypus hollered. "I SAID *ME*! I'M GOING TO DO IT! OUT OF MY WAY!"

Mulberry and Umber started laughing.

"Are you sad?" Umber asked him. "That you're not a prince anymore?"

Mulberry shook his head. "Not at all."

"I'm sorry your mother yelled at you like that." Umber touched his forehead to Mulberry's.

"Maybe I don't care?" Mulberry said. "I'm going to try not to care. I think I did the right thing."

"Me too," Umber said. He looked around. Someone had already found the third council seat that had been removed and three dragons were hauling it onto the dais to put it back in place. Tuatara, Horizon, and Monarch were hugging dragons and making suggestions and trying to listen to everyone at once. Out in the halls, someone started singing a Northern Lights song and several dragons joined in.

I want to fly through the fire
I want to touch the lights in the sky
I want to breathe in the gold and the green
I wish we could be seen
Could be free

CHAPTER 27

Six months later . . .

"Umber!" Quokka came flying into the room. "Umber, it's happening!"

He dropped his clay, and the blobby frog he'd been trying to sculpt went *blorp* into a lump on the table. "Right now?"

"Quick, quick!" She flapped her wings at him and darted out again.

They dove over the balcony and soared down through the castle, weaving around oblivious dragons and finally landing in the doorway of the small Hatchery. Inside, it felt like a tree hollow carefully tended by elegant owls and inventive squirrels. Billows of emerald-green silk covered the windows, where sunlight drifted in.

The floor underfoot was a soft carpet of moss, and each nest was constructed to match the tribes of the eggs — including a pool for SeaWing eggs, a patch of warm sand for SandWings, and a woven hammock for SilkWings. Art made by dragonets in the castle school hung from the walls, a rainbow of colors to welcome new hatchlings.

Since they didn't know what tribes the ancient eggs were from, they'd put them in a WildWing nest lined with moss and leaves and mud. Sora was crouched beside it, peering at them intently.

Mulberry hurried in just after Umber with Paua right behind him. The SeaWing healer had Blob on her back, flapping his tentacles in what looked like wild excitement.

"I can't wait to meet them," Umber said, smiling at Mulberry.

"Me too," Mulberry said, but there was something hesitant in his smile. Umber wondered if he was right that Mulberry had been avoiding him for a couple of days. He had no idea why or what might be wrong.

"There!" Sora said, pointing to the yellow egg. A crack had appeared all along the top of it, and now a tiny snout was trying to poke through. "Should we help? Like a bigwings would? Umber, what do you think?"

"I think we should wait a bit," Umber said. "Let's see if they can get out on their own."

Paua set a gentle talon on the other egg, which was as still and cold as the day they'd taken it from Precipice's cave. "Nothing from this one?" she asked.

Sora shook her head.

"Poor baby," Paua murmured.

"They're probably not siblings," Quokka said. "They could hatch at different times. That one may just take longer."

Paua nodded, but her face was still sad.

Crack went the other egg. *Crickle. Crrrrkkk.*

Umber held his breath as the dragonet inside wiggled, poked, rocked, and wrestled with the eggshell. At last little claws hooked through one of the cracks and started peeling the shell away. Moments later, a small dragonet sat in a chaos of eggshell bits, blinking up at all of them.

She had leaf-shaped wings, a curling tail, webs between her claws, and tiny antennae waving between her horns. She was all the colors Umber had ever seen, red and gold and blue and green, shimmers of rose and lavender, silver spirals along her wings and tail. She lifted her green eyes to meet Umber's and her scales slowly, wonderingly, turned warm mahogany brown like his.

"Oh, wow," he breathed. He held out his front talons and she climbed into them, nestling into a ball.

"She's so tired from all that work," Mulberry said, lightly stroking her forehead. The dragonet went *snrzz,* closed her eyes, and fell asleep.

"Awwww," Quokka said. "OK, Umber, now you can't move until she wakes up."

"Of course!" he said. "I'll sit right here. Wait, are you joking?"

"Maybe," Quokka said, her eyes twinkling. "Aww, think of all the little friends she's going to make!"

Mulberry exchanged a look with Paua and bowed his head. "Would you guys mind if I talk to Umber alone for a minute?"

"Sure," Paua said. "Come on." She waved Quokka and Sora out of the room with her.

"Isn't she the most beautiful dragonet?" Umber blurted as soon as they were gone. Maybe if he kept them talking about the baby, he could stop Mulberry from saying whatever was making him look so worried. "I thought of a name for her."

"Oh yeah?" Mulberry said, smiling as the dragonet wiggled into a sillier sleep position. "What is it?"

"Harmony," Umber said. "Do you think that's all right? Or too sad when we eventually tell her about the village?"

"No, I think it's perfect," Mulberry said. "Umber — I have to tell you something."

Umber's wings drooped. "What did I do?"

"Nothing! Nothing," Mulberry said. "It's not anything you did. It's the prophecy."

"The . . . prophecy?" Umber echoed, thrown.

"My dad's prophecy." Mulberry shifted his wings. "And the message Precipice left."

"What about them?"

"There are some dragons who think Harmony shouldn't grow up here," Mulberry said. "And the other dragonet, if that egg hatches."

"What?" Umber cried. "Why?" He cuddled the dragonet closer and she made a hiccuping purr kind of noise.

"Because Precipice said they have to be taken away, over the Barrier, and that they'll come back in three years," Mulberry said. "And because of the line in the prophecy about danger rising from the past. They think that's about the dragonets."

"How could it be?" Umber said. "They're only babies." *And Harmony is perfect,* he thought mutinously. *She could never be dangerous. Look at her little nose! How could a little nose like that ever do anything bad!*

"I know," Mulberry said. "But a lot of dragons signed a petition, and the Triumvirate decided I should talk to you about it. They think someone should take Harmony — and the other dragonet — across the Barrier to raise them somewhere else."

"That's so unfair," Umber said, fighting tears. *A petition? Has everyone been planning this without telling me?* "They expect her to come get them out of prison, but they don't trust her to live here with them?"

"I think they're just worried," Mulberry said. "They want to follow the admittedly vague, millennia-old instructions exactly, to make sure the spell gets broken."

"But I don't want her to leave." *I love her little claws and her little sweet face already.* Umber's eyes were prickling, but he couldn't reach up to rub them without dislodging the sleeping dragonet. "I want to take care of her and watch her grow up."

"I know," Mulberry said. "That's why everyone thinks it should be you who takes her."

Umber blinked a few times. "Me? By myself?" All those worries about having to be Sora's bigwings — multiply those by a million. How could he raise a dragonet alone?

He'd have no idea what to do. On the other hand, now that he'd met her, he couldn't imagine letting her go without him.

"No," Mulberry said. He cupped his talons under Umber's. "I said if you left, I'd go with you."

"But you can't," Umber said, even though his heart was suddenly thumping with hope. "You're the only connection they have with the outside."

"I'll come back regularly to check on them," Mulberry said. "But I'll live with you and Harmony. There's an island southeast of here where we could go. It's beautiful and safe; there's nothing dangerous or poisonous there, and it's full of the coolest weird birds and giant ferns. You'll love it. I think. Maybe?"

"Hmmm," Umber said. "The last time you offered me a beautiful, safe island, there turned out to be a bit of a catch."

"I knooooow," Mulberry said guiltily. "This one is different, I promise! Or we could go back to Pyrrhia, if you'd rather. You could introduce me to your siblings? Maybe we could take her to your school!" He looked down at the tiny dragonet. "Maybe when she's a little older."

"Pyrrhia should be pretty safe now that the war is over," Umber said. "I mean, how many world-ending prophecies could there be in one dragon's lifetime, right?" He grinned at Mulberry. "I'd love to take you to meet Reed and Clay and Pheasant; they'll *love* you. Although I do want to see these weird birds first."

"And we can bring other dragons!" Mulberry said. "Anyone you want. I mean, I don't know how many of us can cross the Barrier with her. But if you're worried about being lonely, or there's anyone else you think could help us raise her, that's OK with me."

"I'll ask around," Umber said. "Thank you, Mulberry." The idea of leaving the Court of Refuge now that he'd finally settled in was sad, but he knew he could come back. Three years wasn't so long, and then it wouldn't be a prison anymore — it would be another amazing place for dragons to live or visit. And this new picture in his head, of him and Mulberry in a forest full of silver ferns, taking care of a tiny rainbow dragon together . . . that sounded pretty wonderful, actually.

"What do you think about the other egg?" Mulberry said. He picked it up gently and touched it to his snout, then tucked it into the nest again. "I'm worried about it."

"We all are," Umber agreed. "I think we should take it with us."

"I worry about traveling with an egg," Mulberry said, tracing a gentle pattern along its shell. "I'm afraid it could get broken on the way. Don't you think it would be safer here?"

Harmony wriggled around again and closed one of her talons around Umber's claw. He looked from her sweet, roly-poly perfection to the lonely egg left behind and felt like crying again.

"Can't we wait until it hatches?" he said. "I don't want to separate them. And I . . . I want to make sure the other dragonet is all right."

Mulberry leaned against him. "What if it never hatches?" he asked. "I'm so sorry to say that out loud."

"Do you think the petitioners can wait a bit longer?" Umber said. "We could give it another month. And then if that egg doesn't hatch, we'll take Harmony away like they want us to. But we'll leave someone here to watch it — someone who can bring the dragonet to us if it does hatch eventually."

"I think that's fair," Mulberry said. He rested his talon on the cold egg. "I hope you come on out, little dragon. There's a family waiting for you."

That's us, Umber thought, feeling Harmony's wings fluttering in her sleep and the ripples of affection echoing through Mulberry's scales. *A family.*

Umber and Mulberry soared toward the Barrier, and Umber felt a shiver of fear, remembering the lightning-strike pain. *What if this doesn't work? Will it hurt me even worse?*

Mulberry was carrying Harmony, just to be safe. She had her little head poking out of his sling and was making delighted *yeep-burble* noises about flying.

Quokka and Wollemi looked nervous, too. None of them were sure how many dragons could be included in "raising" the egg. But Quokka was so excited about seeing the world outside the Dungeon Isle that she wanted to risk it, and Wollemi had asked to come, too.

Platypus had decided to stay at court, partly to keep an eye on Beryl and Snakeroot's trial and partly to make sure no one else caused trouble for the Triumvirate.

Sora also had chosen to stay, which Umber was sad about,

but he understood. She said she'd watch the other egg, and she and Dugong would bring it to them when it hatched . . . if it hatched. In the meanwhile, she was studying healing with Paua, hoping that one day she'd be able to make up for what she did at Jade Mountain.

And there was one more dragon with them. Claws latched firmly around one of Umber's horns, Nineteen was perched on his head. He could feel it trembling, as if it also wasn't sure whether this would work, or whether the SharpWing would turn into a burned-out hunk of metal as soon as they crossed over.

"Here we go," Quokka said as the Barrier came closer.

Mulberry soared up beside Umber. Harmony waved excitedly, like she had done every time she spotted him on the flight, and he waved back.

Side by side, wing to wing, they crossed the Barrier.

Umber exhaled. He reached up and felt Nineteen pat his talon reassuringly. The little dragon was still alive.

They'd all made it across. They were free.

"All right, everyone," he called, smiling at Harmony. "Follow me."

They swung south and flew away into the sky.

EPILOGUE

"Snowfall?" Lynx padded from the Ice Palace throne room to the queen's chambers, calling as she went. "Snowfall? Or, sorry — Your *Majesty*, will that make you answer? Snowfall?"

Snowfall's little sister was sitting in the doorway of the queen's room, tail curled around her back talons, carving a block of ice.

"Hey, Mink," Lynx said. "Have you seen Snowfall anywhere?"

"No," Mink said with a sigh. "She said she would read me a story and she went to get the scroll and she hasn't come back and it's been *ages*."

"Huh," Lynx said. "That's weird." She sat down next to Mink and gazed along the empty corridor. "I wonder where she went."

Smolder set the tray on Queen Thorn's desk and declared: "TA-DA!" Which was not a word he remembered ever using before Thorn came along, but it felt appropriate to the situation.

She looked up from the list she was making. "What in the — I mean, ahem." Thorn had been trying to use her "queen voice" around him as practice. "Smolder. Dear. What is this?"

"New candy," he said proudly. "I've been experimenting!"

"Oh, yay," Thorn said faintly, but she was fighting back a smile as she studied the concoctions on the tray. "Are they . . . supposed to be that color?"

"That's part of the genius," he said. "You can tell the ingredients by the color. Like that green one is cactus . . . no, wait, that's the other green one . . ."

"I'm going to need you to taste test all of these first," Thorn said. "For poison, of course, not because I suspect they will taste extremely strange or anything."

"I would be happy to," he said with great dignity, "because they will all taste *amazing*. Hang on, I made tea to go with them." He bustled out to the hall and back with the second tray, neatly set with a pot and two teacups.

But when he returned, no one was at the desk. The tray of candy sat abandoned. A corner of Thorn's scroll flapped in the breeze from the window.

"Thorn?" he said, puzzled. "Are you hiding? I promise the candy's not *that* bad."

No response. He set down the tea tray and circled the room, checking behind the tapestries.

"Thorn?"

Smolder went to the window and looked out. There was no sign of the SandWing queen.

Had she actually run away from him? But . . . why?

"Thorn?" he said again, his voice echoing in the otherwise silent room.

A piercing shriek ricocheted through the Sky Palace — a shriek Jasper recognized. He dropped the toy he was mending and sprinted to the throne room. Halfway there, he collided with Prince Cliff pelting toward him, still shrieking.

"Cliff! Cliff!" Jasper said, dropping to his level and catching the dragonet in his arms. "What's wrong? What happened?"

"D-D-Daddy," Cliff sobbed. "Mommy disappeared!"

"What?" Jasper tried to wipe away the prince's tears but they were coming too fast. "What do you mean?"

"I mean she DISAPPEARED! Right in front of me! I was singing her my bestest new song and it's really long and really great and I was at the part that goes *If I were a bird I'd be the kind that could eat you and if I were a fish I'd be a super huge whale and if I were a —*"

"Got it," Jasper interrupted him. "Sounds great, little bug, but then what happened?"

"And she was looking at me and smiling, and then she was JUST GONE!"

"Like she left the room?" Jasper asked. "In a big hurry maybe? Was there a royal emergency?"

"NOOOOOOOOOOOOOOOOOOOOOO," Cliff shrieked. "SHE WENT POOF INTO THIN AIR!" He burst into tears again.

Cliff had a vivid imagination and a tendency to exaggerate, but Jasper believed he wouldn't melt down like this unless something really had happened. He stood up and beckoned to a nearby soldier.

"Summon the rest of the guards," he said. "Search the palace for Queen Ruby. And let me know the moment she is found."

"It's not like Sequoia to be late for a meeting," Cricket said to Sundew. "In fact, according to my notes, she has only ever been late twice. Normally she's here before us."

"Wow, lucky someone is taking detailed notes about that," Sundew teased.

"*You,* on the other talon, are almost always late," Cricket observed, giving Sundew a mock stern look over her glasses. She shaded her eyes to look up at the trees Sundew had grown since yesterday. "These are amazing, Sundew."

"I know," Sundew said, patting one of the trunks. "They would really like me to do something about the very loud birds trying to move in."

Cricket wished she had leafspeak like Sundew. Imagine all the things she could ask the trees! Especially trees that had been around for generations; they must know so much history!

"Who's that?" Sundew asked, pointing. A dragon was hurtling toward them from the north — a HiveWing, although Cricket didn't recognize him.

He plummeted to earth and collapsed, panting, in the

shade beside them. Cricket offered him her water pouch and he waved it away.

"Something . . . terrible," he gasped. "Where's Queen Sequoia?"

Needles of fear stabbed all along Cricket's spine. "She should be here soon. What is it?" she asked. "Is everyone OK?"

"Can only tell the queen," he said, taking the water pouch.

"Nope, no way," Sundew said. "You are absolutely not allowed to sit here expiring loudly and hiding terrible news from us at the same time. Out with it."

He looked at her fierce face, and then at Cricket, who nodded. "Please," Cricket added.

"All right," he said. "It's Wasp."

Cricket found herself reaching for Blue, even though he was on the far side of the lake today. Even before the HiveWing said it, she somehow knew.

"Queen Wasp has escaped."

Pineapple found Jambu hiding at the top of one of the tallest trees in the RainWing village. This was not terribly difficult, as it was Jambu's favorite hiding place, and pretty much everybody knew that. Pineapple lifted one of the giant leaves and sidled up next to him, bumping Jambu's side.

"Did he find her?" Jambu whispered. His scales were dark blue with streaks of green instead of his usual pink.

"I don't think he'll hear you all the way up here," Pineapple pointed out in a normal voice. "And no, I'm so sorry, he hasn't found your sister yet."

"He's SO MAD," Jambu said. "I think her guards are going to be permanently green forever after how he yelled at them."

"He's panicking," Pineapple said. "He's really scared for her. Which I understand — if I couldn't find you, I'd be freaking out, too."

Jambu rested his snout on Pineapple's talons and Pineapple tented one wing over him. "But it's *Glory*. She goes off on missions and has meetings and sees her friends all the time. I'm sure she's fine." Jambu paused for a heartbreaking moment. "Right? You think so, too?"

"I do," Pineapple said. "She's really good at taking care of herself."

They were silent for a little while, each trying not to think of all the things that might happen to a young queen with many enemies.

"It is weird, though," Jambu said, "that that little noisy RainWing is gone, too."

"I know," Pineapple agreed. "They're probably on a quest together, right? That seems like something they would do."

"Right," Jambu said.

"They'll be back any moment," Pineapple said.

"Yup," Jambu said in a more wobbly voice.

"So we don't have to worry," Pineapple said. "I mean, even if someone kidnapped Queen Glory . . . who in the world would also take Kinkajou?"

Sora stepped into the Hatchery and examined the lonely egg in its nest. Still cold. No change in the month Umber had been gone. She sighed and patted it gently. Down the hall, Dugong called and she hurried out to catch up with him.

The egg was left alone.

Night fell. The sounds of dragons in the distance faded as most of them went to sleep and others went night hunting. The halls were quiet.

Quiet . . . except for something breathing.

Something that came through the door Umber had taken to find the SharpWings.

Something that slipped through the silent, deserted halls.

Something that reached the door of the Hatchery.

A shadowy figure crept up to the nest. Gray talons closed around the egg.

"I know you're in there," it whispered. "You're mine now."

The mass of shadows slithered away, taking the egg with it.

The Hatchery was left still and empty in the moonlight.

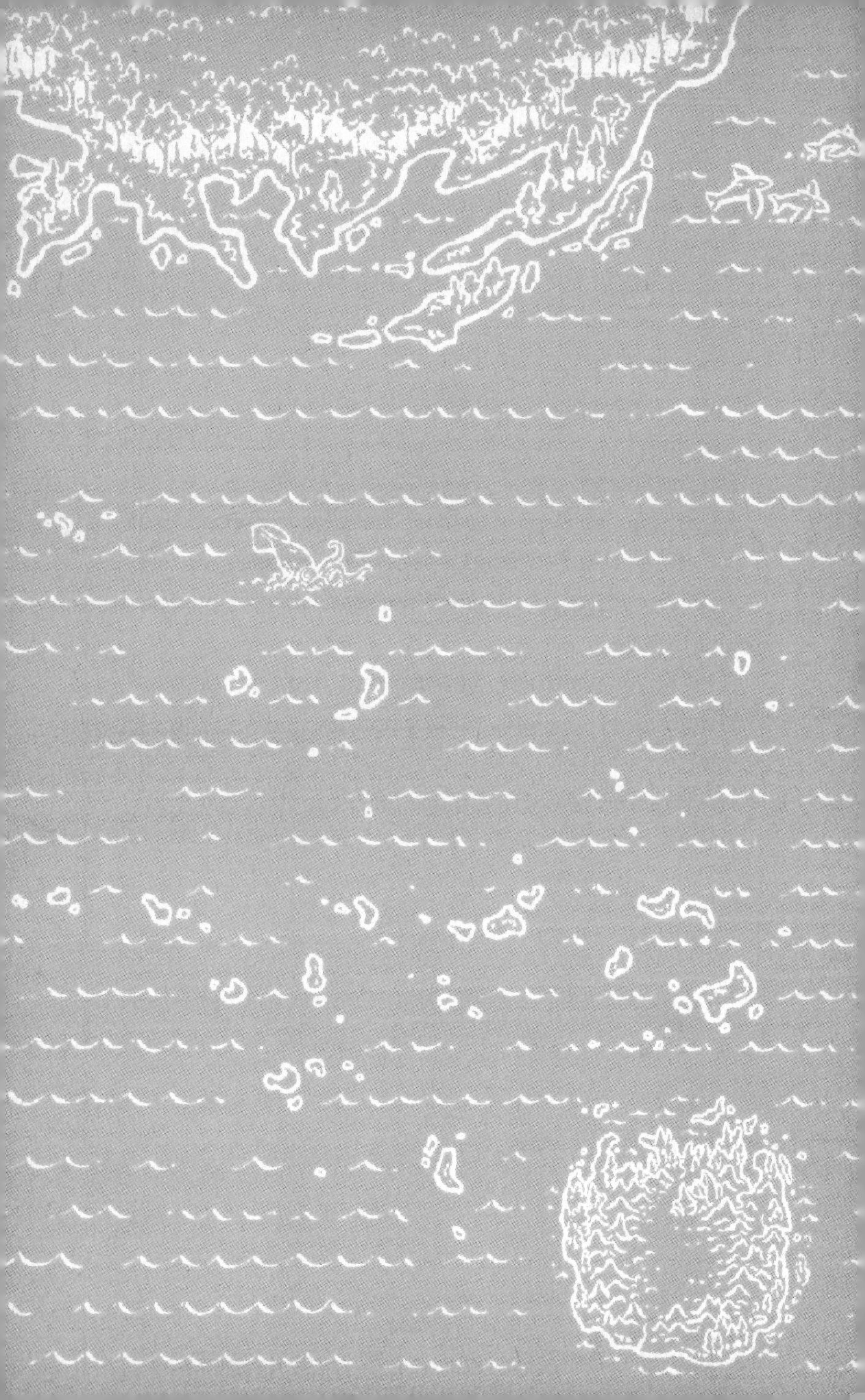

THE FORGOTTEN ISLES PROPHECY

Dragons lost and long forgotten
Abandoned in the sunlit isle
Ruled by power and betrayal
Haunted by an ancient trial.

Lines of blood will hold the key
As danger threatens from the past
And when the claws are at his throat
The hybrid prince will rise at last.

Who springs the trap, who saves the queens,
And which of them is friend or foe?
The smallest claws must choose the path
To right a wrong from long ago.

But is it wise and is it safe
To break the curse, unleash the tide?
What happens when the walls come down . . .
If something else was trapped inside?